OGILVIE
AND THE MEM'SAHIB

Philip McCutchan

This title first published in Great Britain 2002 by
SEVERN HOUSE PUBLISHERS LTD of
9–15 High Street, Sutton, Surrey SM1 1DF.
Originally published 1979 as *The Restless Frontier*
under the pseudonym *Duncan MacNeil*.
This title first published in the USA 2003 by
SEVERN HOUSE PUBLISHERS INC of
595 Madison Avenue, New York, N.Y. 10022.

British Library Cataloguing in Publication Data

McCutchan, Philip, 1920-
    Ogilvie and the Mem'Sahib. - (A James Ogilvie novel)
    1.   Great Britain. Army - History - 19th century - Fiction
    2.   Ogilvie, James (Fictitious character) - Fiction
    3.   India - History - 19th century - Fiction
    4.   Historical fiction
    I.   Title
    823.9'14 [F]

    ISBN 0-7278-5827-0

Printed and bound in Great Britain by
MPG Books Ltd., Bodmin, Cornwall.

Author's Note

The section in this book dealing with the delimitation escort for the High Commissioner owes its birth to the germ of an idea that came into my mind after reading a most interesting factual account by Mr J.E.G. Hodgson late of the Border Regiment (now amalgamated with the King's Own Royal Regt. to form the King's Own Royal Border Regt.). This described an action in which the 2nd Bn. the Border Regiment rendered distinguished service in Waziristan in the mid 1890s when ordered to march as reinforcements in the pursuit of native forces who had attacked the escort. All my characters are of course fictitious as is the way in which I have portrayed the development of the action.

1

THE WOMAN LAY inert across the horse, held in place by the sinewy arm of an Afridi tribesman, one of six riding like the wind itself away from the Nowshera cantonment. The woman was unconscious and blood dripped from a wound in her left shoulder. There was no pursuit: behind them the officers and men of the British garrison slept soundly under the protection of the sentries and barrack guards. The penetration and the attack had been carried out brilliantly and in total silence, the tribesmen mere shadows in the night as they had approached the bungalow, their naked bodies oiled so that they would, if caught, slip easily from the strongest grip. Firearms had not been used; *thuggee* was the safer course, and four privates and a lance-corporal of the 1st Dorsetshires lay dead in the cantonment with cords drawn tightly around their necks, as did the *chaukidah,* the night-watchman, the old retainer responsible for keeping un-desirables from the sahibs' domestic quarters.

The Afridis rode north of Peshawar and its garrison, ul-timately towards the Khyber Pass and the watchful sentries of the Khyber Rifles, high up in Fort Jamrud that guarded the eastern extremity; but well short of Fort Jamrud the riders turned off for the south, crossing the track leading out of Peshawar, to enter Waziristan by ways known only to the men of the tribes, and were soon lost in the hills and the maze of little-used passes into one of the world's wildest areas of savagery. No one saw them go: only the eyes of the hungry jackals and of the scavenging vultures watched, the latter hovering and swooping as the smell of the woman's blood came to them as earnest of a possible meal.

*   *   *

The evening before, James Ogilvie of the Queen's Own Royal Strathspeys had attended a brilliant reception along with his brother officers: a stupendous feast provided by His Highness the Maharajah of Amb for the benefit of the officers of the Raj. Much drink had been available for the guests. Ogilvie, a glass of whisky in his hand, was chatting with the lantern-jawed and voluble wife of a Surgeon Colonel attached to Brigade when he was borne down upon by his cousin Hector, carrying a glass of lemonade with some difficulty through the throng of brilliant dress uniforms.

"An extravanganza, James." Hector bowed to the Surgeon Colonel's lady. "Your pardon, ma'am. I'm interrupting."

"Not at all, Mr Ogilvie, most certainly not." The horse-faced woman gathered up her dress and made for an unoccupied major-general who for no apparent reason had turned up on the North-West Frontier from Calcutta.

"An extravaganza," Hector repeated gloomily.

"As ever in India. The princes are lavish, and generous."

"In their own cause, my dear chap, yes."

Ogilvie lifted his glass and grinned at his owlish cousin. "You mean, I'll scratch your back if you'll scratch mine?"

"An expression I don't care for," Hector Ogilvie said in a distant tone, "but I don't doubt it'll do. Frankly, I'll be glad enough when my duty in India comes to an end," he added, causing James to reflect that the pleasure would not be Hector's alone. "Have you seen Angela? I've mislaid her."

Ogilvie waved his glass towards a corner of the immense, pillared apartment that formed His Highness's throne room. "Over there. Talking to Lord Brora."

"The devil she is!" His face flushed, Hector hurried away looking possessive. Once more, Ogilvie grinned: Major Lord Brora, second-in-command of the Royal Strathspeys, was an arrogant man but could also be a gallant one with the ladies . . . and was a much more prepossessing figure than poor Hector, a Civilian from the India Office in London currently condemned to a year's tour of Indian duty so that he could the better fit himself for his Imperial task of administering the sub-continent from afar. Hector Ogilvie,

8

unlikely son of James's uncle, Rear-Admiral Rufus Ogilvie, was a man of much complaint. He didn't like the climate either in winter, which it was now, or summer; he didn't like the varied smells of Peshawar and he turned up his nose at the natives, from Maharajah to Untouchable—he had had an uncomfortable time in Calcutta, which according to him was full of Untouchables, of which low and smelly class he was to a large extent mercifully relieved in Peshawar. He disliked strong drink, and was appalled by the parties in the various regimental messes as well as by those in the native palaces. He was appalled, too, by the easy way in which officers in garrison drifted into relationships with married women whose husbands were absent, and since his arrival in Peshawar had stuck like a leech, whenever possible, to Angela. Ogilvie wondered, as he had wondered before now, why cousin Hector had ever entered the splendid portals of the India Office in the first place: it was something of an enigma, but was perhaps explained by Hector's love of power and prestige and his preference for the halls of Government rather than the bloody field of action. Ogilvie watched him regain contact with his wife of a little under a year, saw the almost savage glare given him by Lord Brora as Angela turned with a smile of welcome for her husband. Hector's young wife seemed to have that sort of effect upon other men—Ogilvie had noted it more than once in the short time she had been on the Frontier, and was convinced she was innocently and totally unaware of it. Meeting her eye over Hector's shoulder—she was taller than he, almost of James Ogilvie's own height—he saw the response to him in her clear eyes and was stirred uneasily. He frowned: another enigma—why Angela had married cousin Hector! Certainly she appeared fond of him if subdued by him; she looked like a bride still, young and fresh as a flower, and wide-eyed with wonder at all she was seeing along the warring North-West Frontier, the outposts and garrisons of which formed the last defensive line between the Afghan hordes and the British Raj, almost the farthest and certainly the most glittering pearl in the Imperial crown of Her Majesty the Queen-Empress . . . lost in his own thoughts Ogilvie started when he

9

felt the weight of a hand upon his shoulder and turned to find Andrew Black at his side. The Adjutant was looking dour.

"Fiddling while Rome burns, James."

"This?" Ogilvie waved a hand around the expensive throng: there was enough metal in the orders, medals and campaign stars to build a battleship, while the officers' ladies collectively wore a small fortune in gold and rubies, diamonds and emeralds, to say nothing of the romantic splendour of the Maharajah's retinue and of His Highness's own exalted, sky-blue-turbaned person. "It's nothing new or out of the ordinary, Andrew, and nothing's burning that I know of!"

"Maybe. But I smell trouble."

"Where, for God's sake?"

"As yet I cannot say, and I'll thank you not to blaspheme in my presence—"

"I was not blaspheming."

"Or to argue either. My words are a warning, and will be offered to all our officers with special intent for the company commanders such as yourself." Black paused, his dark face somehow menacing as the light from the chandeliers was taken from it by a thick marble pillar inlaid with gold. "The Colonel has seen fit to have a word in my ear. I expect to see sober officers in the morning, Captain Ogilvie. Do you take my meaning?"

"I think so, Captain Black, and I shall abide by it so long as it affects you also. If you take my meaning?"

Black glared, muttered something about insubordination, and turned away sharply, the tartan of the Royal Strathspey swirling around bony knees above legs like spindles. For the third time that evening, Ogilvie grinned. He finished his whisky and set the empty glass down on a side table of solid gold. Andrew Black was a more lucrative prospect than he for the whisky distillers of Scotland, and in the mornings was as ill-tempered from his occasional bouts of abstinence as he was when suffering the effects of over-indulgence. Ogilvie wondered what was in the wind now, if anything; Andrew Black tended to rush towards bad news, and often enough that news had turned out to lie in his mind alone. Ogilvie was not left long with his thoughts: he was approached by a bosomy young lady with a fan and a beaming smile and a heady scent that would have been stimulating had she been of slenderer proportions. As it was, she closely resembled her distinguished father, a portly major-general commanding a division of native cavalry, an officer known to irreverent regimental subalterns as Pigsgut Pomeroy.

"Dear James, I would so like to sit on the verandah, wouldn't you? It's so *nice* under the moon and really it's not awf'ly cold, is it, do you think? I haven't seen you for simply ages, James, in fact Mother was saying only the other day..."

She prattled on; prattle was another of her attributes, but she was a wallflower and Ogilvie felt sympathetic, and also understanding of her mother's guile: as a captain in a Highland regiment of panache, as a single officer, as the only son of Sir Iain Ogilvie commanding the Northern Army in India from Murree, James was a catch and couldn't help but know it and regret it. Few relationships with young women could ever be wholly spontaneous: behind each lay inevitably the web of intrigue and matchmaking that meshed in the social, and often enough the military, life of the garrisons and the hill stations. Only on patrol or in the isolation of an outpost fort or upon the march with one's regiment could one be really at home and at ease ... James obeyed the young lady's wishes and led her out on to the verandah, and spent some half an hour in study of the moon and the low-slung, myriad stars that hung like so many lamps in the night. He felt the keen edge of a cold wind coming down from distant Himalaya, across the foothills to bring the smell of the sub-continent to his nostrils as the sweat of the Maharajah's palace interior dried from the starched shirt beneath the scarlet jacket of his mess dress. Miss Mary Pomeroy evidently had blood less thinned by Indian service than had he.

* * *

"Did Andrew speak to you, James?"

11

"He did." Ogilvie lay back against the leather upholstery of the carriage that, in company with Robin Stuart of E Company, was taking him back after the Maharajah's roisterings to the cantonment on the far side of Peshawar. His mind had not been upon Captain Andrew Black but upon an entertainment presented by His Highness for the gentlemen only: much dusky female flesh had been on erotic display and some exceedingly curious acts had taken place while the drink had flowed freely for the guests—though the Scots officers, mindful of Black's words, had not over-indulged. The atmosphere had been hectic, with a background of throbbing music, and colourful with the varied uniforms of the British and Indian Army units: the Scots tartans, the blue of the gunners, the green of the rifle regiments, the red of the infantry had all added their lustre to the diaphanous and highly-coloured veils of the dancing women as they pranced and pirouetted. Ogilvie's mind was still full of the spectacle, but now he gave thought to Stuart's question. "Do you know what's in the air, Robin?"

Stuart shook his head. "Probably just Andrew fantasising again, old man."

"Shouts of war are heard afar. . .?"

"Possibly. It's what we're here for, isn't it?"

Ogilvie yawned; little more was said as the carriage rolled on beneath the stars, passing through the native city with its drains running sluggishly in their stench along the rutted streets, passing sad bundles of humanity wrapped in rags to slumber the night hours away, passing the odd barking dog, its jaws slavering for food and its eyes bright in the moon. There was an occasional oil lamp burning to light the doorways of the hovels, light that glinted on the shining steel of knives or the dull metal of antiquated rifles. Peshawar at night was a place of potential danger for the traveller and men on foot kept well clear of its alleys; but mounted or carriage-borne officers of the British Raj in uniform were normally allowed to pass unmolested: the risk of vengeance was potent in the native mind, for the great Queen-Empress in Windsor Castle was immensely powerful and extended full protection to her armies overseas; though she might turn

12

a blind eye to the robbing of a drunken private soldier who had asked for it, any attack upon authority passing upon its lawful occasions would bring down much wrath and many bullets. So the carriage passed in safety through Peshawar and on to the British cantonment some three miles westward towards the frowning sides of the Khyber Pass.

* * *

Ogilvie awoke bleary-eyed to the strident voice of the bugles blowing Reveille throughout the cantonment, bringing men awake in the barrack-rooms to tumble out and wash and grumble their way to early-morning parade to be inspected by the section sergeants and corporals, to show clean rifles and shaven chins. Ogilvie lay in his *charpoy*, listening to the sounds from the square—the rattle of equipment, the stamp of feet, the shouted commands. When his native bearer brought hot water, he got up and walked in his dressing-gown on to the verandah and stared out into the cold and freshness of the pre-breakfast hour. Across the square he saw Lord Brora pacing the parade with the Adjutant: those two were up bright and early! Something must be in the air after all. As Ogilvie watched, Mr Cunningham, the Regimental Sergeant-Major, came briskly from the direction of his bungalow, marching as straight as a ramrod with his pace-stick beneath his arm. As the RSM gave himself an eyes right and snapped to the salute on passing the second-in-command and the Adjutant, he was hailed by Brora and altered course to halt before the officers, slamming his boots into the ground and saluting again. The three men were still in conference when Ogilvie turned away and went back into his room: water could grow cold, and the morning was undoubtedly a chilly one. Breath steamed from the parade-ground. At breakfast there was, as usual, silence except for the discreet movements of the Corporal of Mess Servants and his native staff, offering food and coffee from white-gloved hands. Most of the officers were in fact invisible behind newspapers, many of them ancient ones that had travelled the long sea route from home and acted as shields

13

to morning privacy rather than as purveyors of news. Captain Black finished his breakfast just as Ogilvie entered, and nodded a good morning as he passed. At one end of the table the great bulk of Lord Brora loomed, solid and scowling as he glared over the top of an old *Morning Post* to seek out more marmalade.

"You."

Ogilvie lifted an eyebrow. "Me, Major?"

"No, blast you. You!"

The Corporal of Mess Servants hurried across and stood at attention. "Yessir?"

"*Yes, My Lord.* Don't you ever damn well *learn,* man? My Lord in the Mess, sir on parade. Next time you'll go before the Colonel." Brora tapped the sticky silver pot before him on the table. "Marmalade. See that it's kept filled. And wipe the damn thing."

"Yes, My Lord." The Corporal snapped his fingers at a bearer. "*Jaldi!*" His tone was fierce; the bearer salaamed twice, once towards the Major sahib, once towards the Corporal sahib. The silver vessel was filled with trembling fingers and set before the Major sahib, who sat in a frigid silence, glaring from angry accusing eyes. Breakfast proceeded to a sound of munching and coffee-drinking. The start of one more day in India . . . but before the meal was finished the Corporal, who had had words with a runner in the pantry, had approached each officer and had bent respectfully to deliver a message.

"Beg pardon, sir. The Colonel's compliments, sir, and he'd like to see you in the battalion office at nine-thirty sharp, sir."

* * *

In the battalion office there was a buzz of conversation while Black, having counted heads, went off to report to the Colonel. Talk was stilled when Lord Dornoch entered with Brora and Black. The three officers walked to the Colonel's desk and arranged themselves on chairs behind it. Before sitting down, the Colonel wished his officers good morning

14

and then pulled out his pipe. "You may smoke, gentlemen," he said. He filled the bowl and puffed to the strike of a match. Many other pipes and a few cigarettes were lit: the air grew thick as Dornoch went on, "I'll be brief and to the point, for you're about to be busily employed." He ran a hand over his moustache. "Last night, at the Maharajah's palace, Captain Black acquired some information that may or may not be genuine, but which has already been passed to Brigade and is being forwarded by the telegraph to Murree. At this moment, we await the GOC's reaction and possibly his orders." Dornoch paused. "Captain Black overheard two kinsmen of His Highness . . . it seems that word has leaked through the grapevine, at any rate to native ears in the first place, that a serious boundary dispute has occurred in Waziristan—in the vicinity of Mana to be precise. I think you all know what that means, gentlemen. It can be put in a nutshell: trouble. Trouble that will initially be our concern, since we're the stand-by battalion. . ."

As Dornoch continued speaking, giving his orders for the battalion to be brought to instant readiness to march out if required, Ogilvie felt a shiver of excitement mixed with apprehension run along his spine. Waziristan, that remote and mountainous country to the south and west of Peshawar, was wild, desolate, a terrible place for a winter march, a land of many feuding tribes such as the Afridis and the Mahsuds who were ever individually at each other's throats and collectively at the throats of the Raj. A sizeable boundary dispute would not be easily settled and the regiment would be likely to mourn many deaths by Christmas if they were ordered out to exert the interest and authority of the Raj. Mana was around a hundred miles as the crow flew—longer via the high passes, with the Tochi River and its tributaries to cross. This would be no ordinary patrol and could lead to a confrontation with tribal power that might involve the whole Peshawar garrison if things went ill for the Raj in its mediation attempts. Much would of course depend on the mood of the *maliks,* the local headmen, and that mood was always unpredictable except in so far as it was seldom friendly towards the Raj. Lord Dornoch was not as brief as he had promised: Surgeon Major Corton of the Medical Staff caused delay. There were a number of sick and a number of those recuperating were on light duties, and there was a shortage of medical supplies such as would be needed on the march into hostile and cut-off territory. These had of course been indented for to Brigade but had not yet arrived . . . Brora was heard to remark loudly that here was a case of damned inefficiency if ever there was one, and it was clear that he was metaphorically pointing the finger of blame at Corton rather than at Brigade. Lord Dornoch took the fuse from an explosive atmosphere.

"We all know what the supply situation's like. I shall have words with Brigade at once. I—" He broke off as the door opened and a subaltern saluted. "Yes, what is it, and who are you?"

"Second Lieutenant Roberts, sir, Probyn's Horse . . . from Brigade, sir. I have despatches, sir." At Dornoch's nod, the subaltern marched forward and handed a sealed envelope to the Colonel. Frowning, Dornoch slit it and read, then looked up. He appeared shocked.

"Thank you, Mr Roberts. I have despatches in return, and you shall wait." The Colonel got to his feet. "Orders, gentlemen, and the speed with which they have come from Murree indicates their urgency. Sir Iain has had similar information from the Political Department that confirms the word to Captain Black, and the High Commissioner is proceeding into Waziristan to sort out the dispute. He will take a Delimitation Escort, and we are ordered to form part of a brigade that will provide that escort." He turned. "Captain Black, we're ordered to be ready to march by noon. We move south by way of the Kohat Pass, at the southern end of which we'll rendezvous with the remainder of our brigade who'll march out from Kohat to join us under Brigadier-General Norris. We're to be brigaded with a battalion of the Punjab Frontier Force and one of Ghurkhas, and I'm told we're required as stiffeners for the native troops."

"I trust that guns and cavalry will be provided, Colonel?"

"Yes, yes, the Kohat contingent will join with a cavalry

16

squadron provided by the Guides, and a battery of mountain guns." Lord Dornoch paused, his face serious. "Thank you, gentlemen, that's all. Make your reports as soon as possible to the Adjutant, if you please." He lifted a hand to Ogilvie. "Captain Ogilvie, I'd be obliged if you'll remain behind a moment."

"Yes, Colonel."

The officers left amid a buzz of conversation: the general feeling was that Dornoch's manner had been unduly sombre. When they were alone Lord Dornoch pulled at his moustache, an expression of extreme gravity on his face. "I have bad news for you, James. Family—though not immediately close, I hasten to add. The fact is, the despatch brought other news. There was an attack upon the Nowshera cantonment during the dark hours after the palace reception—five bodies, six with the *chaukidah,* found when the guard changed, all killed by *thuggee.* A British subject was taken—or at any rate is missing, and there were signs of a struggle and some blood."

"My cousin, Colonel?"

Dornoch shook his head. "Not your cousin, James. Your cousin's wife . . . a lively and likeable young woman to be sure. I'm very sorry."

Ogilvie's face was white. "And the reason, Colonel? Has any reason emerged?"

"No, but there's a very clear connection. Your cousin . . . the Government in Calcutta had in fact decided already to appoint a commission to enquire in general terms into boundary matters in Waziristan, and your cousin was to have been one of the commissioners. Word may have leaked, and the result is kidnap."

"To put pressure on Hector, Colonel?"

"Very possibly, and on the High Commissioner too, for a woman's life can't be held lightly. It's nasty, James." Dornoch gave him a direct look. "Well, what's your wish? I'm prepared to excuse you escort duty if you feel you can be of assistance in Nowshera. It's up to you."

2

JAMES OGILVIE RODE out alone for Nowshera while the regiment prepared to march south. Hector was family and would need his support: his father, indeed, would expect no less than that he should give it. At Division in Nowshera he reported to a staff captain and was admitted to the presence of the Lieutenant-General Commanding Her Majesty's First Division, Lieutenant-General Francis Fettleworth. With the Divisional Commander was Hector, his face white, his eyes red as though from weeping. All Hector's pomposity was gone: Ogilvie saw him as he had seen him as a small boy, visiting the Ogilvies' home at Corriecraig Castle in distant Scotland: a small boy, plump and sailor suited, who had lost a toy boat on Loch Rannoch and had howled his head off.

"Well, Ogilvie. A sad business and a serious one for the Raj."

"Yes, sir." Ogilvie turned to Hector. "I'm sorry, old chap. I don't know what more to say . . . except that I'm here to help in any way I can."

There was no response from Hector other than a nod: he seemed completely distrait. Fettleworth blew through the trailing ends of a white walrus moustache and said, "Patrols, Ogilvie, search parties. They're being organised. Care to go with one?"

"Whatever is most useful, sir. My Colonel has released me from regimental duty."

"So I understand. Well, you've been in India a long time, Ogilvie, you know the Frontier better than many of the officers in my Division. What do you suggest may have been the course of events since Mrs Ogilvie disappeared? Mr Ogilvie, I think perhaps you should explain all the circumstances as you found them, to your cousin."

"Yes." Hector's voice was low and thick. For a moment he put his face in his hands, then seemed to stiffen a little and looked up at his cousin with pain-filled eyes. In a halting voice he told his story: after their return from the Maharajah's palace he and Angela had gone straight to bed in their adjoining rooms, which gave on to the bungalow's verandah. The doors and jalousies had been closed, but he had heard no sound of their being opened by any intruder: he was a heavy sleeper and was tired. Nothing had been known until the guard-change, when the bodies had been discovered, and then he had been at once awakened by the Sergeant of the Guard and had gone with the orderly officer to Angela's room. The door from the verandah had been open, swinging slightly in the dawn breeze. The bed was awry, with the sheets trailing to the floorboards, and there was a trace of blood on the ground, and some of the furniture had been displaced and a chair overturned. That was all. There had been an immediate search of the bungalow and the go-down where the native bearers and sweepers lived, and of the vicinity. Nothing had been found: Angela had gone, leaving no clues.

"We'll find her," James Ogilvie said.

Fettleworth nodded. "Indeed we shall. No stone left unturned, Mr Ogilvie, I promise you. Especially where a woman's concerned, the Raj responds quickly."

"It'll be too late, General." Hector's tone was flat.

"Upon my word it will not!" Fettleworth said stoutly.

"She'll be tortured . . . she won't stand that for long."

"Even the tribesmen respect women," James said, with a glance at Fettleworth as though appealing to him to support a necessary untruth. "She won't be harmed physically, Hector."

Hector's eyes blazed and his white face flushed to an unhealthy colour. "I don't want stupid palliatives, James. You've always thought I knew nothing of India, haven't you? I'm not as green as you imagine . . . I know what the natives are capable of. We're not all wrapped in cottonwool in Whitehall, and since I've been out here I've heard more than you think. I'm not a damn—"

19

"Yes, yes, Mr Ogilvie." Fettleworth gave a loud cough and made a rasping sound in his throat. "India's India, of course, we'll not deny that." He stopped and once again blew through his moustache as though suddenly conscious of having uttered a non-profundity. "Everything that can be done will be done, you have my word. I feel what has happened to be my own responsibility and matters will be put right. And while we await the results of the patrols, Mr Ogilvie, we must also await something else."

"Something else?"

Fettleworth got to his feet and walked over to a wide window overlooking the green patch of grass in the centre of which the Divisional standard flew from its flagstaff; turning again, he looked upwards and met the stern, framed gaze of Her Majesty the Queen-Empress, staring down at him from the wall opposite. As ever, that imperial gaze affected his emotions. He cleared his throat. "We must await word from the persons who have removed your wife, Mr Ogilvie. Soon they must utter, and tell us their demands."

"You think they'll have demands?"

Fettleworth tugged at the neckband of his scarlet tunic. Mr Ogilvie was a fool. "Of a certainty they'll have demands! These things are never done without reason behind them, you may be sure. When the demands come, then we shall have more to go on."

Hector stared. "What do you suppose the demands might be, General?"

Fettleworth pulled for a moment at his moustache, his eyes cold and bleak. "You are about to sit on a boundary commission, Mr Ogilvie, and I'm bound to see a link." He paused. "What would be your reaction ... if your wife's kidnappers put pressure upon you and your colleagues to find in favour of some persons as yet unknown?"

*   *   *

James Ogilvie and Hector walked alone in the grounds of Divisional HQ. Hector's response to Fettleworth's question had been indirect; he had said, properly enough in his

20

cousin's view, that it was now his duty to ask Calcutta to remove him from the boundary commission. Fettleworth had at first been dubious, saying that to do such would be to play to some extent into the hands of the kidnappers, to admit their power to control events and to admit it pointlessly since the effect would be much the same whether or not Hector remained a member of the commission: the pressure would still be upon the Raj. But he had eventually agreed, for it was obvious Hector would not only be useless but would also be a confounded nuisance and an embarrassment. Hector's request would be passed via the Army Commander in Murree who was already, as it happened, hastening in person to Nowshera by the railway for words with his nephew—this had been intimated by the telegraph from Rawalpindi where Sir Iain had been about to inspect the troops in garrison. Walking beneath some trees that gave a degree of shelter from a cold wind, James Ogilvie did what he could to offer hope and comfort. Certainly the Frontier was a big area to cover, certainly the kidnappers could have ridden north or south, or west into the Afghan hills, though it was unlikely they would have risked entering the Khyber Pass with its many forts friendly to the Raj. But Peshawar and Nowshera were strongly garrisoned and more troops could be sent speedily from Murree and Rawalpindi and Mardan. Ogilvie did not add that no general would too far deplete the northern garrisons by sending out patrols in sufficient strength and numbers to weaken his base; nor did he add that patrols could be cut up to a man and never return to Peshawar to report. It had happened before and would happen again in this wild land where the bullet came without warning and the knives sprang like magic from the scrub and the sides of the passes, and the cord of *thuggee* could be whipped around even a horseman's throat before he had heard a sound or felt a movement from the man who had dropped upon his horse from a tree or overhanging jag of rock. Although all this remained unsaid, Ogilvie had the uneasy feeling that his cousin was possessed of much more imagination than he had suspected.

"Find her, James," Hector said in a tight, too-controlled

21

voice, a voice that was in basis as brittle as the morning frost. "She's like a child . . . and not strong. Not strong at all. So — thin." And so trusting too, James thought to himself, remembering her eyes of the night before. Wherever she went she saw no evil, but God alone could tell what she was seeing now. He felt a lump in his throat and his vision misted. Find her he would.

* * *

The 114th Highlanders, The Queen's Own Royal Strathspey, marched out of cantonments at noon precisely behind the pipes and drums, kilts a-swing round knees still brown from the blazing suns of the last summer season, rifles at the slope until the order should be passed by Lord Dornoch to march at ease. The side-arms in their brightly polished scabbards bumped the pleats of the kilts as the step was called by the section sergeants. From ahead of the Colonel and Lord Brora, riding with the High Commissioner, Sir Lawrence Bindle, the wail of the pipes swept back upon the marching files, stirring and haunting, warlike yet sad, as the cantonment and the troops in garrison who had turned out to cheer them on faded away in the dust behind. The tune was "The 79th's Farewell to Gibraltar"; it beat out strongly as Captain Black came riding down the line from the van, face haughty, eyes sharp for any slackness of dress or marching. The NCOs and men were ready for the expected, and Black could find no fault. He spurred his horse back towards the van, where he joined the Colonel.

"All well, Andrew?"

Black saluted. "Yes, Colonel."

"A devilish business!"

"And a damn pretty filly," Brora said.

The Colonel turned his head. "I dislike your choice of word, Major."

"Never mind the choice of word, my dear sir, if I find her I'll slit the damn guts of the buggers who laid a hand on her last night! And I'll tell you something else as well: I realise that our orders are for Mana and a peaceful exort, but *balls*

22

to our orders if we should happen to raise the scent of the wench—which is a word I trust you'll like better than filly, my dear sir!"

"Thank you, Brora. I think you've said enough."

"If you say so, Colonel." Brora's eyes flashed, and he exchanged a look with Black. Black thereafter avoided the Major's eye: he was unsure of his ground as between the Colonel and the Major, who were ever at loggerheads since Brora's brief and unfortunate command of the battalion in the absence of Dornoch in hospital some months before. It made it hard for an Adjutant to please both at once, and often Black sighed for the return from the dead of John Hay, an ineffective Major but an easy man to deal with, and a mild one. Brora was an aristocratic swashbuckler, and Black, with his background of moneyed trade, felt more ill-at-ease with him than he did with Dornoch, equally an aristocrat but not by any means a swashbuckler. Brora, Black felt, would have made a first-class buccaneer in the days of ocean piracy... meanwhile the advance on the Kohat Pass continued and after a few more minutes Lord Dornoch passed the word for the battalion to march at ease. As the order went down via the Adjutant, the company commanders, the Regimental Sergeant-Major and the colour-sergeants, rifles left the shoulders and were hung from their blanco-ed slings, the neckbands of the khaki-drill tunics were thankfully loosened and voices lifted in song: at first, bawdy song, and loud. A roar from Mr Cunningham almost reached the van.

"Stop the filth, d'ye hear me? This is no' an ordinary march, it's a Delimitation Escort and we have the High Commissioner wi' us."

There was some muttering, but the song changed. In the van Dornoch suppressed a smile and thanked heaven for his RSM. Sir Lawrence Bindle wore almost continually pursed lips, and was in truth little different from Hector Ogilvie. As the afternoon shadows lengthened the air became colder with the sun's westerly decline over the stark Afghan hills. A halt for resting of men and horses was called soon after the column turned southwards and came into the Waziri

23

heights, and under the care of the scouts and picquets pipes were lit and smoke rose blue over the fallen-out line and feet were eased from heavy boots. The respite was brief, for there was yet much distance to be covered to the vicinity of Kohat, but it was not too long before the battalion went into their night bivouac before entering the Kohat Pass which the Colonel preferred to traverse in daylight hours.

* * *

The single shot came like the crack of a whip, shattering the night's brooding silence. From the hillside the body of a picquet tumbled, head-over-heels, sliding down and bringing small boulders and stones with it in a cascade of debris. Everywhere men came awake, rubbing the sleep from their eyes and seizing the rifles which were ever at their sides. Mr Cunningham, who seldom seemed to sleep when on the march in hostile territory, was the first to reach the body. He bent for the heart and found no flutter.

He straightened. "Dead," he said. He looked around, saw nothing. There were sounds from the hillside as the picquets still on post searched for the man who had fired.

Brora came stalking up, a revolver in his hand. "What is it, Sar'nt-Major?"

"Private MacFarar, sir, C Company, shot dead."

"How d'you know he's dead, Sar'nt-Major?"

"Why, sir, I—"

"You're not a medical man, Sar'nt-Major, rouse out the Surgeon at once."

"But I—"

"Do as you're told." Lord Brora swung away abruptly, peering about and lifting his revolver. Cunningham, an angry man, shouted for a runner. In the meantime, the company officers and colour-sergeants were forming the men up for the defence of the bivouacs and for a search of the hillsides; and while this was going on a flaming torch was seen to be descending from a lofty crag on the eastern hillside, a torch that swung out widely to drop between the bivouacs. The moment it was seen an intensity of rapid fire

24

was opened on its spot of origin by the rifles and the Maxim detachment, who had their gun ready assembled for night fighting. There was a loud cry and another body tumbled, crashing down the slope to lie with spread arms and legs and a turban soaked in blood from a split skull. Several men ran towards where the torch had landed and was still sputtering. It was attached by a long cord to a stone, and to the stone was tied a square of goatskin. As a lance-corporal removed the goatskin from the stone, Lord Brora appeared.

"Hand me that."

The lance-corporal saluted. "Sir!" He passed over the skin, and Brora bent to examine it in the light of the native flare.

"By God!" he said, and straightened. He said no more, but made at the double towards the Colonel. "A message from the damn natives, in English." He shouted for a guard lantern, and one was quickly lit. In the guttering yellow light Dornoch read out the words burnt with red-hot iron into the skin.

"To the British High Commissioner and escort. The woman will die if you advance further." Dornoch balled the skin in his fist, and looked up. In the lantern's light his face was strained and old.

"Well, Colonel?"

Steadily Dornoch said, "We must continue. We are under orders from Murree, not from Waziristan."

"It'll be the High Commissioner's decision."

"I am the military commander here, Brora—"

"But his is the mission. He may consider it more prudent to abandon it. Nevertheless, I agree with you, Colonel. We should not be dictated to and be seen to give in—that way lies eventually the end of the Raj."

Dornoch seemed dazed. "But that poor young woman—"

"My arse to that, Colonel," Brora broke in loudly. "The filly's safe for a while yet. These buggers are wily and artful — they won't throw down their own wicket by killing their hostage so early. Let us go to Sir Lawrence and put our views with force."

* * *

25

In the late afternoon, with all plans made as far as they could be at this stage, James Ogilvie had ridden out westerly from Nowshera with a reinforced cavalry patrol found by a squadron of the Bengal Lancers. With him went two mountain guns, stripped down with their parts distributed with the ammunition on the backs of the mules. Further patrols had been sent out to north and south; the easterly direction, which was not considered a very likely route for the kidnappers to have taken since it led into British garrisoned territory, would be covered on the off-chance by units from Army Command at Murree. Ogilvie's task, outlined to him by Brigadier-General Lakenham, Fettleworth's Chief of Staff, was to follow the westerly track through to Fort Jamrud and look for any spoor that might yield up a clue and, if he found such, to follow it up after sending back a mounted runner with a report. He had carte blanche to pursue any track anywhere north or south of the Peshawar to Fort Jamrud route and even, if he thought fit, to enter the Khyber Pass itself. The word had gone out that Angela Ogilvie was to be found at all costs; no effort in terms of men or animals, ammunition or supplies was to be spared. Her safety was vital for the Raj and any patrol that picked up her trail would have the fullest backing from Murree and the other garrisons by way of reinforcements to be despatched immediately their need was notified. Available at this immediate notice were full battalions of the Dorsetshires, the Duke of Cornwall's Light Infantry, the Manchesters, Hampshires, and Middlesex together with half-a-dozen Indian Army infantry battalions plus three cavalry brigades, guns and support columns including signal companies, engineers and field ambulances.

"Enough to have pleased the Duke of Wellington himself," Sir Iain Ogilvie, who had arrived shortly before his son's departure, had said. "But the tribes can still win so long as they can keep hidden. It's touch and go, James. Do your best."

"I shall, sir."

His father's eyes had been a trifle moist. "Damn it, she's only a child. It's a filthy country at times, James. Her father's one of my and your Uncle Rufus's oldest friends." He had said no more, had simply given his son a firm hand-clasp. But when James Ogilvie glanced back as he rode away with the squadron he was aware of a blank look on his father's face. He thought: the old man's suddenly aged . . . he's getting long in the tooth for the strain of high command, and it doesn't help when it comes so close to home.

3

IN HIS BIVOUAC, Sir Lawrence Bindle, his holstered revolver laid acorss his knees, looked shaken and undecided, cheeks puffy and pale behind the stubble peeping through. "I'm not a man of action," he said. "You are, Colonel. What d'you advise?"

"My instinct's to go through, Sir Lawrence."

"And mine," Brora said loudly. "We have the strength, and we shall join our brigade the other side of the Kohat Pass."

"But that's not quite the point—"

"The orders from the GOC were clear enough: a full effort. And full backing." Brora's voice rose even higher. "It's permission to slaughter the damn natives willy-nilly and teach 'em a lesson they'll not forget!"

Sir Lawrence lifted a hand. "Please, Lord Brora, allow me to continue. You must not lose sight of my special mission, which is essentially one of peace. I enter Waziristan simply as an adjudicator, to settle a dispute between two opposing tribes, two opposing aspirations for land. The military power represented by yourselves is here only as an escort, at any rate in the first instance. And, of course, there is the lady who is the subject of this communication—"

"Precisely!"

"I cannot put her in danger of her life, Lord Brora."

"You'll not do so any more than she is already, and has been since the moment she was taken."

"The message reads that Mrs Ogilvie will die if we advance. In my experience of India, which is longer than yours, Lord Brora, the natives do not make empty threats —especially the Frontier tribes. You would agree, Colonel?"

28

Dornoch nodded heavily, shadows passing across his face as the light from the guard lantern flickered. There was a stir of wind, a sound of desolation, and from the distance came the mournful hooting of some night bird that had found its prey and was making a kill. Killing was the very essence of this lonely land ... Dornoch said, "Yes, I agree in general, but I think not on this occasion." He put the point Brora had made earlier: the natives would not precipitately despatch a valuable hostage. He put another point as well: his battalion was currently and undeniably under orders to act as the Delimitation Escort for the High Commissioner, but such did not relieve him of his duty to act in accordance with the spirit of the overall order from Murree, which was to spare no effort to find and rescue Mrs Ogilvie.

"Who could well be not far away, Sir Lawrence."

"Not far?" Bindle raised his eyebrows. "How likely is that proposition, d'you suppose?"

Dornoch shrugged. "Not very likely, I admit, but it's a possibility I can't ignore."

"You would see no conflict with your orders to act as my escort?"

"No, Sir Lawrence, I would not."

"Then I'm sorry, but I do. The two cannot be compatible." The High Commissioner lifted a hand as Brora attempted to interrupt. "Suppose you send out search parties, Colonel ... suppose they become involved in fighting? What happens to my mission then, if my escort fires perhaps on one of the parties with whom I am here to negotiate? What will be my use then, as an adjudicator?"

Dornoch said quietly, "I'd not propose to detach patrols specifically to search, Sir Lawrence. Others are doing that, and I would certainly not wish, for instance, to delay your arrival at Mana—"

"Then what *do* you suggest?"

"Simply that we continue, and disregard the goatskin— in Mrs Ogilvie's interest. I'm convinced they'll not carry out their threat yet, and I believe that if we advance as ordered they'll in fact take pains to preserve her life until she can be of more use to them than she can be at this moment. Also, if she is being held in the vicinity, then there's a chance she'll continue to be near us."

"Possibly, possibly. A difficult situation, gentlemen, a difficult decision... I would like guidance from Calcutta."

"Calcutta's a long way off," Brora said tartly.

"The telegraph—"

"Is also a long way off, at Peshawar, and we have not laid a field telegraph for the simple reason that the natives would have cut it the moment we were out of sight along what's an unprotected track. And a runner would delay us for too long." Brora turned to the Colonel. "I have pre-empted, no doubt, what you were about to say yourself, Colonel. I apologise."

*   *   *

Dornoch, who had in fact made up his mind as to his course of action, had been fully prepared to enforce his decision and to over-rule the High Commissioner; but some further persuasion did the trick. The orders were passed for the regiment to move towards the Kohat Pass at first light, with picquets out and scouts extended ahead. As the sky lightened, the bugles blew and the Scots eased themselves from their bivouacs and after a hastily-taken wash in a stream, and breakfast from the field kitchens, they were fallen in and formed into column for the march. The pipes and drums played them on towards the high sides and sinister gloom of the pass. There was no sign of human life and no repetition of the previous night's goatskin threat; but just before moving out Lord Dornoch had sent back three mounted men, a lance-corporal and two privates, each of them carrying copies of a despatch for Division. As the van of the advance came beneath the shadows of the pass, the pipes and drums continued playing, giving heart to the marching files as the heights took away the climbing sun and the wind blew cold along the rock-strewn track beneath. Still no one was seen; but there would be watchful eyes along the peaks and behind boulders on the steeply-sloping sides where the picquets doubled to protect the column from flank attack, doubled until they reached the sanctuary of rough *sangars* from which they could watch the hillsides behind the sights of their rifles. The unseen native eyes would be reporting their progress, sending the word on from peak to peak that the Raj was coming through. When the column was deep into the pass, something happened: as in the night before, there was the crack of a rifle, quickly followed by another. From half-way up the hillside a turbaned figure rose, clutching at its throat; its back arched and, screaming, it toppled and rolled down towards the track, bounding from the boulders in its path. From a *sangar* one of the picquets looked down, his rifle smoking still. The native fetched up almost at the feet of Black's horse, and as the Colonel lifted a hand to halt the column the Adjutant dismounted and bent over the bloodied, trembling figure.

He looked up. "Alive, Colonel—just."

Lord Dornoch turned in his saddle: the Surgeon Major was already coming up. Corton carried out a quick examination. "He hasn't long, Colonel."

Dornoch, his face stiff and drained of emotion, nodded. "The Sar'nt-Major—quickly." A runner was sent down the column at the double, and within the minute Cunningham was puffing up and slamming to the halt and the salute beside the Colonel's horse.

"Sir!"

"Mr Cunningham, that man—that native. He's to be made to talk—you've had success at that in the past. You haven't long. Find out what he knows of Mrs Ogilvie."

"Sir!" Another salute, and Cunningham turned about, his face set like the Colonel's. Then he squatted on his haunches beside the dying man, looked up at the waiting runner, and gestured for the man's bayonet. Drawn from its scabbard, the gleaming blade was handed down. Pointing it at the face, Cunningham began talking in Pushtu, rapidly, urgently and with threat in his tone. After a while the bayonet moved and there was a cry that ended in a throaty bubbling. There was a bloody froth. Corton, who had turned and walked away during the questioning, turned again as he heard the sound and came hurrying back. He bent, then looked up. "All right,

Sar'nt-Major. Enough's enough." There was a silence, then Corton looked up once more. "He's dead, Colonel."

"Thank you, Doctor. Well, Mr Cunningham?"

"Not a word, sir."

"I see. Thank you, Mr Cunningham—a distasteful job, I know." Dornoch glanced at Lord Brora. "Move out, if you please, Major."

The order to resume the march was passed; the pipes and drums sounded again, to beat off the rocky slopes and fill the pass with martial sound. No one enquired as to the body's burial: such was unnecessary. The bones, when left bare by the vultures already clustering in a black cloud overhead, would be of themselves a warning message to the enemy. Without further incident the Royal Strathspey continued through the Kohat and came unscathed to the southward and into more open but still rocky and desolate terrain with high mountains all around in the great distances, peak upon peak, range upon range to every point of the compass. Ahead there was an immense cloud of dust and as it was seen, so also was a subaltern from the scouting party seen, riding back to make his unnecessary report.

The rider halted. "The brigade, Colonel, out of Kohat."

"Thank you, Mr MacTaggart. Captain Black, the signallers, if you please. There's sun enough for the heliograph. My respects to the Brigadier-General, and an identification of my column."

"Very good, Colonel." A runner was despatched and shortly after he had doubled away the mirrors of the heliographs began their winking. The columns converged, and Brigadier-General Norris was seen to be cantering ahead of his troops with his Brigade Major and a subaltern. Riding ahead himself, Dornoch saluted and said formally, "Colonel the Earl of Dornoch, sir, joining your brigade with the 114th Highlanders."

There was a friendly nod. "Delighted to see you, Colonel, though I fear it'll not be for longer than it takes me to pass your orders."

Dornoch was surprised. "You have fresh orders, sir? I was to accompany you to Mana."

32

"Yes, indeed. Army Command's changed its mind—I shall take over the High Commissioner, with yourselves replaced by the 2nd Border Regiment who will join from Dera Ismail Khan when I reach Mana."

"And us, sir?"

"You're to be detached to back up the Kohat garrison and join the search for Mrs Ogilvie, Colonel—"

"Good God, we might just as well have been left in Peshawar to probe south from there!"

"Not so. There's a need for you in Kohat. The garrison's depleted and it's considered a likely area."

"To find Mrs Ogilvie?"

The Brigadier-General nodded. "Fresh information has come to hand, it seems. You'll be fully informed by the Political Officer . . . feller called Blaise-Willoughby, sent down from Nowshera a few weeks ago."

* * *

Ogilvie had ridden the day before with his cavalry patrol along the whole route to Fort Jamrud: an officer of the Khyber Rifles had come down to greet his arrival in the lip of the pass. There was little to report on either hand: no unidentified persons had entered the Khyber below Fort Jamrud, and for his part Ogilvie had picked up no leads. The rifle subaltern, however, had a piece of information that might be worth following up: a Pathan had ridden out of the pass a few hours earlier from Afghanistan with two other horsemen. Riding apparently in peace, he had not been interfered with. Many of the tribesmen from the Afghan hills had relatives inside the Frontier, and it was customary to allow latitude for their visits; but on this occasion the NCO of the native guard had been curious enough about the man's splendid accoutrements, and impressed enough by his imperious bearing, to talk about it after being relieved.

"And the result?" Ogilvie asked.

"A very clear description. He wore gold earrings with medallions dangling, medallions bearing a boar's head motif—like a crest. The same motif appeared on the haft of

33

his dagger. He was tall—exceptionally tall. And he didn't wear the usual filthy goatskin coat, either. He had a cloak of some sort of maroon cloth, with gold thread worked into it—"

"And you identified him?"

"Yes, I did. Murrum Khan, basically a horse-thief and gun-runner—"

"Who would have been better arrested?"

The subaltern shrugged. "I suppose so, but in point of fact he's done nothing against the Raj specifically and I doubt if I'd have arrested him even if I'd been there myself and recognised him. Most of the bloody Pathans are horse-thieves and gun-runners, aren't they?"

Ogilvie grinned. "Well, that's true! What's different about Murrum Khan?"

"I didn't know this at the time, as it happens, but he's a kinsman of Dostman Khan, the chap that's behind the boundary dispute down Mana way."

"Is this on your file?"

"No. My NCO recognised the name when I told him. He has a second cousin—I think I'm right in saying—who's married to the aunt-in-law of Dostman Khan's wife's niece. Something like that. My NCO has never met him, but he's heard of him via the family." The subaltern paused. "There's something else as well: *badal* may come into it."

Ogilvie's eyes narrowed: when the Pathan invoked *badal*, the tremendously important concept of ultimate revenge, then murder became inevitable. The subaltern elaborated: Dostman Khan's father, now dead, had killed Murrum Khan's elder brother in a dispute over a woman. Ogilvie asked, "Have you reported this to Peshawar?"

"I was about to. I'd only unravelled my NCO's story just as you came in sight."

"Then I suggest you report at once."

"I'll do that, providing the field telegraph's not cut again —"

"If it is, send a runner. I'd advise your Commanding Officer to treat that as an order from Division, and waste no more time." Ogilvie spoke harshly: in his view there had been an appalling slackness, a lack of proper vigilance on the part

34

of Fort Jamrud's garrison. He went on, "Murrum Khan . . . which way did he ride from here?"

"Along the track for Peshawar—"

"I didn't meet him."

"There's a pass to the south, the Rahkand Pass—"

"Yes. I shall ride along it, into Waziristan. The message to Peshawar quickly, please."

"You think there's a connection with Mrs Ogilvie?"

"I don't know, but I do know this: if she's got mixed up in *badal*, if she's going to drop between two factions looking for revenge for wrongs—or trying to avoid its results—then it's going to go hard for her and she's likely to be killed the moment British troops approach wherever she's being held." Ogilvie swung his horse and rode towards the Squadron Commander of his patrol; after they had had words Ogilvie and the Bengal Lancers turned away, back in the direction of Peshawar, and rode fast for the Rahkand. Ogilvie's heart was like lead: his words to the rifle subaltern had been only too true. *Badal* was always a killer, and was the one thing that precluded all attempts at reason. Angela could well become a helpless pawn in the dreadful game of *badal* . . .

* * *

The Royal Strathspey marched with their drums beating into the native city of Kohat, to be met by an Assistant Provost Marshal who directed them to the British encampment beyond the outskirts to the east. Awaiting them in camp was the familiar figure of Major Blaise-Willoughby of Lieutenant-General Fettleworth's divisional staff. With him on his shoulder, Dornoch saw, was his pet monkey, disrespectfully named Wolseley after the Army Commander-in-Chief in Whitehall. As Blaise-Willoughby approached in unmilitary fashion, Wolseley nibbled at a nut and scattered fragments of shell over Blaise-Willoughby's appallingly crumpled suit of *mufti*.

"What's in the air now, Blaise-Willoughby?"

"A smell of monkey, sir. Wolseley needs a bath—but I digress and apologise for it."

35

"For the smell?"

"For the mention of it, sir, in an ungentlemanly way. I suggest your battalion makes camp, and that we talk in privacy while they make it."

"With my second-in-command and my Adjutant."

"Oh, by all means," the Political Officer said in a distant voice, sounding put out. He stared at the other two officers, a touch of disdain noticeable. "Captain Black, isn't it?"

"Yes," Black answered shortly: he disliked monkeys and unsmart officers who had defected to the ranks of the Civilian establishment. "We have met, Major Blaise-Willoughby."

"Yes. And?" Blaise-Willoughby raised an eyebrow at the second-in-command.

"Major Lord Brora. It's not only your damn animal that needs a bath—so, by God, does that suit of yours!"

* * *

"Colour-Sar'nt MacTrease!" The Regimental Sergeant-Major's voice was a bellow that seemed to strike against the Waziri hills and come back in loud thunder. "A word in your ear, if you please."

MacTrease marched up smartly and stood at attention. "Sir!"

"You will have words with your company, Colour-Sar'nt, and tell them to modulate their voices when referring to the Divisional Political Officer."

"Aye, sir—"

"He is a *gentleman,* Colour-Sar'nt, even though he serves now in a Civilian capacity, *not* a whatever it was I overheard loud and clear. Mr Oscar Wilde is not a subject I wish to hear spoken of, do you understand?"

"Aye, sir, I do that."

"Very well, then." Cunningham relaxed a little. "I don't deny the accuracy, just the stressing of it in a loud voice. Major Blaise-Willoughby has a job to do and I for one wish him luck with it, bloody monkeys notwithstanding!"

"So do I, Sar'nt-Major—"

"*Sir* on parade, Colour-Sar'nt MacTrease, and we are on parade now, a parade to make camp. It will be done smartly. There are native units adjacent, and I will not be made a laughing stock before natives. Straight lines, Colour Mac-Trease, and dead even spaces—you'll pass the word round. I'll be checking distances myself, with the RQMS. Understood?"

"Aye, sir."

"Very well, then." Cunningham turned about smartly and marched off, back straight as a rod, free arm swinging from the shoulder. MacTrease stared after him thoughtfully: old Bosom was being unusually unfriendly. It was, MacTrease thought to himself, the atmosphere . . . the kidnap by thugs of a young lady with regimental connections was having its due effect on tempers and reactions. The regiment was a family in its own right; so, in a much larger sense, of course, was the Raj itself, and this sort of thing diminished the Raj and its power. That affected them all, from the Viceroy down to the newest joined recruit from the home depot . . . Mac-Trease shrugged, and marched away with his pace-stick to haze the section sergeants and junior NCOs, who in their turn would harry the poor suffering privates into precise tent placement. It wasn't only Bosom Cunningham who had the good name of the regiment at heart.

4

IT WAS AN unhappy conference, one that brought bad news for Lord Dornoch: Blaise-Willoughby reported that word had been received via the telegraph from Division of Ogilvie's contact with Fort Jamrud, of the entry into India of Murrum Khan—and of the fact that subsequently Ogilvie and his patrol of the Bengal Lancers had, apparently, vanished.

"Easily enough done," Dornoch said, frowning. "Why your seeming inference that harm's come to them?"

Blaise-Willoughby laughed and stroked Wolseley's hairy back. "Harm's easily done, too! But the facts are these: Captain Ogilvie was known to have the intention of entering the Rahkand Pass into Waziristan. When this news was to hand, General Fettleworth ordered out a regiment of cavalry with attached guns to ride to his assistance—"

"Had Ogilvie asked for this?"

"No, I gather not," the Political Officer said, "but we all know what Bloody Francis Fettleworth is like, I think. Can't resist a show of force . . . anyway, the cavalry found no sign of him right the way along the Rahkand or in the vicinity of the Waziristan end of the pass—"

"Understandable, surely?"

Blaise-Willoughby shrugged. "True, it's a big area, but Bloody Francis's reinforcements couldn't have been all that far behind Ogilvie, and there was one suspicious circumstance reported back to Division by a mounted runner: there was a cast shoe on the track inside the Rahkand."

There was no need for elaboration: no cavalryman, indeed no mounted infantryman who understood horses, would have ridden on in the circumstances. If the refitting of the shoe was impossible, the horse would have been walked all the way back to base if necessary; but no dismounted trooper had been seen.

"Man could have been intercepted by a Pathan and killed," Brora said.

"Yes, he could. I'm not saying positively that harm's come to Ogilvie's patrol."

"I take it," Dornoch said, "it's not because of the possibility that it has, that my orders have been changed?"

"Not directly. You're here—you've been as it were checked in your southward advance—to cover the Waziristan end of the Rahkand and parts adjacent and find Mrs Ogilvie."

"This is on account of the man Murrum Khan?"

"Correct, Colonel."

"I think you'd better tell me about him, Blaise-Willoughby, before we go any further."

"Right, I will." Settling Wolseley comfortably, the Political Officer proceeded with his exposition. Murrum Khan, who should undoubtedly have been apprehended before passing easterly of Fort Jamrud, was a man of great influence amongst the tribesmen, a stirrer of trouble wherever he went, a ruthless man dedicated to self-aggrandisement and to harassment of the Raj whenever he saw the chance. It was, Blaise-Willoughby declared, a certain wager that if he was not already the mainspring of the boundary trouble in the Mana area, then he would be seeing to it that he became such; Brigader-General Norris had been informed of the man's entry into India and of the inherent dangers. Murrum Khan, Blaise-Willoughby said, would in the process of thrusting his fingers into the pie add to his personal dimension in the esteem of the tribesmen of at any rate one of the opposing sides—and, if he could outwit and outmanoeuvre the Raj, possibly of both.

"And the outmanoeuvring's to come via Mrs Ogilvie?" Brora asked.

"It's very possible—indeed likely."

"Then it's a case of find this Murrum Khan, find the filly?"

Blaise-Willoughby's smile was enigmatic. "Never assume the native's simple, my dear Brora. There's no black and white out here—in a metaphorical sense, of course—"

39

"For God's sake," Brora snapped, "talk English! What's all that supposed to mean?"

"It means, if I must put everything into words of one syllable, that Murrum Khan's much too wily to be close to his hostage, if that's what the lady's to become, and frankly I'm working only on guesses so far. She'll be held somewhere distant, yet handy." Blaise-Willoughby waved an airy hand. "Your oyster's a large one, Brora. You haven't the world, but you have a sizeable chunk of Waziristan." He paused, eyeing Brora mischievously: the two were poles apart in character and approach, already full of mutual dislike. "I know you've not been long in India, my dear chap. You'll learn much in the next few weeks—"

"Not from you, at all events."

Blaise-Willoughby shrugged. "Be naive if you wish, it's not my funeral. I only try to help by attempting to instil a *soupçon* of guile into regimental officers—"

"Bosh! If an officer can't be forthright and honest, what does he become, what's he worth to an army in the field? Guile my arse." Lord Brora got to his feet, breathing hard. "I am Lord Brora. I insist on fighting clean. Guile's not for the field, it's for pimps' parlours. I wish you good-day—with your permission, Colonel, I have duties to attend to."

Dornoch, the twitchings of a smile playing about his mouth, nodded. "By all means, Major."

Brora turned for the tent-flap; as he bent to leave, the Political Officer, his face pale, spoke venomously. "I shall not forget your words, Lord Brora—"

"I am unrepentant."

"I have a long memory . . . like the elephant. I trust you enjoyed your sojourn with the Supply and Transport, Lord Brora?"

Brora straightened. His face had gone a deep red and his eyes bulged, bright blue anger signals flashing at the Political Officer; but he caught the warning stare from Dornoch and contained his temper with an effort. Without a word he turned away and thrust his large frame through the flap and out of the tent. He seethed away: the past was back with a vengeance, the recent humiliation when at Sir Iain Ogilvie's

40

instigation, no less, he had been temporarily seconded to the S & T, a damn lowly bunch, to superintend the journey of a contingent of elephants to the domains of the Rajah of Rangapore, a sop arranged by Captain Ogilvie to bring a rebel back within the Raj! It had been a shameful business and a direct result of his having done his duty in arraigning Captain Ogilvie before a General Court Martial that had had the crass stupidity to reject his charges almost out-of-hand... Lord Brora, smelling nepotism all the way, had suffered an appalling journey to Rangapore. As for Political Officers, they could give themselves fancy titles if they wished, but they were no more than damn spies in reality.

*   *   *

The cave-mouth was well hidden: across its entry stood a hefty boulder, screening the black hole from all passing sight but allowing the ingress and egress of persons prepared for a tight squeeze. Inside little light penetrated, and the air was foul. Immediately behind the boulder, just within the cave, a man stood guard with a curved dagger thrust into a cartridge belt and a bayonetted *jezail* sinister in the crook of his arm. Though he stood where he could get, as it were, first sniff of such air as came through, he seemed not to mind the stench too much. The stench would get worse, far worse: it came mostly from death. The cave was deep, running back into the hillside's rocky strata for more than a mile, penetrating far below the summit like the great system of caves and pot-holes beneath Ingleborough in the West Riding of Yorkshire; and there was much room in its cross-passages and extensively-opening caverns to house the dead as well as the living. A squadron of cavalry of the Indian Army consisted of three British officers, four Viceroy's Commissioned Officers, a hundred and ten native other ranks and seventy-two followers, with one hundred and eighteen riding horses, sixty pack mules and two riding camels. True, the special patrol that had been ambushed and heavily out-numbered in the Rahkand Pass had not been of such great

41

size: there had been no followers and no transport train attached, while the squadron itself had not been up to strength. Nevertheless, the knives and the *jezails* had been busy and all prisoners save the one had been despatched most expeditiously and the bodies of men and animals rolled down a slope that led to a wide surface hole connected to the main cave system. Reaching the bottom, they had been dragged by sweating Pathans with hooks and ropes into the side passages and caverns; what the sentry's nostrils picked up now was the smell of blood: soon the putrefaction would set in. But for now just blood, and the metal of the guns, which had been dismantled to seal the total disappearance of the British patrol and had been cast down the slope behind the corpses. All this, James Ogilvie knew: he had seen much of it and had heard the rest after he had been manhandled to the slope, tied hand and foot and lowered down the shaft on the end of a rope. Once down, he had been seized by four armed Pathans in stinking garments and carried to a recess at the side of the main passage where he was thrown down, still bound, to lie under guard of two men. The only sounds now were of their movements and voices as they exchanged occasional words of Pushtu but said nothing of any help to their prisoner.

Time passed: how long, Ogilvie could only guess. He lay in pain from wounds received and from the binding ropes that were drawn over-tight, in misery approaching despair as he went over and over the massacre, blaming himself, wondering how long it would take Bloody Francis in Nowshera to react to the non-return of his patrol.

*　　*　　*

At sundown that day Lieutenant-General Fettleworth was enjoying a *chota peg* in his private quarters with his Chief of Staff and complaining of the lack of news from all the various probes that he had ordered.

"Someone must have found something, Lakenham."

"There was the cast shoe, sir."

"Yes! I know. And then what? Damn silence, that's what!

What's become of the unit I ordered out to reinforce young Ogilvie?"

Lakenham stifled a sigh. "They were the ones who reported finding the cast shoe, sir."

"Ah, yes. And they were who?" '

"Probyn's Horse, sir."

"H'm." Fettleworth took a mouthful of whisky and lifted the glass to study the golden glow against the lamp on a table beside him. "Don't know what we'd do without the Scots, hey, Lakenham?"

"Fine regiments. . ."

"Well, yes, them—but I was referring to the whisky." Fettleworth frowned, and eased his stomach a little in the chair. "Talking of Scots regiments, what about Dornoch's lot?"

"I told you, sir, Blaise-Willoughby's spoken to Lord Dornoch—"

"Yes, so you did. Yes, indeed. Well, they're the right regiment in the right place at the right time—what? We can be sure they'll do their best—after all, the name of Ogilvie . . . d'you follow me?"

"I do, sir, but—"

"When I've the time, I'll write a memo on security of married quarters, *all* married quarters, not just the military. Remind me of that, Lakenham. Damn Civilians! Blasted inefficiency, losing that poor young woman—and just look at the hoo-ha it's put me to!" Fettleworth scratched his chin, lifting his face like a bulldog to do so. "Before long I'll have everyone on my back—the Commander-in-Chief, HE, Whitehall and the Prime Minister, even Her Majesty I dare say." Fettleworth turned as a bearer came in and made a low salaam. "What is it?"

"Dinner, General sahib."

Disregarding the native, Bloody Francis spoke again to his Chief of Staff. "Drink up, Lakenham, and we'll fill the inner man. I'm dashed hungry—*dashed* hungry! It's all the pressures, y'know. . ." He heaved himself to his feet and ushered Lakenham towards the dining-room. Conversation at dinner was limited: Fettleworth was ever a hearty trencherman, and his wife, who could normally be relied upon to entertain guests with chatter, was away, somewhat unseasonably to be sure, in Simla. Fettleworth concentrated therefore on the food and cleared his mind of the worries of command: he'd done what he could.

*　　*　　*

A man came at last to Ogilvie, a tall man though far from splendidly dressed. He stood in silence, smiling down, teeth very white in a dark, handsome face, clearly visible in the light from a lantern set on a pole beside Ogilvie's recess.

"Murrum Khan?" Ogilvie asked.

The man shook his head, his smile disappearing. "Not Murrum Khan, sahib. I am called Razjah Shah. But you shall tell me what you know of Murrum Khan."

"I know nothing of Murrum Khan beyond his name."

The smile came back. "Yet you ask if I am he. I am not a fool, sahib, nor am I a fat and slothful Hindu. I am a Pathan, a warrior. Our way is to strike, and strike hard as I have already done. If you do not speak of Murrum Khan, I shall strike again, and this time at you." From the folds of his garment he brought a long knife, and drew the end across Ogilvie's cheek, not deeply but enough to sting. "Now, sahib. Murrum Khan."

No harm, perhaps, would come of the truth. Ogilvie said, "He has ridden out of the Khyber, and is believed to have entered Waziristan."

"By way of the Rahkand Pass, and you were in pursuit of him?"

"Yes."

"Why, sahib?"

Ogilvie didn't answer. The Pathan's smile was still in place, and he shook his head slightly as he said, "I shall tell you: because you believe he knows the whereabouts of the Englishwoman, Ogilvie mem'sahib. The wife of your cousin of the boundary commission." He paused. "I see surprise in your face that I know your name, Ogilvie sahib, but you

44

must realise that men can talk, and some did so before they died."

"Under torture."

"Yes. War is war, Ogilvie sahib, and exists only to be won. Now I shall tell you more, which perhaps you do not know: Murrum Khan has not the woman in his own hands yet, but soon will have unless I can prevent the happening, the transfer—"

"You?"

"I, Ogilvie sahib."

"You are yourself friendly to the Raj?" Ogilvie asked, lifting a sardonic eyebrow.

The smile widened. "That you shall find out. So often events dictate our loyalties, for we are largely nomads, and must do as needs be at the time. More I shall not say, except this: soon now you will move from here, since this place may be known to Murrum Khan, who is no stranger to this side of the Afghan frontier."

He went away; the guards and the lantern remained, and after a while food was brought, and water, and Ogilvie's wrists were untied. While he ate the guards stood with their *jezails* pointed at head and stomach, the sharp ends of the rusty, snaky bayonets only inches from his nose. The food was scanty and the meal was soon finished and another period of silence and inactivity began, and once again Ogilvie's wrists were bound with the rope. He thought of Hector's wife: so far there were no clues but he had a feeling he was close now to learning more and that soon there might even be a contact with her; that gave hope. He wondered continually how Angela would be standing the strain of captivity and perhaps brutality. James Ogilvie had first met his cousin's wife in Simla, whilst on local leave at the hill station; though her father and his own father were old friends, Angela had been a child when James had last been at home at Corriecraig, and he had no recollection of a visit from her—a matter for regret, he had felt when Hector had arrived with her in Simla. She was friendly with everyone and was a favourite with the elderly officers to whom she seemed to bring back a touch of their youth: many gallantries had been accorded her. Yet, in spite of this and in spite of the propensity of Simla tongues to wag in gossip over even the most innocent of friendships, the ladies of the hill station had nothing but good to say of young Mrs Ogilvie, and this James considered a major triumph on Angela's part. Almost every other woman in Simla had had her reputation shredded by Mrs Colonel This and Mrs Major That: jealousy was Simla's watchword, and gossip the inevitable outcome of sheer boredom in a way of life in which there was no work whatsoever to be done. Angela had enjoyed her first experience of Simla, but James was certain that its new delights would fade quickly if she had to be there for long; Hector's duties, however, had taken him back to Calcutta and then on to Nowshera. James Ogilvie had missed Angela after she had left in the bullock cart for the railway junction at Kalka; and had somewhat moodily cut short his own leave and returned early to rejoin his regiment and expend some of his energies in polo and pig-sticking, envying his cousin his luck in the marriage stakes. There were few females of interest in Nowshera and Peshawar, or in Simla either: those bored, sharp-tongued military wives and their jolly daughters who almost knew more about their regiments than the husbands and fathers did . . . James, however devoted to the army, had no wish to marry it.

His thoughts of Angela were roughly interrupted when Razjah Shah returned, striding into the circle of light from the lantern. He said, "The time to move has come, Ogilvie sahib." He gave an order in Pushtu and the guards bent and hoisted Ogilvie to his feet, untying the ropes from around his ankles but leaving his wrists secured. A smelly but concealing goatskin coat was thrown over his uniform. The lantern was taken from the pole and Ogilvie was marched away down the main cave towards the entrance. Squeezing round the great boulder, he emerged into darkness to find more ready *jezails* with bayonets fixed.

A voice said in Pushtu, "Come, follow me." Urged on from the rear by the bayonets Ogilvie moved behind the man who had spoken. There was a cold wind; the night was icy. Through the darkness Ogilvie made out horses, some score of them waiting in a semi-circle around the boulder-hidden entry. Ogilvie was led to one of these horses and swung up into the saddle along with a rangy Pathan who put strong arms around him after tying a filthy rag in place as a gag. More Pathans mounted and then Razjah Shah emerged from the cave and swung himself into the last remaining saddle. He lifted an arm and called out, and the cavalcade got on the move through the night, descending swiftly to the track below and riding towards the south. The horses' hooves had been muffled and there was scarcely any sound, and no sign of life but for their own. Ogilvie sat helpless with his wrists still tied and the sinewy arms of the Pathan holding him close to a stinking body.

*　　*　　*

In the Kohat encampment, patrols of the Royal Strathspey had been detailed and had marched out by nightfall to scour the inward end of the Rahkand all the way from the Kohat Pass itself, leaving the Scots' lines depleted and too open to surprise attack for Lord Brora's liking. Blaise-Willoughby had left during the afternoon, remarking to the Colonel that he had matters to attend to in the city of Kohat.

"More spying, no doubt," Brora said that night in reference to the Political Officer's intentions.

"Bad blood doesn't help, Major," Dornoch said mildly.

"Nor does rudeness. Feller's a boor, a cad and a damn bounder. Within the hour he'll be rootling about in the brothels of Kohat like a pig in its sty."

"Live and let live, Major." Dornoch, his voice quiet and level still, raised a hand as Brora began to interrupt heatedly. "That is an order, and you'll do well to heed it. Do you understand me? Major Blaise-Willoughby has an important job to do and we must be of mutual help."

"Firmness is needed now, Colonel. Not guile and jiggery-pokery."

"Then how would you handle this?" Dornoch asked.

"Mount a counter-threat. Threaten somewhere—Kohat

47

city if you like—with the guns. Blow it to smithereens if Mrs Ogilvie's not handed back unharmed."

Dornoch smiled. "The idea's not without its attractions for me, Brora, I admit, but it would in fact be fatal and we must both recognise it—"

"Why so, Colonel?"

"Because the area's like tinder, that's why. We should light no sparks. To destroy—even to threaten to destroy—a native city that may have no connection with the kidnappers would cause the trouble to spread throughout India, far beyond—"

"Villages are laid waste from time to time, are they not?"

"Occasionally, yes, as part of a punitive expedition."

"Then it's simply a difference of scale."

"I disagree," Dornoch said. "Along the North-West Frontier the infrequent burning of a village is seen as an expected punishment for some specific act against the Raj. To shatter a town by gunfire before there has even been a death would be viewed quite differently—"

"But if that death should come, it will be too late!"

Dornoch spread his hands. "True. We must bank on it that the death won't come—we must wait, and keep our powder dry until more is known, and in the meantime search as diligently as we can. We must do nothing to make harder the High Commissioner's task, either—that's important."

"But the filly—"

"What happens or does not happen to Mrs Ogilvie is wholly dependent upon the fate of the boundary dispute, and that means the High Commissioner, Brora. Don't lose sight of that, and remember something else: India's changing— not fast, not much, but change is in the wind and some of it has settled on the land already. Our footing here has never been entirely sure since the Mutiny. The Political Officers today are possibly more germane to our problems than the soldiers are!"

Lord Brora made no reply but turned away rudely and pushed through the tent-flap into the darkness, thinking slanderous thoughts about such as Blaise-Willoughby. Sighing in frustration, Dornoch set about drafting orders for

48

the morrow, which was likely to be a repeat of today: patrols and more patrols, and very probably nil reports coming back when they marched in again. After a while the Colonel drew his watch from a pocket and threw down his notes. He went outside the tent and stood in silence as the bugler sounded Last Post. Then, a moment later, he heard the first wail as Pipe-Major Ross blew air into the bag beneath his arm, and squeezed. In accordance with regimental tradition, the Pipe-Major marked Lights Out with the gut-twisting strains of "The Flowers of the Forest". A lump came to Dornoch's throat as he listened. That same tune had been played by the regiment over the Heights of Abraham within sound of the closing ears of Wolfe; it had stolen over the bloodied battlefield of Waterloo. But it was Scotland that came back tonight to Dornoch, Scotland that he had not seen for many years; Scotland and the men of the 114th Highlanders who had fallen in action under his command throughout the long years of Indian service, men who would not march back again to the depot at Invermore when at last the regiment took the troopship for home. Sad thoughts and nostalgic ones: Dornoch was almost glad when the pipes had finished playing.

*   *   *

Into the smelly alleys of Kohat a man came furtively: slinking along by the running sore of the open drain, keeping in the shadows of the hovels as the moon's light stole down. He was thin as a rake and poorly clad for a cold night; the face was cadaverous, the nose hawk-like, the eyes piercing as they met the moonbeams now and again. The man carried no *jezail,* no firearms at all, but a knife was handy in the folds of his clothing and would be used if necessary. As he made his way along he heard regular footfalls and a clink of equipment and then, fortuitously, the moon lit upon marching men, and khaki, and Lee-Enfield rifles: a patrol from a British regiment, ensuring the peace of the native city—at any rate, on the surface of the public face. The man saw the entry to a cross-alley ahead, and moved for it swiftly and silently. Unseen, he dived down into obscurity, and the British soldiers moved on past, their sounds fading behind in the night. The man continued his journey, only to be impeded again: Kohat had its share of persons anxious to rob even those who appeared of little wealth. Those with wealth did not move around at night alone, and the choice of victim was thereby restricted, and even a poor man might possess an *anna* or two. The footpad struck swiftly from a black hole that passed for a doorway, but the hawk-nosed man was quicker. The knife came out and thrust upwards into the throat, and there was a gurgle and a fountain of life-blood, and the man pulled out the knife and moved on. The body fell in a heap, the head drooling into the open sewer, to lie there until the city's sweepers should be prevailed upon to remove it from human sight, and its stench from human nostrils. The hawk-nosed man vanished again into the shadows, and went by way of many alleys and cross-passages until he stopped by a thick wooden door bound with brass.

Here he knocked three times and waited, his eyes casting glances all around as though attack might come before he was admitted. The door was opened to him by Major Blaise-Willoughby.

5

"HOLD!"

Razjah Shah's voice was not loud but it carried back; his upraised hand was faintly seen, at any rate by the forward riders. The cavalcade halted, the breath of the horses steaming in the chill night air. They were on high ground and open to the wind. Ogilvie could make out nothing ahead but the scrub and rock of a barren land looming through the night. The leader rode back and faced his followers.

"It is below us now. I have seen lights. Here we part for a while." He spoke in Pushtu. "The British officer sahib comes with me and will be guarded by the three men as already told. The rest of you will ride on and take our horses with you."

No mention of where they were to ride to, no mention of what it was that lay below with lights: Ogilvie's guess was a native village, or perhaps a bandit camp. He found himself lifted down from the horse and set on his feet, once again with bayonets close. Figures loomed through the darkness: the leader spoke again, this time in English. "It is near to journey's end, Ogilvie sahib. There is to be no sound if you wish to live." The men moved closer with their *jezails* and Ogilvie was pushed ahead along a sloping track, and a moment later he saw what the tall man had seen: lights below, just a handful of them but widely scattered: the place they were coming to was clearly bigger than a mere camp. More than the lights he could not see: there was no moon now. Heavy cloud lay across the sky, moving fast before the wind but being backed up by more rolling cloud out of the north.

The downward journey was taken carefully, with hands holding fast to the prisoner. As the ground levelled out they

51

came to some isolated hovels; they went on past these and began to enter what seemed to be a small town nestling behind its walls at the foot of the mountain range, a small valley community. Here the wind was less, but the air as cold with a hint of snow to come out of the wind blowing across the peaks from the foothills of Himalaya. The men moved swiftly, like fleeting shadows, deeper into the town; at the corner of an alley a man met them.

"Come. . ."

He turned away and was followed. At the end of the alley was a crumbling building, its windows gaping, its stone broken and jagged, a staircase bare to the elements. The party was led into this semi-ruin, tramping through dust and debris and decay. The disturbance brought fragments down like rain, with larger pieces of masonry that fortunately fell free of the intruders but made noise enough to waken the dead, Ogilvie thought. In a place that had been a room the guide stopped in the darkness and swept debris aside with his foot until a square had been cleared and a trap-door lay revealed. The foot tapped twice, then once, then twice more: the trap-door swung open on a counter-balancing weight, and steps were seen.

"Down, Ogilvie sahib."

Ogilvie obeyed; all the men came down behind him except the guide; when the trap-door had been shut his feet were heard again, scuffing the concealing debris back into place.

*   *   *

In the Kohat morning, after the Union Flag had been hoisted to the flagstaff and the colour guard marched away with the pipes and drums, Major Blaise-Willoughby and Wolseley the monkey rode out again from the city and, passing the guard tent to the salutes of the sentries, were met by Lord Brora, who was on a tour of inspection of the regimental lines.

"Ah, Lord Brora. A very good morning to you."

Brora looked the Political Officer up and down. "I trust

you've come from your damn spying to apologise for your remark of yesterday?"

"No."

"It was in filthy taste," Brora stormed, his face red, "and I *demand* an apology. If I don't get it, I shall make representations to Division and have you damn well recalled out of my sight!"

Blaise-Willoughby smiled and shifted Wolseley to a more comfortable position on his shoulder. "How will you do that, I wonder?"

"Via the telegraph from Kohat, of course."

Blaise-Willoughby's eyes narrowed. "To use my name on the telegraph would be foolish, but I believe you're fool enough to do it all the same. As for me, I have my duty to consider. You have my apology, as abject as you'd like."

"And for your remarks just uttered."

"And for my remarks just uttered. Where's your Colonel?"

"In his tent."

"Thank you."

The Political Officer rode on, wearing an expression that Brora considered supercilious and impertinent. At Dornoch's tent Blaise-Willoughby dismounted and took off his hat to the sentry's salute. Hearing sounds, the Colonel put his head from the flap and once again Blaise-Willoughby removed his hat.

"Good morning, Colonel. I come with tidings."

"Do you indeed. Come inside."

Blaise-Willoughby entered and was bidden to a canvas camp stool. Dornoch asked crisply, "Well?"

"Last night," Blaise-Willoughby said, "a man came to me. As a matter of fact, I was expecting him—if not his news."

"A native?"

"One who passes as such," Blaise-Willoughby answered obliquely. "I prefer his identity to remain with me."

"Your privilege, Major."

Blaise-Willoughby leaned forward and spoke quietly. "This man has been in the field—in the field in *my* terms, that is—for some weeks past. He's learned some interesting facts, Colonel. He has learned that a bandit by name Razjah Shah is concerned in the boundary dispute around Mana. More recently, in fact only yesterday, he learned that your Captain Ogilvie and his cavalry patrol had been ambushed and taken by this man Razjah Shah—I hasten to add that Ogilvie is alive and kicking. I'm sorry to add that his patrol was slaughtered to a man after the ambush."

"Good God!" Dornoch's face had whitened beneath its sunburn. "What . . . where is Ogilvie being held, Blaise-Willoughby, do you know that?"

"No. Only where he *was,* as last known by my man. He was to be moved. My man didn't know where to."

"No clues?"

Blaise-Willoughby shook his head. "I'm afraid not, Colonel. Frankly, I can't even make a guess. Waziristan's an easy enough place to vanish in—as don't we all know! However, I'm able to make certain conjectures in the broad sense."

"Well?"

"This bandit, Razjah Shah, is known to the Political Department and so, of course, is Murrum Khan. Now, Razjah Shah, although a Pathan as is Murrum Khan, is of the Mahsud tribe. Murrum Khan is an Afridi." Blaise-Willoughby paused. "You follow, I think, Colonel?"

"Indeed I do. Murrum Khan and Razjah Shah are on opposing sides of the boundary fence—of the current dispute? Is this the fact?"

"Yes," Blaise-Willoughby answered. "And more than that: if Murrum Khan has a hostage in the form of Mrs Ogilvie, then so now has Razjah Shah in the form of her husband's cousin! And I don't like it one little bit. Young Ogilvie and the girl are going to be somewhat nastily played off against each other as counters, I fear . . . and somewhere in between is the greater consideration of the security of the Raj."

Dornoch, who was lighting his pipe, looked sharply over the bowl. "Do I understand you right, Blaise-Willoughby?"

"I fear so, yes. There must never be a breach . . . the administration can never allow any thin ends of wedges, Colonel, such that could become levers."

"I'd prefer plain language, if you please, Blaise-Willoughby."

"Very well, Colonel." The Political Officer got to his feet. "The considerations of the Raj must come first. You'll not disagree with that, I know. Unless a double rescue can be brought off, it may become necessary for one or other of the parties to be—"

"To be left to it?"

"To make a sacrifice, Colonel. Even both of them. I'm sorry." Blaise-Willoughby put a steadying hand on Wolseley's rump. "I shall be making my report to Division at Nowshera, and no doubt there'll be a reaction from General Fettleworth. Good-day to you, Colonel."

Blaise-Willoughby left the tent; Dornoch listened to the hoofbeats as man and monkey rode away towards Kohat. Dornoch felt a shake in his hands; Blaise-Willoughby was a cold-blooded man, as cold as a fish, and a schemer . . . but that was not fair, of course. Political officers had to be schemers, to be such was part and parcel of their trade, a trade that Dornoch in fact liked as little as did Brora. Of course the Raj must come first: that was why they were all in India. Ogilvie would realise that as well as anyone else, and would make no complaint about it, but the young woman was in a different category. And Bloody Francis Fettleworth? What would be that reaction when it came? Dornoch believed he could sum it up in advance: it would follow precisely along the lines of Blaise-Willoughby's recent utterance. But of one thing Dornoch felt positive: Fettleworth would still use every endeavour to get the woman at least to safety, and if he failed he would mount the biggest punitive expedition ever seen upon the Frontier—for what that would be worth after the event.

Dornoch left his tent and stood looking along the precisely-spaced regimental lines, at parties of men going about their work at the ammunition and supply train, at men cleaning rifles, at the Farrier-Sergeant and his section tending the hooves of horses and mules, re-shoeing where necessary, while the menial tasks that in military stations in white countries would be performed by fatigue parties were carried out by the lowly natives of the camp followers. A peaceful, workaday scene, with a wintry sun shining down from a clear sky to bring a touch of warmth to the northern chill. But all around stood India, the immensity of the great sub-continent brooding in its age-old silence, brooding as though biding its time... Blaise-Willoughby was right! Dornoch's own words to Brora came back to him starkly: India was changing, and no person would be more aware of that than the officers of the Political Department whose ears were ever to the ground. New ideas were stirring, new faces of native power were emerging with clamouring voices, voices that spoke in the bazaars and in the hills against the British Raj and to whom each small victory would be manna from heaven. Certainly no breach must come! The integrity of the Raj must stand four-square or it would go piecemeal.

Dornoch braced his shoulders and turned to his native runner, standing obsequiously by the sentry. "Go to the Adjutant sahib speedily. I wish all officers and the Regimental Sergeant-Major sahib to attend outside my tent."

*   *   *

The word spread fast after the conference: Dornoch had given no orders that it should not, and in fact preferred his men to know the facts rather than be misled by rumour. The mood of the Scots was grim and determined; James Ogilvie was a well-liked officer and this business had now come even closer home. Vengeance was firmly in the air, and the opinion was freely expressed that Northern Army Command in Murree should draft in more troops and saturate the whole area. More cautious voices suggested the truth: that Waziristan was much too vast a territory for even the total strength of the combined Murree and Ootacamund commands to cover in such a way that every hole, every crevice and every town hide-out could be found and searched. The natives were as ever wily, and would contrive to keep one jump ahead. Wiliness was better met by wiliness, a task that no regiment was equipped to carry out; which put the matter firmly in the hands of the Political Department, whom not a man amongst the Scots trusted. They were a dodgy, lot, and too clever by half, and had opted for the Political as being a softer billet than the field and the cantonment.

In the meantime the patrols continued, fresh ones going out as tired men marched or rode in with their nil reports.

*　　*　　*

In the cellar below the derelict building there were three apartments, damp and dirty and smelling of all manner of unpleasantness. In one sat three Pathans with knives and *jezails,* and a crone, as old as the surrounding hills, dressed in black that was green with an age that came close to rivalling her own tally of years. Her face was seamed, the eyes coal-black and bright in the beams that struggled through the oily fumes from a lamp set on a chair. She sat against the wall like a carven image of Methuselah, her bottom on the damp bare earth, seeming scarcely even to breathe. In the next apartment were heaps of sacking that did duty as makeshift beds, also set on the bare earth, and a young woman, modestly veiled, with a baby in her arms being gently rocked and crooned to sleep. It was to the third apartment that Ogilvie had been taken; still with his wrists tied behind his back but the goatskin garment now removed, he looked around in the flickers of a kind of Aladdin's lamp, a wick in a boat-shaped vessel containing tallow. The apartment was quite large, and in the centre was sunk a pit the bottom of which he could not see from where he stood. Over the pit a beam ran, just below the ceiling, and on this beam was rigged a runner with a pulley and hook dangling from it. As Ogilvie waited at knife-point the pulley was hauled along the runner, a rope was placed around his chest and pulled taut under his bound arms, the slack was taken up by two of his escort, and he rose in the air. He was then pushed along the runner until he was positioned over the pit.

Then the lamp was brought closer and set in a niche in the wall close to the pit. Ogilvie looked down: at first he could see nothing but thick blackness. The pit was deep. Then he made out smooth sides, sides with no purchase anywhere—they could almost have been of polished rock. Razjah Shah lifted the lamp from its niche and held it over the lip of the pit.

"Look," he commanded.

Ogilvie looked downward again. He could hear a curious rustling now and could begin to see something heaving and undulating: snakes, very many of them, small but no doubt deadly, writhing, some of them attempting to climb the smooth sides, and failing, and dropping back, and trying again. This was not an unusual ploy of the Frontier tribes but it was nonetheless scarifying for that. Ogilvie clamped his teeth, and felt a horrible crawling in his flesh.

Razjah Shah smiled, his teeth shining in the lamplight. "It is my hope you will not become their meal, Ogilvie sahib. Such would be an ungallant ending for an officer of the great Queen-Empress." He gestured to the two tribesmen on the end of the rope; Ogilvie was lowered until his head was below the rim of the pit, and then the rope's-end was turned up around the beam and secured. Restless sounds came from below, louder and closer now, and stench arose. It was warm in the pit. Fear of the revolting gripped Ogilvie. His throat went dry, his tongue seemed to swell in his mouth. As if from a great distance above him the voice of Razjah Shah came again: "Ogilvie sahib, here you shall remain until my negotiations are finished. If success comes, you will be free to live and to rejoin the Raj. If there is no success, you remain. Before we leave this place, the rope will be cut, and you will fall to the snakes."

When the voice stopped, sounds of departure came down followed by the slam of a heavy door and then the creak of locks and bolts. The light remained to flicker in its oily fumes from the niche in the wall.

*   *   *

The night's calm broke under the impacting clamour of horse's hooves moving at the gallop: in the Royal

58

Strathspeys' camp the Sergeant of the Guard ran full belt towards the sound as a shout came from the picquet on outpost duty. The sergeant himself made the challenge.

"Halt!" His voice carried strongly; the hoofbeats slowed and stopped in the darkness.

"Who comes there?"

"Friend!" It was a breathless, urgent shout.

"Advance, friend, and be recognised."

Two men rode forward, tattered men whose uniforms were dark with sweat as they came under the light from the guard lantern held aloft by the sergeant: the uniforms of the Raj on native bodies, a lance-*duffardar* and a *sowar* of the Guides. Up behind the sergeant came the Regimental Sergeant-Major as the camp began to stir.

"Sar'nt Anderson, what have we here?" Mr Cunningham turned to the lance-*duffardar*. "Let's have it quickly."

"Yes, Sergeant-Major sahib. We come from the brigade that is marching on Mana, sahib. There has been very heavy attack . . . we are the only men remaining of the squadron, which was destroyed when great shells exploded in our midst, sahib." The man's eyes were still wide with shock. "The position is most serious, sahib, and the Brigadier-General sahib wishes reinforcements speedily."

The Regimental Sergeant-Major gave a brisk nod. "You'll come with me at once to the Adjutant, the both of you. Carry on, if you please, Sar'nt Anderson." He turned and saluted as the Subaltern of the Day came up at the double; he reported what had happened. "Will you deal with it, sir, or shall I?"

"You took the report, Mr Cunningham, so I'll leave it to you while I check the outposts."

"Sir!" Cunningham saluted again, then raised his voice. "All you men, there, back to your tents and get some sleep. It'll maybe turn out the last you'll get for a while." Marching smartly to the Adjutant's tent, he shouted Black to wakefulness.

"What is it, Mr Cunningham, for heaven's sake—"

"Begging your pardon, Captain Black, sir. We must go immediately to the Colonel." Cunningham explained briefly, and Black grumbled himself to his feet and pulled on shirt and trews, tunic and boots. When awakened in his turn, the Colonel's response to the lance-*duffardar's* full report was fast.

"A message to Division via the telegraph at Kohat, Captain Black. You'd better ride yourself—and report also that I must wait for my extended patrols to come in before I move. Mr Cunningham, see the men from the Guides are examined by Dr Corton and then fed and bedded down till morning."

"Sir!"

"Warn all companies at first muster, to prepare to move out if so ordered by Division. And my runner to Lord Brora. I'd like words with him at once." Dornoch had scarcely finished when the tent-flap was thrust aside and the Major entered, hair tousled and an open dressing-gown flapping about his large body. The RSM left the tent with Black and the two cavalrymen and Dornoch said, "Bad tidings, Major. The column's been cut up en route for Mana. Among other things, they're left with no cavalry."

"And we're wanted as infantry replacements? That's—"

"As reinforcements in the action. The Brigadier-General's holding on."

Brora stared. "Then had we not better get on with it at once?"

"Not until the patrols are in, and I think not until we're ordered out by Division."

"You mean we sit on our arses while a British brigade's cut to pieces?" Brora's voice was loud and angry. "Balls to that for a start, Colonel! I'll not have it said that the 114th refused to fight!"

"There is no refusal to fight and I object most strongly to your insinuations. I shall not march without my patrols, which leave me currently with so little strength as to render me useless to any brigade—"

"You—"

"And I have to remember our priority orders, which were to extend patrols to locate and rescue Mrs Ogilvie." Dornoch was white with anger. "You will hold your tongue from now on, Major, or you will be relieved of your duties as my

60

second-in-command and held in arrest in Kohat while we march out—if that is what we're ordered to do. Do I make myself quite plain, Major?"

Brora's face suffused, but he held his tongue. Swirling his dressing-gown, he turned and stormed out of the Colonel's tent. For a moment Dornoch put his head in his hands; to be up against one's second-in-command was a devilish trying experience and one that was of no help to discipline or the conduct of a regiment in the field. Then he stiffened; difficult subordinates were part and parcel of the tribulations of command and had to be accepted as such, and no man among his Scots was in any doubt as to who commanded the regiment.

*　　*　　*

Andrew Black waited in Kohat while Dornoch's message was transmitted to Division, waited while Bloody Francis Fettleworth was awakened from his slumbers and pulled his thoughts together and sent post-haste for his ADC and Chief of Staff. Waiting, Black dozed. When he was roused with the Divisional Commander's reply the dawn was breaking. Black mounted and galloped back to camp, where he handed Fettleworth's orders to Lord Dornoch. Those orders held a touch of not unprecedented ambiguity: on the one hand Lord Dornoch was told to march to the assistance of Brigadier-General Norris as soon as he had re-mustered his patrols, and was to attempt to rendezvous with the 2nd Border Regiment who had already reached Kajuri Kach on the Gomal River en route for Mana; their Colonel would be contacted by the field telegraph laid from Dera Ismail Khan—if it had not been cut by the men of the tribes—and ordered to deviate and force-march north towards the map reference of Norris's brigade. So far, so good and clear: but Fettleworth thereafter was covering himself nicely and in effect contradicting his own orders: Lord Dornoch was to bear in mind that the withdrawal of his regiment would leave an important part of Waziristan uncovered in regard to the search, which was also an urgent matter. Units currently in

61

the Nowshera district could not be spared as replacements. Dornoch was to use his discretion and act as he thought best after taking into account all the circumstances. There was an informative footnote to Fettleworth's orders: as of the time of origin of his message, there had been no approach made by any persons who might have either Mrs Ogilvie or Captain Ogilvie in their hands.

6

ONE WAY OF complying with Fettleworth's ambiguous orders
would be to march out towards Brigadier-General Norris
whilst at the same time leaving enough men behind to
maintain patrols on a skeleton basis; this Lord Dornoch
rejected the moment it came into his mind. To march on
relief with a depleted battalion, to go against what he had
himself said to Brora during the night, would be to fail the
Brigadier-General and also to leave no backbone for the
patrols should they come back to camp with information
that would need following up. To split one's force was, to say
the least, inadvisable and would serve neither objective
properly. Dornoch made up his mind speedily: he would
obey the first part of the orders, and march. To allow a
British brigade, and even worse the High Commissioner, to
be cut up by rebels would most certainly set the Frontier
alight in the present situation. But even as he made the
decision in his mind, he was uncomfortably aware that he
might to some extent have allowed Lord Brora's insubor-
dinate remarks to affect his judgment. He faced the Major
squarely as he gave his orders.

"We shall move out, gentlemen. When the last of the
patrols reports back, they are to be given a meal and allowed
one hour's rest. Then the battalion will be paraded in
marching order and formed into column of route." He pulled
out his watch and addressed the Adjutant. "I shall speak to
all officers and senior NCOs in ten minutes' time, Captain
Black."

* * *

Ogilvie's chest was sore from the rope's pressure as he

hung over the pit, waiting helplessly. Above him in its niche, the oil lamp flickered, casting yellow light that penetrated a little way down the walls of the pit, just enough for its loom to show the ever-moving surface of the horror below, the undulations as the snakes heaved and twisted and reared their scaly heads. After a while the light dimmed, gave a few hiccoughing flickers, and died.

The darkness made Ogilvie's flesh creep, as though the snakes were already upon him. He was enveloped in their curious smell, like a smell of death and decay and corruption. It was all he could do not to cry out; he clamped his teeth and sweated. After a long, long time as it seemed, he heard the sound of the door's bolts and lock, and it opened, and light stole in behind it. It remained open and he heard footsteps retreating and a minute later returning. More light came in: above him the oil lamp was lifted and oil was poured in and it was re-lit. Bending his head backwards he was able to make out a figure, and then he heard a creaking noise and found his body moving slowly upwards, inch by inch: he was being wound in by a handle, as though he were a bucket down a well. When his head came level with the lip of the hole, he saw the young veiled girl whom he had noticed on his first arrival. He could see little of her features, but was aware of a slim body behind the voluminous garment she wore.

In Pushtu she said, "Food, sahib. Eat."

"How?" he asked.

"I shall feed you." She squatted by the edge, and he saw the bowl in her hands. With slim brown fingers she picked out meat—chicken, it tasted like, with rice which she crammed into his mouth. Then she turned aside and reached for a pitcher, and poured water into her cupped hand and tilted it towards his mouth, and he drank, one handful after another, gratefully.

"You have had enough, sahib?"

"Yes, thank you. How long have I been here?"

"I do not know, sahib."

"And Razjah Shah—when will he return?"

"This also I do not know."

"Do you know where he has gone?"

"No, sahib, this I do not know."

Like hell you don't, he thought. He tried once more. "The English mem'sahib . . . do you know where she is?"

"I know of no English mem'sahib." The girl got to her feet with a swift, graceful movement. "Now I go."

*　　*　　*

By devious ways Razjah Shah had entered Thal on the Kurrum River and had gone alone to the house of a kinsman on his mother's father's side. This kinsman, a small, dark man with glittering eyes, knew well enough why he had come and wasted no time.

"You seek the woman, cousin, the mem'sahib from Nowshera."

"Yes. Do you know where she is?"

There was a shrug of indifference. "It is possible. There have been rumours."

"Of Murrum Khan?"

The eyes flickered, and discoloured teeth showed in the lamplight. "Of Murrum Khan, unloved of Allah."

"And of me also. And of you."

"Yes. Praise be to Allah."

"Praise be to Allah." Razjah Shah bowed his head in reverence. "Where is Murrum Khan, cousin?"

A dreamy look came into the glittering eyes, and for a moment they shifted away while the thin shoulders shrugged: Razjah Shah recognised the signs easily enough. The small man said apologetically. "In Waziristan is much poverty, also hunger. Not enough crops, not enough goats. I have much need of a hundred goats, cousin."

"A hundred goats?" Razjah Shah laughed, a sound of scorn. "Never have I heard such a thing! You are my mother's father's nephew . . . one's kin does not make demands such as this, cousin."

"Yet there is the need, cousin. I am sorry."

"I cannot spare a hundred goats."

"You are a rich man, cousin. Your kin suffers much poverty and deprivation—"

"Because of the British, not because of me."

"Because of the British, yes, this is so. Yet there is talk of possible happenings at Mana, and I believe you to be concerned. If matters go as you wish, you will become a richer man." A touch of steel had crept into the tone. "Without your help, your kin in Thal will grow poorer."

Razjah Shah made an impatient gesture. "Very well. Forty goats."

Hands were raised to Allah. "Forty goats!"

"Some in kid."

"Cousin, forty goats is far from enough even if all were in kid."

"Fifty goats..."

A compromise was reached at sixty goats with ten nannies guaranteed to be in kid, delivery to be made after Razjah Shah had satisfied himself that Murrum Khan was indeed at the place yet to be revealed by his kinsman. "Now, cousin: where is Murrum Khan?"

"Murrum Khan is to be found in a disused fort belonging to the Raj... one mile north-east of the village of Takki, which is—"

"Takki I know, and the fort. Murrum Khan is both daring and brazen, to make such use of a British fort!"

"The British go there no longer, cousin."

"Even so..." Razjah Shah stood up and laid a hand on the haft of his dagger. "May Allah look with favour upon you, cousin. You have been helpful and I shall not forget."

The small man bowed his head meekly. "More help will come, more information if there are more goats ... word of the movement of British soldiers..."

After further satisfactory haggling, Razjah Shah rode out of Thal and outside the town he rendezvous-ed with his followers. Takki, which was some forty miles due north of Mana, was no more than twenty miles west of Thal and could be quickly reached, though not before the dawn. Razjah Shah deemed it more prudent to approach the fort during the hours of darkness and made his plans accordingly. For now it was back to the cellar; and at the next night-fall he would ride for Takki.

* * *

Sweat poured from Ogilvie as he became aware of a shift in his position: his midriff, as he had seen when looking down, had moved just a little relative to the slant of the oil lamp's beam. A little more of himself was outside the direct rays.

He was very slightly lower, very slightly closer to the probing horror below.

There was only one conclusion: the rope was tending to stretch under the continuing pull of his weight. Either that, or it had been damp and now was dry. His sweat blinded him, running into his eyes. He called out loudly: they would not want him to die yet, his potential use was in being still. No one came: the pit itself held down his shouts and muffled them. There was increased movement below, an extra surge, he believed, in the hideous undulations. Very gradually the lamp's shadow moved up his body: the skirt of his tunic could be seen no longer now. He bent his knees, lifting his feet clear, and held his posture while he shouted again and again, and no one came through the locked and bolted door. Minutes passed, his legs grew heavy... heavier until he could hold them up no more and the muscles relaxed in instinctive desire to ease the agony. As his body swayed a little on the rope he felt the scrape of his feet across moving things, and a dry sound of rustling, and something fell across his boots.

He screamed: and then lost consciousness.

* * *

The regiment had moved out of camp as ordered, towards the map reference as indicated by the lance-*duffardar* from the Guides. This reference put Norris's brigade in a mountain pass about half-way between Kohat and Bannu—thirty miles approximately of appalling terrain south-west from the encampment. With forced marching Dornoch reckoned he could arrive by noon the following day; but, as he remarked to the Major as they rode together in the van, he would arrive with exhausted troops that might be little succour to a heavily engaged brigade.

"They're Scots, Colonel."

A frown passed across Dornoch's face. "I'm well aware of that. Even Scots can tire."

"Not when brought alive by the pipes."

Dornoch made no response: there was, in fact, a good deal of truth in Brora's dogmatic-sounding statement. The pipes often enough wrought miracles, but Dornoch failed on this occasion to see them as sufficient to rally men dog tired from slogging all night and next morning through the rocky passes. If he was to arrive even as late in the day—and in the engagement—as noon, there would be scant time for rest en route, and horses as well as men needed rest. . .

Brora spoke again. "Colonel, have I your permission to speak to the company commanders personally?"

"To what end, Major?"

Brora blew out his cheeks. "To what *end,* my dear sir? Why, to ensure the men put their best foot forward and that there are no damn slackers and drop-outs—*that's* what end!"

"Then it's not necessary—"

"But—"

"They know the facts. They don't need to be reminded, Major. I'll not have them hazed."

"Colonel—"

"Save your breath for the ride, Brora. I have first-class men and the best NCOs in the British Army, under the best Sar'nt-Major. Hazeing is not officers' work, Brora. Mr Cunningham can be relied upon to do all that's necessary."

"So you do not give your permission?"

"No."

"Then," Brora snapped, "upon your head be it, if we fail to reach Brigadier-General Norris in time!"

Dornoch turned and stared at the Major. "I am the Colonel," he said simply. "Everything's upon my head, is it not?" For a moment Brora met his eye, then turned angrily aside, blowing through his drooping moustache, and rode on in silence. Dornoch felt immensely depressed and even felt dislike for his own class. Money and privilege . . . not a poor man himself, his wealth could not bear comparison with Brora's. Perhaps there was something wrong with the system after all . . . whilst the possession of wealth made for independence of spirit, which in itself was no bad thing and prevented a weak toadyism sullying the army, it could work the other way also, which was a bad thing when it came to officers like Brora who were impetuous and in Brora's case too often stupid in addition. Private means could be a two-edged sword, breeding arrogance as well as independence. Dornoch sighed; it had to be borne and for the sake of the regiment his hand upon the Major would need to be firm when they came to action. The Colonel's thoughts moved on: a lot would depend upon the Border Regiment, the men from Carlisle and England's north-west corner already on the march to Mana from Dera Ismail Khan. If the diversionary order from Division had failed, as fail it easily could, to reach them and deflect them northwards, then the Royal Strathspey must needs go in alone and the casualties must be heavy. In the meantime, however, there were heartening sounds coming from the marching Scots behind as in the last of the daylight their voices were lifted in song.

*　　*　　*

Opening his eyes, Ogilvie found himself lying on his back beside the pit, free now of the rope from which he had hung. Faces peered down, among them Razjah Shah's. There was a smell of gunsmoke, and there was some pain and blood, as though a bullet had grazed his right thigh, as in fact was the case.

"We were just in time, Ogilvie sahib," Razjah Shah said. "I myself shot the snake that had climbed, then you were at once hauled up. One more minute, perhaps . . . that would have been sad."

"Indeed it would," Ogilvie said sourly. "You, no doubt, would have wept like a woman over the loss?"

69

The native smiled. "You are brave enough, which is a thing I admire. No, I would not have wept, though I might well have thrown my watchmen to the snakes for not being wakeful, since I assume you would have called for help when the rope stretched."

"I did."

"But now all is well for you."

"For how long?"

"That shall be your decision, Ogilvie sahib. The snakes wait still." Razjah Shah squatted beside Ogilvie. "I seek your help. I believe you will give it . . . not only because of the snakes that wait."

"Then why?" Ogilvie attempted to sit up, but was pushed flat by one of the men. A knife was brought out and held with the point towards his throat.

"You will wish to assist the Raj, Ogilvie sahib."

Ogilvie laughed. "As you yourself do, Razjah Shah?"

"Perhaps so, perhaps not. Or perhaps this: for certain purposes the welfare of the British Raj runs parallel with my own. Do you understand, Ogilvie sahib?"

Ogilvie narrowed his eyes, staring thoughtfully at the native leader. "It's possible, Razjah Shah. Do you refer to Murrum Khan and—"

"And the mem'sahib, the wife of your cousin—yes, that is so. I know where Murrum Khan is hidden, and the mem'sahib will be with Murrum Khan. Progress has been made, and with your help more can be made."

Ogilvie asked, "Is the mem'sahib alive, Razjah Shah?"

"I have not heard otherwise. Why do you ask?"

"Because I have been told that *badal* is involved in the boundary dispute, that Murrum Khan seeks revenge for an elder brother killed by the father of Dostman Khan who is behind the Mana dispute. This you knew?"

Razjah Shah nodded. "All this I knew. Why should the mem'sahib suffer on account of the father of Dostman Khan?"

"When *badal* is involved, as of course you know, many die. Many become involved who were not involved in the first place. Dostman Khan will know by now that Murrum

70

Khan is in Waziristan and seeks vengeance. Dostman Khan will protect himself. Does your information say if there has been any attack upon Murrum Khan?"

"It says nothing of that, Ogilvie sahib, but I realise that there is much truth in your words. It is partly because this is so, that there must be no delay."

"You intend to attack yourself, Razjah Shah?"

"Yes—"

"And take over the mem'sahib?"

"Yes. I understand your quandary, Ogilvie sahib, but the mem'sahib will fare no worse with me than with Murrum Khan and will be protected from *badal*. I ask you to show me your trust."

Again Ogilvie laughed. "Why should I do that, Razjah Shah?"

"Because you have no alternative. Think, and you will realise. The snakes wait . . . and the mem'sahib is in more danger where she is than if she were here."

"And the snakes?"

Razjah Shah seemed to understand. He met Ogilvie's eye steadily and his tone was solemn when he went on, "She will not go to the snakes. You have my word, this I swear upon the Prophet and upon the souls of my fathers. I shall make a bargain with you, Ogilvie sahib. Do you wish to hear?"

"Go on."

Razjah Shah got to his feet and stood looking down at Ogilvie. "When the mem'sahib is in my hands and has been brought here, an exchange will be made. For her—you! The mem'sahib will be escorted in safety to the track running from Fort Jamrud to Peshawar, and left to ride in peace to your British garrison. You shall remain as my hostage—and the teeth of Murrum Khan will be drawn. Are you agreeable to this?"

There could be only one answer; Ogilvie nodded. He believed that in this at all events Razjah Shah could be trusted. The advantages to the native of depriving Murrum Khan of his bargaining power vis-à-vis the Raj were clear and obvious, and there was another point that Razjah Shah had not mentioned: the release of Angela Ogilvie would go much in his favour when the Raj came to consider the distribution of land should new boundaries be agreed in the district of Mana. Ogilvie said, "You asked my help, Razjah Shah. Have you more to ask?"

"I have. Let us go more comfortably to consider this." Razjah Shah gestured to his followers. They moved back, and Razjah Shah himself assisted Ogilvie to his feet, and they went through the door, away from the horrors of the pit, into the adjoining room where chairs were set. Razjah Shah faced Ogilvie across a table. He said, "I have been given certain tidings of your British soldiers, Ogilvie sahib. Do you wish to hear?"

"Yes."

"Between this place and Mana there is an engagement of a British brigade of foot-soldiers and cavalry and the forces of Dostman Khan. With this brigade is your High Commissioner. The battle has not gone well for the Raj, and from Kohat is being sent a battalion of the men in skirts, the men who fight like devils. It is possible that these men are of your own regiment, Ogilvie sahib. So much I know or conjecture. It is necessary that I know more, since Murrum Khan may move to a new hiding-place if the troops of either the Raj or of Dostman Khan should threaten to come too close. In that would lie continuing danger for the mem'sahib, and for my own future plans. You understand?"

"What is it you ask of me, Razjah Shah?"

"Your knowledge of the dispositions of the Raj, Ogilvie sahib. As accurately as possible. . . I must know the places beside Kohat whence reinforcements may be sent for your High Commissioner, also the strength of forces in your garrisons in Waziristan, and the likely tracks along which your patrols will be operating. If you do not know all this in detail, you as a soldier will be able to make estimates. Such will be of help."

"To free my cousin's wife from Murrum Khan?" Ogilvie's tone was sardonic.

"That is so."

"I think you take a sledgehammer to crack a nut, Razjah Shah! The men of the tribes such as yourself are well

72

accustomed to sneaking through the British lines and snatching persons and arms away—just as the mem'sahib was snatched in the first place from the Nowshera cantonment." Ogilvie paused, and leaned across the table. "There is something else, is there not, something further that you seek? I shall make a guess at what this is: you seek information so that you can assemble your own tribal warriors from Afghanistan, who will filter through the passes and over the mountains and form your army in Waziristan! Is this not so, Razjah Shah?"

The native smiled blandly, and nodded. "Your guess is good. What you have said comes near perhaps to the truth. It is for you to consider, and come to a decision. This decision must be made quickly in the mem'sahib's interests."

As he had done in the pit, Ogilvie broke out into a sweat. He was in something of a cleft stick: the information sought by Razjah Shah, if given, could lead to a charge of rendering assistance to the enemy if ever he got back again to Peshawar. But Angela counted also, and might well be under torture for all he knew: Hector, her husband, as a highly-placed Civilian from Whitehall, knew many things about the administration of the Raj, more than the military knew about future policy, and Murrum Khan might well try to pick the brain of a hostage so close, or least by proxy of marriage, to the seats of power in the land of the Queen-Empress. Nevertheless, duty and training and upbringing held: officers did not part with information, and in this instance to attempt to fob Razjah Shah off with false information must rebound upon him soon enough, and very likely upon Angela as well.

"I'm sorry, Razjah Shah," Ogilvie said quietly, looking the native in the eye. "You ask the impossible. For my part, I believe you both can and will find the mem'sahib without my answers to your questions." He paused. "If there is any other help I can give . . . if you will tell me where Murrum Khan is hidden, then perhaps I can advise you on a more restricted basis, by indicating any danger in the vicinity, perhaps?"

Razjah Shah frowned and his eyes shone with anger; but he said, "To tell you cannot be of harm, I think. Murrum

73

Khan is occupying an abandoned fort to the north-east of Takki, which is—"

"A British fort?"

"Once a British fort, Ogilvie sahib, yes."

"Fort Canning, named after a former Viceroy."

Razjah Shah's eyes widened. "You know this fort?"

"I have served there. I know it well." Ogilvie's voice held sudden excitement. "I know how it can best be attacked, and with a small number of men such as you have here. My knowledge—"

"Will for the time being prove more helpful, I think, than the broader information! I can trust you, Ogilvie sahib?"

"In regard to the mem'sahib, yes. Further than that, no."

Razjah Shah gave a deep chuckle and his eyes sparkled. He reached forward and laid a hand on Ogilvie's shoulder. "You shall be most closely watched, I promise you! You shall ride with us tonight, Ogilvie sahib."

7

THE REGIMENT HAD so far made good time, but the resulting effect upon men and animals was plain to see: as the dawn came up in the east it lit the straggling column, the stumbling, weary men, the sagging heads of the horses and the transport mules as they plodded on between the boulders and the desolate scrub. The pipes and drums were silent; by now the regiment was not many miles from its objective, and there was no point in sending ahead the warning of their coming; even though they had probably been reported onwards by the enemy's scouts along the high peaks, Dornoch would not take an additional chance. As that dawn broke, the Colonel turned in his saddle to look along the column, shading his eyes against the first rays of a hard sun.

"We must rest them, Major."

"We must consider the time, Colonel."

"I do not propose to send them into action on empty stomachs," Lord Dornoch said curtly. "Captain Black, I shall halt the column for long enough to take breakfast. Pass the word for the field kitchens to be set up the moment the men fall out."

"Sir!" Smartly, Black saluted and turned his horse. As he rode down the column, Dornoch lifted a hand high, then brought it down. The long column shambled to a halt and without waiting for the order the men fell out, many of them collapsing on their faces beside the terrible track, feeling some of the weariness drain away as they gave themselves up to the comparative comfort and relief of the hard ground. The Regimental Sergeant-Major took the opportunity of sprucing himself up with the aid of his bearer, and of using a pool of water between some rocks to shave. Thus tidy, he marched along the column giving words of encouragement to the men. Meeting the Adjutant, he slammed his feet to the halt and gave a swinging salute.

"Good morning, Sar'nt-Major. The men are a mess."

"Not surprising, sir, not surprising at all."

The Adjutant pointed with his riding-crop. "That man. His kilt's around his waist. It's not decent. Take his name, Sar'nt-Major." Black rode on, slowly and haughtily, looking down his nose. Cunningham, breathing hard, approached the miscreant, a lance-corporal.

"Don't chance your stripe, Corporal Mathieson."

"Sir!" Mathieson started to get to his feet, but Cunningham gestured him back. "What's the trouble, sir?"

"Your kilt, man! Now rectified. The Adjutant wants no public demonstration of what highlanders wear or do not wear beneath the kilt—that's all." Cunningham passed on, leaving a softly swearing Scot; the name would be conveniently forgotten and Black could do what he bloody well liked about it. Cunningham liked a smart regiment, but there were limits, and pinpricks could become bayonet thrusts when men had been pushed to their full extent. Always with a Scottish regiment the hand of command and discipline had to be sensitive to atmosphere: Scots could never be driven stupidly, and Black could often be as stupid as the Major if not as rude . . . the RSM blew out his cheeks as he marched along, left-right-left to his own internal voice of command. Warrant officers such as himself had much to sort out between officers and men and as a result were frequently the butt of both, but he could take any amount of that. What mattered was the regiment; and by this evening's sunset the regiment might well be sadly mauled and there might be many graves to dig in the hard Waziri hills, many hastily-constructed crosses to be planted to mark a sacrifice in the Queen's name. Cunningham gave himself a shake: action was action and they were trained to it and would acquit themselves as well as ever.

There was a sound and a smell of frying, a welcome one. There were steaming mugs of tea, and after a while there was conversation and some laughter from the men as smoke rose from pipes, trailing upwards, blue in air that was almost dead still as the wind was taken away by the high, rearing mountain peaks. Trestle tables were set up for the officers, with deck chairs to sit upon. Coffee was brought by the bearers, and fried eggs and bacon. With his coffee Lord Brora lit a cigar and slumped back in his canvas chair, his long legs stretched out before him. As he puffed at the cigar there was a sharp crack and the end of it seemed to explode in his face. A ball of smoke was seen from one of the peaks as Brora leaped to his feet and shook a fist in the air. Down the column the NCOs shouted the men off the track and into such cover as they could find, while the sharpshooters took post behind boulders and opened on the spot where the smoke had been seen.

"I'll be buggered!" Brora said loudly. "Where the devil are the damn picquets?" He glared upwards. The picquets in the *sangers* had in fact fired only seconds after the shot, but the sniper seemed to have got away with it: a *jezail* was brandished from the peak and a jeering shout came down. Fire was opened again, but the Pathan dodged back into cover and the bullets pinged uselessly off the rock. A moment later there was another shot from above, though the man had not reappeared, and one of the cooks at the field kitchens spun round, knocking over a pan of fat. There was a shout for stretcher bearers, and two men ran up with a *doolie* into which the wounded soldier was lifted: the bullet had entered his shoulder. While Surgeon Major Corton sterilised his instruments and began the unanaesthetised extraction, the orders came down by bugle to prepare to march. The field kitchens were packed away and quickly the regiment was once again on the move: Lord Dornoch's decision had been to join the main action as soon as possible rather than be pinned down and wait for more bullets. For a while there was no more firing, but as they moved along the pass the odd isolated *jezail* cracked, and the picquets were kept busy on the hillsides as they ran and scrambled ahead to clear the slopes for the advance.

Brora looked towards the Colonel. "The pipes, I think?"

"Not just yet, Major."

"Why not, my dear sir? Damn it, we've been spotted, have we not, the buggers'll know we're coming!"

"The effect's better when held to the last moment. Major, I've had years of Frontier fighting and I know the Pathan as well as anyone. The pipes will remain silent until I give the order, and Pipe-Major Ross knows my mind as well as I do myself."

They rode on, Brora looking stiff and angry and with a sneer twisting his lips. Dornoch speculated on the current position of the Border Regiment, pushing north from Kajuri Kach on the Gomal. They were going to be most mightily welcome if they turned up in time: one battalion would help, two might decide the outcome. Might: the Pathan was always a tough fighter, and this time the prize was great. As the advance continued the sniping from the heights died away altogether. To Dornoch it was almost as though the Pathan saw no point in wasting ammunition on a column that night in any case be marching to its extinction.

*　*　*

"Here we halt, Ogilvie sahib." Razjah Shah, riding up alongside in the night, laid a hand on the bridle of the horse that carried Ogilvie, who was tied as before. His uniform was once again hidden by the goatskin. "We shall dismount and go forward on foot, and in silence. The horses will remain here, with four men to guard them."

"Will you detach the frontal assault party now?"

Razjah Shah nodded. "Yes. They will ride on farther yet, then converge on the fort dismounted."

Ogilvie was set on his feet, his wrists remaining bound. With no time lost the horses of the dismounted men were led into the lee of a cleft in the hillside, and the fifteen men who would ultimately approach the fort on their stomachs rode off. The remaining half moved forward, mere shadows in the dark, behind Razjah Shah and Ogilvie. For many past miles a careful watch had been kept for any sign of men extended by Murrum Khan as sentries—though in fact Ogilvie, who had picked up remembered landmarks and bearings some way back, had not expected any watch to be set so far out from Fort Canning. Now, as they began to close the perimeter of the area which, when directly under British control, had been regarded as the outer defensive line, the watch was even more painstaking and the men moved like ghosts, careful to make no sound at all as they trod the rough ground, careful to keep in the shadow of the hillside and out of the moon's beams.

After an hour's slow progress they came within sight of the mountain track's end: from some quarter-mile ahead, as Ogilvie knew, that track left the hills and started the precipitous descent into the broad valley in the centre of which lay Fort Canning. He was about to whisper this information to Razjah Shah when the native leader put a hand on his arm, lightly.

"Stop, Ogilvie sahib, and keep very still and silent."

"What is it?"

"On the peak to the left . . . a man. Stay here." As Razjah Shah moved invisibly away, making no sound, Ogilvie screwed up his eyes and searched the peak. He could see nothing, though the rocky jags stood out fairly clear in the hard moonlight. Nothing but those jags . . . certainly a man could as it were melt into the rocky outlines if he were able to remain still enough, but the smallest movement could betray his presence to sharp eyes. Razjah Shah must have very sharp eyes indeed . . . Ogilvie shrugged and waited with the others, none of them stirring but remaining like carven images in the darkness. There was a sigh of wind, a cold wind that eddied along the pass and rose now and again to a whine as it curled its icy fingers around the high places to bring a reminder of Himalayan snows. A timeless part of the globe, and time tonight seemed to merge into past centuries . . . when Razjah Shah at last returned, he returned as silently as he had gone, making Ogilvie start as his whisper broke the intense stillness.

"All is well, Ogilvie sahib, and we go on."

"What did you find?"

"Two men, both now dead. I believe the way is clear."

"There'll be more at the entry—I warned of this."

"True. They also will die."

"You sound confident," Ogilvie said. There was no response. The tribesmen moved on again behind Razjah Shah and Ogilvie, as slowly and as carefully as before, taking no chances. They approached the break in the hills, the point where the track descended, and in so doing came to the point of most danger. At a word from Ogilvie, Razjah Shah ordered his men down on to their stomachs and himself brought out a knife and cut the rope away from Ogilvie's wrists.

"Now there must be full trust, Ogilvie sahib," he said. They crawled on, a painful process over the hard, stony track. Ahead now, they could see the stark outlines of the fort below, far below, its walls and battlements and its guard tower silvered by the moon that spread a blanket of light over the entire valley and the surrounding peaks. With difficulty they moved down the sloping track until, rounding a bend between rocky sides, they came to more open ground where, at a signal from their leader, they moved aside into boulder-strewn scrub that would give them a degree of cover and prevent an over-swift descent that might well alert the men they expected to find farther down. When they had moved some three hundred yards towards the valley, Ogilvie reached out for Razjah Shah's shoulder.

"Ahead now—you see? The upstanding rock. That's it."

Razjah Shah stopped and spoke a few words of Pushtu to his followers. At once a sideways movement began, the men fanning out to right and left. When they had gone down far enough, they would converge on the rock and mount an attack from either flank. Razjah Shah and Ogilvie moved on behind, still flat on their stomachs, clothing and skin ripped by stones and thorns. There was a rattle as some rock debris was loosened to fly down the hillside: there was a savage intake of breath from Razjah Shah. Ogilvie, watching out ahead, saw, or fancied he saw, some movement at the right-hand edge of the great rock beside the track. A man, alerted by the small give-away sound?

There was no turning back now.

As they crawled painfully on, the man below was confirmed as such: a figure moved out from the rock's lee, tall and ragged, garments blowing out along the wind, his *jezail* and its snaky bayonet clear in the moonlight. Then something seemed to be hurled from the shadows like a rocket, and the sentry vanished. There was a short scream that ended in a gurgle, and on its heels another man came out from the rock, moving fast, but not moving for long: from the left flank Razjah Shah's men came in quickly with moonlight glinting on their knife-blades. The second man died as quickly as his comrade.

Razjah Shah gave a sound of triumph. "Now the way is clear," he said. "Come!"

With Ogilvie he rose from his stomach and together they covered the last stretch to the rock on their feet but bent double: it was possible, though Ogilvie thought unlikely, that they might be seen from the fort. In safety they reached the rock where they were rejoined by the men of the flank attacks.

"The bodies?" Razjah Shah asked.

"Already dragged into the entry."

The leader nodded and followed Ogilvie behind the rock; on the side facing the valley there was a wide hole, large enough to admit a man with bowed head. The two went in, and Razjah Shah struck a flint and lit a torch that flamed and smoked foully in the enclosed space. The bodies of the dead sentries lay huddled in a corner; stones and debris were being piled on them. The walls, black shiny rock, reflected back the torch light; at ground level there was another hole, a smaller one, and beyond it a smooth downward slope that seemed to travel into the very bowels of the earth.

"It looks difficult," Ogilvie said, "and it is, but it can be done. When you're half-way, Razjah Shah, it will be well to remember what I told you: that I myself have made the whole passage in safety."

Razjah Shah laughed. "You think I am frightened, Ogilvie sahib?"

"No. But I think you may come to believe that the tunnel has no ending! The way is long."

There was another laugh, a sound of scorn and confidence. The leader gestured Ogilvie to enter the inner hole, and, once again on his stomach, he did so, feet first. Next came Razjah Shah himself; the others followed, some of them looking not so ebullient as Razjah Shah, their eyes rolling as they committed themselves and their fate to the unknown. Behind them the loom of moonlight faded from the entry, as did the smoky fumes of Razjah Shah's torch, now extinguished. For a while they moved fast, finding the value of the British officer sahib's strictures that their feet should go first and their bodies follow: that way, they had more control of their movement and could check their sliding progress over smooth rock when it became necessary. It was an unnerving and totally helpless feeling as they sped willy-nilly to the earth's fiery stomach, leaving behind them the good fresh air and open skies.

*   *   *

Towards the previous noon, not far to the southward of Fort Canning as it happened, the Royal Strathspey had seen the advanced scouts of the warring levies ahead, natives highly situated atop the pass, armed with *jezails*. As these men were engaged by the picquets, the Colonel in the van saw the rising blobs of smoke as word of their coming was signalled onward. He turned to the Adjutant.

"Sound the Stand-to, if you please, Captain Black."

Black saluted. "Sir!" He called to the bugler; a moment later the strident, brassy voice spoke loud and clear, echoing out along the pass.

"And my compliments to the Pipe-Major. The pipes and drums to commence."

"Sir!" Black passed the word by runner, and the Colonel glanced quickly at Lord Brora, who was muttering something about it damn well being time ... Brora's face was alight and savage, and already his revolver was drawn. A moment later that revolver was thrust back into its holster, and Brora reached down for the leather scabbard that bumped along his horse's flank. He drew his highland broadsword, its blade flashing in the sunlight as he whirled it exultantly around his head. In the marching files behind bayonets had been fixed and the rifles, with their slings tightened, had been removed from the "march-at-ease" position and were ready for the order to open. In the centre of the advance the Maxims' crews had their guns ready to blast into the native hordes when the column extended, with plenty of ready-use ammunition boxes broken open and at hand in the limbers. At the tail and in comparative safety the commissariat and transport mules plodded on ahead of the rearguard; along the flanks the colour-sergeants of companies encouraged and exhorted and kept the step going with their shouts and their pace-sticks, their crimson sashes bringing touches of brilliance to the humdrum khaki mass of men, khaki that was itself lightened a little by the tartan of the Royal Strathspey as the kilts swung to the step. That step lightened noticeably, and chests swelled boastfully, as the pipes and drums beat out along the pass, thrown back upon the marching column by the rock sides, a very real sound of war and glory. In accordance with regimental tradition the first tune to be played as action approached was "Cock o' the North". The battalion swung on defiantly to the rescue of the brigade and the High Commissioner; and as the sound of the embattled guns blazed down from ahead Pipe-Major Ross changed his tune to "Highland Laddie".

> Oh where and oh where,
> Is your Highland laddie gone?
> He's gone from bonnie Scotland
> Where noble deeds are done,
> And it's oh, in my heart,
> I wish him safe at home. . .

Once again Dornoch gave a brief glance at Lord Brora. The Major's lips were moving: he was singing to himself and his eyes were shining. Dornoch smiled slightly; he loved the pipes himself. So far he had not seen his second-in-command in action: in the Mess, in cantonments in general, the man was a boor and a bully. But he had the air of a man whose best side would show itself in action, and for that Dornoch was truly thankful. Compactly, the column moved on: Dornoch had the feeling that in a sense they were moving into a situation not unlike that faced years before in the Crimea by Lord Cardigan and his light Brigade. However, what was to come was inevitable: the pass, as indicated by close study of the maps, was the only approach from easterly to the brigade's position, and once in it there was no turning aside to the flanks, and there was no cover. And currently there was no sign of the Border Regiment, whose field telegraph, it now seemed confirmed, must have been cut before the message came through from Bloody Francis in Nowshera. Such was the luck of the soldier. As Dornoch turned to look back along the column, there was a shout from the Major.

"Scouts coming back, Colonel!"

Dornoch turned again, eyes front: the subaltern with his scouting party was pounding back at the double, and as he came rushing on he fell in his tracks, his body crashing into a boulder and blood spurting like a fountain from his neck. All at once the peaks along the sides seemed to sprout men, and a sustained fire was poured down, while from ahead came the roar and blast and flame of heavy gunfire.

8

AFTER THAT FIRST sliding descent, the tunnel flattened and the going became a good deal harder and disadvantages were found in the feet-first progress. The air grew thick, and bodies grew wet with sweat that ran into the eyes and blinded them with muddy grit. It began to seem as though their journey really was into some red-hot interior of the planet; even Ogilvie, with his knowledge that the end of the tunnel must come in time, began to feel a kind of desperation brought about by the enclosing walls of rock and the fact that there was not room enough to reverse his mode of progression. If one of the Pathans should panic, all hell would be let loose; but Pathans did not panic easily—not, that was, on the surface. Allah or the Prophet alone could tell what the effect of subterranean confinement might bring to the superstitious mind! Ogilvie tried to concentrate his thoughts ahead as he dragged himself along: the objective was all that mattered and somewhere, not far ahead by now, Angela would—he hoped—be found alive and well. He prayed that she might be; and hoped that Allah also was playing his part in keeping Razjah Shah's powder and flints, charges and explosives dry and intact for journey's end. When the journey ended, it would end in a wall built during the British occupation of Fort Canning to seal off the tunnel. This had been built partly in order to keep out any tribesmen who might penetrate and partly to permit the construction of a chamber below the fort for combined defensive and disciplinary purposes: the chamber had been divided into an underground armoury and magazine on the one hand, and cell accommodation on the other. There was a heavy wooden door, and danger would lie in the blowing of it if the charge should be too big. Ogilvie, however, was reasonably confident that he could prepare a safe charge and tamp it well down; Razjah Shah had agreed with him that it was unlikely Murrum Khan would yet have assembled enough weapons and explosives to need the use of a magazine. Nevertheless, much of this was, of necessity, based upon hope and guesswork; and one of the imponderables was whether or not the explosion would alert the natives in the fort above before the infiltrators were ready for the next move. The one defence against that was sheer speed after the event.

Razjah Shah's voice came from the total blackness: he was suffering acutely. "May a thousand asses defecate upon Murrum Khan. It will give me much enjoyment to slit his throat!"

"Try to discipline yourself not to, Razjah Shah. It is important that he should live to talk."

"For the Raj?"

"For the Raj, perhaps. Also for you."

There was a grunt. They moved on as fast as possible. The air was growing foul and there was an immense lethargy in their aching limbs; to push and drag was a tremendous effort and every part of their bodies was lacerated and grazed by the unevenness of the walls and floor once they had come to the flat section. It was akin to medieval torture; but they held on in the knowledge that to go on was considerably easier than to retreat. Ogilvie listened abstractedly to the scrape of the Pathans' ancient rifles along the floor of the tunnel, at the clank of the heavily loaded bandoliers. The time factor was much on his mind. It was to be hoped that by now Razjah Shah's surface party would have completed their stealthy crawl towards the fort. Everything would depend upon the co-ordination of the attack on two fronts.

They crawled on, closing their objective inch by inch. At long last Ogilvie felt the tunnel widening out, and he passed the word to the others to keep as quiet as possible. Soon he was able to stand up, a process that he took carefully in the pitch darkness. He heard the small sounds as the rest of the party emerged, heard Razjah Shah's whisper in his ear: "The light now, Ogilvie sahib?"

"Yes."

A flint was struck and a tallow candle was lit. The resulting shadows were eerie, scarifying. There was a total silence but for the breathing of the Pathans. Ogilvie looked around: the end-chamber was as he remembered it, a circular cavern of some fifteen feet diameter, with the one door leading into a passageway between the cell accommodation and the armoury. He put his ear to the door and listened: he heard no sound—but the door was thick.

He turned to the native leader. "The explosives, Razjah Shah."

Razjah Shah reached into his voluminous garments and brought out gunpowder in four goatskin bags; one of his followers produced more bags, this time filled with workable clay; another brought out pieces of goatskin and canvas in strips and squares and oblongs. Ogilvie set to work preparing the blasting charge, a tricky process with the flickering candle held close to the explosive material. When he was ready, and when another man had prepared the clay, he set the charge on the rock floor at the door's foot, against the woodwork: to blow the lock would be pointless, for at any rate under British occupation there had been bolts at top and bottom and a heavy beam set across the middle. With the charge in place and a short powder-trail laid into the cavern, the clay was applied, packed in tight, and then the layers of goatskin and canvas were placed across.

Ogilvie beckoned to four of the Pathans, and spoke in Pushtu. "All the rubble and loose rock you can gather," he said. "Lay it against the skins, and build it up well to cover them and help contain the explosion when I light the fuse-trail."

They set to, their lean dark faces devilish in the candle's glow. They worked fast, keen enough to be above ground again; quickly, as effective a casing as possible was run up, and the pieces of skin and canvas vanished, leaving only the powder-trail visible. Ogilvie took the candle from Razjah Shah. "In a moment," he said, "I shall touch the flame to the powder. We shall have ten seconds, no more. Much rubble will fly . . . there may be injuries. You must all go into the tunnel and crouch on the floor and cover up your heads as well as you can. Your heads to the tunnel entry, your rumps to the explosion. Go now, and go quietly."

The men moved hastily into the tunnel. When the last man had vanished, Ogilvie gave it fifteen seconds more, then bent with the candle to the end of his fuse-trail, and touched the burning wick to the powder. It caught first time; as soon as he saw the spark move, Ogilvie ran for the tunnel and got down on hands and knees. He had scarcely done so when the charge blew: in the confined space the noise was tremendous, battering at the ear-drums like an artillery barrage in the field. Debris flew everywhere, and the acrid powder-smoke spread from the cavern along the tunnel. Back through the smoke crawled Razjah Shah's men, cannoning into one another as they came into the cavern. The smouldering edges of the hole in the door gave them their bearings. Razjah Shah struck his flint again and the candle was re-lit. They got to work like demented men with knives and daggers and bayonets, expecting a rush of the fort's defenders at any moment. The hole was quickly widened out enough and Ogilvie pulled his body through and stood up in the passageway. The others came through behind, and Ogilvie gestured towards a flight of spiral stone steps at the end of the passage. As he did so he felt Razjah Shah's hand on his arm. Looking down, he saw the British Army revolver in the Pathan's other hand.

Razjah Shah passed the revolver to him. "You shall lead, Ogilvie sahib, and you shall not lead unarmed."

"You trust me, Razjah Shah?"

"You have given your word as an officer sahib. You will not break it. When the need to be armed ceases, the revolver will come back to me."

Ogilvie held out a hand and shook that of Razjah Shah. He said, "Now we must not delay. Remember, at the top of the steps, we come to the stables and through them to the open courtyard." He went for the steps, the Pathan's revolver in his hand with the hammer drawn back, and climbed fast. There were sounds from above, becoming audible as he climbed: the movement of horses in their stalls, and some whinnying, and the pull of halters against ring-

88

bolts. The climb was a long one, but was taken in short time, and all the men had ascended into the stable area when human footsteps were heard, and gruff voices came, and then a lantern was seen, held high above a man's head and guttering in a wind blowing coldly in from the courtyard. Razjah Shah dropped to the ground and Ogilvie and the others followed his motion. The Pathan leader crawled silently through the mixture of straw and droppings, the noise from the horses increasing as they became more uneasy, concealing the approach of the infiltrators come from the depths of the earth.

The man with the lantern halted just behind the row of horses, the light bringing up his puzzled frown as he looked to right and left. But not for long: like a striking snake Razjah Shah rose behind him and plunged his dagger centrally between the shoulder-blades, twisted it and withdrew it dripping blood as the man fell with no sound beyond a harsh cough that sent more lifeblood gushing from the mouth. The guard lantern had fallen with him, and the glass had shattered. Flame was already curling into the straw and taking hold. Razjah Shah called out to his men, and at once they freed the horses and gave each a stinging smack on its rump. As some of Murrum Khan's men appeared, entering the stables, the terrified horses plunged out with forelegs a-flail, some of them rearing up with flashing hooves, at least one of which found a target and smashed a head like an egg-shell. Razjah Shah seized one of the horses and quietened it; mounted, he rode out into the courtyard, a scimitar whirling around his head, a figure of sudden vengeance that had sprung from nowhere, his wild tribesmen behind him with their bayonetted *jezails*. At a shout from Razjah Shah, just as the fire took a firm grip of the stables and began to billow smoke and flame, one of the Pathans raised his *jezail* and loosed it off into the air. Immediately from beyond the high walls of the fort a sound arose in response to the expected signal: high shouts of war and of determined men, accompanied by a fusillade of bullets that smacked into the outer walls by the guardroom or snicked over to break slivers from the stonework inside. Razjah

Shah, bent low over his horse as fire came from the defenders emerging from the one-time barrack-rooms, spurred for the gate where he dismounted. Scimitar in hand, dripping blood from men hacked at as he went along, he lifted the great beam that secured the gate, throwing the latter back on its hinges. As he shouted his internal attack force aside, his surface party stormed in through the gate behind a hail of bullets.

*   *   *

It was all over very quickly: surprise, as ever, was proved the best of weapons, and the burning of the stables helped as it spread throughout the fort. It was victory, but one of doubtful value: a thorough search of the fort revealed no British mem'sahib, no prisoners at all, and no Murrum Khan. Razjah Shah, his face grim and forbidding, had one of Murrum Khan's chief lieutenants brought before him, held fast by two Pathans. Outside the burning fort now, he glanced at Ogilvie's face in the red glow. "Your pardon, Ogilvie sahib. The man is now to be made to talk."

"Torture?"

Razjah Shah nodded. "You are not a part of British India at this moment, Ogilvie sahib. It is my fiat that runs now, and for all our sakes I must have the truth, but I shall save your face." He gave an order in Pushtu and the captive was dragged away. Razjah Shah rode after him, still holding his scimitar. The group faded into the shadows. Soon screams came back, screams of torment and agony that chilled Ogilvie's blood. Then silence, followed by groans, then further screams and after them silence again. Razjah Shah came riding back; there was a strip of flesh hanging from the tip of his scimitar, and there was no captive. He met Ogilvie's questioning eye.

"Food for the vultures," he said. "But before he died, he spoke! We ride again, Ogilvie sahib, as soon as my horses rejoin us." He swung towards the north, and put a hand to his mouth. A long cry rang out, high and vibrant like the call of some great bird, a cry that carried into the distance of the hills to be answered by a similar one from afar where the reserves had been held behind with the horses.

Razjah Shah turned back to face Ogilvie. "Our ride will be to the south. Murrum Khan left many hours ago for the town of Mana itself, with the mem'sahib. It will be a long ride and must needs be a fast one, or I fear much for the life of the mem'sahib once the bargaining starts."

*   *   *

The Royal Strathspey, marching as it were into the very mouths of the guns, had suffered badly in the first assault: before the ranks had scattered by order of the Colonel to find what cover they could where there was virtually none, the rebel artillery had caused upwards of two hundred casualties all told, including forty-three blown to pieces as the pounding shells exploded to scatter case among the Scots. All around them when they had had the time to notice had been the remains of the shattered squadron of the Guides Cavalry, men and horses lying in blood and spilt guts and brains. Here and there an arm or a leg hung upon a bush or a jag of rock; an appalling sight in which to engage the enemy. But morale and discipline had held, and from somewhere along the line the pipes had played on to give heart to the sorely struck battalion. The Maxims had gone into stuttering action immediately, pumping and swinging over the Scots to find targets amongst the enemy gunners, whilst the picquets had been strongly reinforced by men who climbed towards the heights to bring rifles to bear more closely upon the attacking native infantry along the peaks. Support had come from the Brigadier-General, whose force was evidently in being yet: his guns had opened down the pass, sending shells into the rebel artillery positions, but it had been a sadly depleted bombardment and had not lasted long, though in fact the native guns fell silent afterwards.

"I think Norris has not many guns left," Dornoch said breathlessly to his Adjutant, his face showing pain: his left arm hung by his side, limp and bloody.

91

"No, Colonel." Black added, "I'm fearful of the outcome, I must confess—"

"And your suggestion is?"

"A strategic retreat, Colonel."

"From an impossible position?"

Black nodded. "Yes, Colonel."

Dornoch's voice was brisk, though there was a wince in it as his arm swung to a sudden movement. "No situation is totally impossible, Andrew, certainly not this one, and in my view there is no such thing as a strategic retreat. A retreat is a retreat and in this case it would leave the brigade in the lurch." Dornoch stared ahead along the pass to where it was effectively blocked by the rebel gunners. "They've ceased firing, which probably means a parley. In my view there's nothing to parley about, but it gives us a breather."

"Yes, Colonel, and—"

"Send Mr Cunningham to me, and Lord Brora. And all company commanders. At once!"

"Very good, Colonel." Black shouted at the runner waiting beside his horse, and the man went off at the double. The Regimental Sergeant-Major was the first to come up and salute.

"Sir!"

"Mr Cunningham, how are the men?"

"In good heart, sir."

Dornoch's eyes narrowed. "You're wounded, Mr Cunningham."

"It's nothing, sir."

"You'll have that shoulder seen to nevertheless." The Colonel turned as Lord Brora rode up, to be followed by the company commanders. They made a tattered, blood-streaked band of officers but there was no defeat in their faces. Dornoch said, "Gentlemen, we have a respite. It'll not last long. While we have it, we shall act. I intend to scale the heights and get the battalion beyond the ability of the rebels' guns to bear. Action will be carried on atop the pass. Mr Cunningham, you'll split the battalion in half, one to scale the northern side, one the southern."

"Sir!"

"It'll be a hellish job, but will be done. I shall command the southern half, Lord Brora the northern. You, Sar'nt-Major, will come with me. Captain Black goes with Lord Brora. All understood?"

"The wounded, Colonel—"

"Yes, indeed. They'll have to be carried in *doolies*. I'll not leave any man behind. I'm afraid the dead must wait."

"Until after victory?" Brora asked.

"Until after victory, Major."

Brora gave a loud laugh. "You are over hopeful, I think, Colonel, but damned if I don't admire your spirit!"

Dornoch stared, sensing a kind of impertinence, but said nothing; in any other subordinate the remark would indeed have been impertinent, but Brora seemed to be a law unto himself and probably considered his words polite enough. Dornoch said abruptly, "Very well, gentlemen, make your dispositions immediately. A to D Companies south, remainder north. You have three minutes precisely, then I shall sound the Extend, and that will be the signal to advance from the flanks. And good luck and success to you all."

Salutes were exchanged, and the officers broke up to move at the double for their companies. Dornoch sat on his horse like a ramrod, watching his men, casting a glance towards the enemy whose guns remained silent still. It was an almost uncanny silence in the middle of an action, and Dornoch was puzzled: something odd was in the air, and it might prove to be the emergence of a flag of truce and a demand for surrender or it might not. Certainly the enemy must be thinking the British were in that impossible position claimed by Andrew Black! As a medical orderly came up, Dornoch dismounted and allowed his arm to be splinted and bandaged. This work was in progress as the three minutes ended by Dornoch's watch and he gestured to the waiting bugler. The notes echoed out harshly and at once the battalion moved to the flanks and sprang up to climb, moving nimbly with ready rifles and the bearers with the *doolies* coming on much more slowly as they lifted the wounded onward. As the movement was seen the gunfire started again and shells whined down the pass. Dornoch urged the medical orderly

93

to hurry and as soon as his arm had its bandage in place he went at the double for the southern flank, leaving his horse with the other animals. Case and fragments of rock and earth flew everywhere and there were many more casualties. Along the peaks the rebel levies were again in action, pouring down their rifle fire on the climbing Scots. Men rose in the air, arms flung wide, to come off the steep slope and fall outwards, plunging down into the pass below. First to reach the top, a colour-sergeant died with a bayonet through his throat, the blade coming out bloody the other side so that for a moment he hung like a rag doll speared by a sadistic child. Dornoch, in much pain from his arm, sweated and climbed. By dogged determination not to be bested, by guts and courage, the Scots on both sides pounded and dragged themselves to the top, and re-formed; disciplined rifle-fire now battered at the enemy, while in the pass the artillery stood helpless to intervene, their barrels unable to elevate so far. Dornoch, advancing in the van of the southern flank force, looked across to the north: Brora was running ahead in great leaps like a stag, his broadsword awhirl about his head. Even over the rifle-fire Dornoch could hear his shouts and yells as he encouraged his half-battalion on, his big body a prime target that yet seemed impervious to the native fire. As the advance continued amid the highland oaths and cries, the rebels began to press back. Coming farther westwards, Dornoch caught a glimpse of the brigade below in the pass: they had been caught in the worst possible sector, a place where any flank movement was sheerly impossible: the rock sides, if anything, leaned outwards, their tops overhanging the deep cleft in the hills. There seemed to be an enormous number of dead men and horses, Dornoch noted, and shattered guns and limbers: the brigade had been almost cut to pieces—but it was fighting still. Two guns were firing down towards the rebel artillery, and the rifles were in action too. Dornoch turned his attention back towards his own regiment: their progress was slowing as rebel reinforcements came in to join their fellows on the heights, and the Scots' casualties were mounting.

Dornoch found the Regimental Sergeant-Major beside

him. He said sadly, "We're hard pressed, I fear. Perhaps I was wrong to try."

"You were not, sir. You were not! There's not a man who'd agree with that, sir!"

Dornoch sighed. "I think the dead would, poor fellows ... but I appreciate your remark." He held out a hand and speaking again addressed the RSM by his regimental nickname. "We've served together for a long time, Bosom. I appreciate all you've done for the 114th." There was a lump in his throat as he shook Cunningham's hand, and he couldn't go on.

Cunningham pressed the hand warmly. "Never say die, sir." All at once he stiffened and said, "Wheesht, Colonel! Listen, sir. D'ye hear what I hear?"

Dornoch listened, then picked up the distant sound. Over the thunder of the guns below and the sharp crackle of rifle-fire he identified the sounds of a British regiment on the march, the notes of the fifes and drums sweeping down from ahead—the Border Regiment marching in from a westerly approach to form a pincer movement on the rebel hordes. Dornoch stopped and beat time with his cane as the fifes and drums came up more strongly to the tune of the regimental quickstep:

> D'ye ken John Peel
> At the break of the day,
> D'ye ken John Peel
> When he's far, far away
> With his horse and his hounds
> In the morning. . .

95

9

WITH THE ARRIVAL of a second British battalion to reinforce
the brigade, much of the heart had seemed to go out of the
rebel infantry attack. The heights were thereafter quickly
cleared by the Scots, the natives melting away into the hills
and leaving their comrades still in the pass to fight it out with
the newcomers. As the men of the Border Regiment halted
and opened fire with rifles and Maxims, with their attached
battery of mountain artillery quickly assembling their pieces
and opening in support, Lord Dornoch was already leading
the left half of his battalion back to the point where they had
climbed out of the pass. The Scots scrambled down the
hillside like goats, slipping and sliding, to engage the rebel
gunners from the rear as their artillery was turned on
Norris's still beleaguered brigade. The Scots charged along
the pass with bayonets fixed, yelling and shouting like
demons as the pipes and drums played them on. From the
northern heights Brora's half battalion poured down a
concentrated fire on the gun teams, and by the time Dornoch's companies had reached the gunners, half lay already
dead behind the breeches. Hand-to-hand fighting started, a
murderous business and a bloody one as the knives and
bayonets grew red in the sunlight. Looking up at one
moment, Dornoch saw Brora leading his men back to come
down into the pass and join the action at closer quarters.
Such of the rebel infantry as had not fled from the peaks was
pouring down now to the assistance of the guns, and no
doubt Brora had seen this from his higher position, and no
doubt also saw the difficulties of finding the right targets in
the mêlée below him. Brora came down the hillside like an
avalanche, picked himself up and ran like the wind towards
the fighting. He came up and joined the Colonel with his

broadsword whirling and as Dornoch looked round he saw a turbaned head roll and bounce from the rocks littering the floor of the pass.

"He was about to have you, Colonel. With that splinted arm you're not safe, and I suggest you retire to the doctor's care."

"I'm all right," Dornoch said briefly, "and the doctor has other things to do. What's the situation ahead, did you see?"

"The Borderers have matters nicely in hand."

Dornoch nodded: tactically, everything was now to the British advantage. With the main body of the brigade in the centre, the rebel force was now hemmed in on both sides of it and it must be merely a matter of time and attrition. At the Scots' end, the guns now stood silent; but not for long. As the native crews were killed or captured, the Scots took over. Though not artillerymen and with only a basic, rudimentary knowledge of heavy guns, they handled the pieces well enough. As the shells from their own guns landed amongst them, the rebel infantry, massing for a charge down the pass, wavered and then turned and ran, yelling, back into the ready barrels of Norris's brigade. Dornoch waved his broadsword ahead and called for the bugler. The Royal Strathspey, advancing once again as a battalion, ran for the enemy's unprotected rear.

Twenty minutes later, as the defeated natives fled from a scene of appalling carnage, Dornoch and the Colonel of the Border Regiment closed the Brigadier-General from their opposite sides. Norris's tunic was blood-soaked and his face was white, but he was still in command as he shook the hands of the two colonels.

"Thank God," he said, and turned to his orderly officer and Brigade Major. "Sound the Cease Fire."

"No pursuit, sir?" Brora demanded loudly.

Norris lifted an eyebrow. "Pray who are you, sir?"

"I, sir, am Major Lord Brora, second-in-command of the Royal Strathspey—"

"And not long on the Frontier, I assume! In these hills pursuit is useless, and I have to reach Mana with the High Commissioner."

"Is he all right, sir?" Dornoch asked.

"Yes," Norris answered briefly. "And your battalions, gentlemen?"

"Badly cut up," Dornoch said.

"Colonel Hinde, your Borderers?"

"As the Scots, sir—there'll be a sad count."

The Brigadier-General nodded. "I don't need to say how sorry I am. My own casualties have been very heavy, I'm afraid, and the burials . . . this ground's too hard in winter. We've not far to go to clear the pass westwards—you'll confirm that, Colonel Hinde, I think?"

"Yes. Four miles, no more. The natives chose their ground well enough!"

Norris swayed a little; his Brigade Major put out a steadying arm. "My apologies, gentlemen, I think I have lost blood. The men will rest for half an hour but the picquets must be maintained, of course . . . after that time the dead will be placed on the mules and camels and the column will march out with them. As soon as we come clear of the pass they'll be buried in open ground where there is less rock. Carry on, if you please."

The colonels saluted. As they turned away to their battalions, the Brigadier-General slumped on to a camp stool opened for him by his orderly officer. Dornoch walked slowly towards his Scots and passed the orders. What he saw around him was terrible: the dead lay everywhere, both British and native, loyal man and rebel, with the clouds of vultures gathering, black above the pass. The very earth seemed red; and in the pass was gathering gloom as the sun declined. Dornoch walked on, hearing the cries of wounded men, of men with arms and legs severed by the rebel blades, of men on the point of death, men for whom the medical parties could do nothing. He walked down to the place where for the Scots the action had started that day, the point where he had split the battalion for the climb to the heights. All along the track lay bodies. Going sombrely back towards Brigade he met the Regimental Sergeant-Major.

"A sad day, Bosom."

"Aye, sir, but when all's said and done, sir—we won."

Dornoch nodded. "Yes, we won." His voice was bitter. A

high price had been paid, but it was no more than a deposit on somebody's land holding—and they had yet to reach Mana for the High Commissioner to hold court and make his decisions on that! Dornoch said heavily, "The British soldier is the world's maid-of-all-work, Sar'nt-Major. Sometimes I wonder he puts up with it all!"

"Aye, sir. But—it's a matter of pride, sir, is it not?"

* * *

During the half-hour's rest, rum was broken out and issued, a quarter of a mug for each man. It was warming and it helped, so did the words of praise from the Brigadier-General, who cast aside medical advice and rode along the pass to talk personally to the men. He was proud of every one, and said so, adding that he believed the way would now be clear for Mana, that the enemy had expended his force and lost it in the place most propitious for him, and would be in no position to strike again along a less amenable part of the route. After this Norris assembled the officers and announced that interrogation of the prisoners had revealed that the attack had come from the Afridi tribe: although the prisoners didn't know, or wouldn't reveal, the whereabouts of Murrum Khan himself, it was fairly clear that his were the forces and that he was attempting to assert his strength and settle the boundary dispute favourably to himself by despatching the High Commissioner to his Maker in advance of mediation.

"Somewhat foolishly," Norris said, "since High Commissioners can be replaced, but it's well in line with the Pathan outlook that sees military victory as decisive." He smiled wanly. "I suppose we do too, but at least we're able to look beyond it, and see that the element of decisiveness is often illusory." He pulled out his watch. "Time passes, gentlemen. I shall sound the Advance in fifteen minutes."

The officers dispersed and the men, having had their half-hour's respite, were fallen in and sent about the business of gathering the dead on to the transport animals and manning the *doolies* for the carriage of the wounded who could not walk. In fifteen minutes precisely the bugles sounded from Brigade and the regiments moved out with their silent burdens, led by a solitary drummer of the Borderers, a poignant beat to keep the step going. From the centre, behind the Brigadier-General and his staff, Pipe-Major Ross blew a haunting highland lament, a sound that brought a prickling to the eyeballs of the Scots as they marched in sad procession out from the enclosing walls of the pass. Once into open country it would become a matter for the pioneer sergeants and for all men capable of wielding pick and shovel or of fashioning with the bayonet's blade rough crosses from any pieces of wood that could be mustered after the cairns of stones had been set in place.

*　　*　　*

Razjah Shah had said the ride for Mana would be a fast one: it was. They rode in silence, concentrating all their energies on their objective. Ogilvie's wrists had been left free: he was a firmly trusted man now, one who had kept his word and had brought about victory over the holders of Fort Canning. For his part Ogilvie was willing to trust the Pathan leader, and had no doubt that in his turn Razjah Shah would honour his side of the bargain and allow Angela to go free once he had got her away from Murrum Khan. All help Ogilvie could give, that he would give, and never mind that Razjah Shah was as sworn an enemy of the Raj as was Murrum Khan himself.

Good progress had been made by the time the sun came up; they halted a while to rest the horses and to eat a frugal meal of berries and mushy rice that had been brought ready boiled from the cellar hideout, now many miles to the north. Water-bottles were refilled from a stream and then they mounted and rode on; there was some deviation resulting in a loss of time when the necessity arose to ford a tributary of the Indus River. As that afternoon the sun went down the sky, they entered a narrow defile, filled with rock and much overgrown with scrubby trees. The men were forced to dismount and lead the horses on. Razjah Shah brought down curses upon the delay, savagely: there was, he said, no other way through the mountains at this point and the track they were using was in fact one that had been disused for many years except by bandits such as himself, and that only rarely.

"Where does it come out?" Ogilvie asked.

"In the plain which we must cross to reach Mana by the fastest route." With his men, Razjah Shah hacked away at the scrub, forcing a passage. The horses could scramble through behind only with great difficulty; there was much time lost. Working desperately, Ogilvie thrust through with the others, using a heavy-bladed, very sharp knife to hack away at the branches that seemed covered throughout their length with some of the worst thorns he had ever experienced, thorns that ripped at his flesh and uniform and brought a good deal of blood. An hour passed . . . two hours, three hours, the men taking only brief rests. From Ogilvie sweat poured freely though the air was bitterly cold; at last he saw, or thought he saw, the end of the defile ahead. There was more light and he believed open country was in view. He turned and called back to the Pathans behind him, then went on hacking at the scrub. A last effort and he was through, and standing on high ground just outside the defile, looking down a steep track to the plain—and seeing something that brought a mixture of emotions: a swirl of dust extending for something like a mile, a snake making its way along the track . . . a military formation of perhaps brigade strength, men and guns and animals on the march.

He stood there with thoughts crowding . . . a moment later he heard the sound, sweeping up towards him as an unheard order was given, the unmistakable sound of the pipes and drums. Fresh sweat broke out. Unless there was an almighty coincidence around, the Royal Strathspey was down there with the marching column! No more than perhaps a couple of miles distant . . . with luck he could make it, or at least attract attention.

But to what end? It would scarcely help now for Razjah Shah to be taken by the British, or for time to be spent in questioning and in making decisions afterwards. In Ogilvie's view Razjah Shah in freedom offered the fastest route to

Angela's safety; and besides there was the clinching factor anyway: he had given his word. That word held until his cousin's wife had been set upon her way back to safety in Peshawar.

Ogilvie turned away and went back into the defile.

* * *

Lord Brora lowered his glasses with a savage movement. "He's gone, Colonel. Turned aside. I tell you it was Ogilvie. A kilt, below a filthy goatskin jacket! I have not a shadow of doubt."

"Then he will show again, Major. Of that *I* have no doubt . . . unless he's under duress."

"Duress my arse. He's got free! He was entirely alone. I had a fine view!"

"Which no one else had. The distance is too great for certainty."

"Am I to be blamed for sharp eyes, Colonel? Is no blame to be given to those with blinkers when they should be keeping watch on the flanks? Damn it, that's no way to conduct a column in hostile territory—"

"Thank you, Major, that's enough said. The light is none too good, but you are convinced you saw Captain Ogilvie. Very well! I am *not* convinced yet—"

"For God's sake, Colonel, how many kilted officers do you expect to find wandering about Waziristan and turning their backs upon British troops and buggering off into cover?"

"Major—"

"It's damned fishy, Colonel, damned fishy. I'd like to know how you explain it away."

"I shall make no attempt to do so until Ogilvie rejoins—"

"Which I think he will not!"

"Or until he at least reappears, Major, when I can see for myself. In the meantime you may send a runner to Brigade with a report of a sighting on the right flank."

Brora snorted and called up a runner. As the man doubled away Brora and the Colonel rode on in a tense silence, with Black hovering on the flank. Time passed; there was no reappearance of the kilted figure. Brora began to make ominous sounds and Dornoch said, "Well, I agree there's to be no reappearance, Major—"

"Quite! And much time wasted, if not by you then by the Brigadier-General."

"For whose order we must still wait."

Brora's mouth closed like a rat-trap. They rode on; within the next few minutes the orderly officer was seen riding down from Brigade. He pulled up his horse beside the Colonel and saluted.

"The Brigadier-General is about to halt the column, sir. Will you please detach a company to form Mounted Infantry on mules and extend to the right flank to investigate the sighting?"

Dornoch nodded, and turned to the Adjutant. "Captain Black, detach Ogilvie's own company. Major, if you wish to satisfy yourself once and for all, you have my permission to ride yourself in command."

Brora's arm rose to the salute; it was a somewhat ironic gesture, and he was smiling in a sneering way as he gave it. "My thanks, Colonel. I shall not be long." He turned his horse and rode down the column towards B Company a little way behind the Adjutant. The mules were led up from the transport section at the rear of the battalion and, clumsily in their kilts, the NCOs and men mounted and were reported ready by the Colour-Sergeant.

"So many sacks of potatoes, Colour MacTrease," Brora said disagreeably. He pointed with his riding-crop. "That peak there, some two to three miles away by my estimate. We are to close it as fast as possible—I hesitate to use the term gallop in connection with mules, but gallop we must try to do. Understood, Colour MacTrease?"

"Aye, sir." MacTrease hesitated. "And when we get there, sir?"

Brora stood in his stirrups, his eyes challenging and angry. "When we get there we dismount and climb and we carry out a search for no less a person than Captain Ogilvie, whom I happened to see briefly through my field glasses a long enough time ago to make our task doubly difficult. Carry on, Colour MacTrease."

Brora swung his horse and touched spurs to its sides. He went off fast to the flank, the animal's shoes striking sparks from the stones in the track as it obeyed the prick of the rowels. He had soon well outpaced the obstinacy of the flap-eared mules behind.

*   *   *

Ogilvie had made his report of British troops below, and in return Razjah Shah's handclasp had been warm. "Your word is an honourable one, Ogilvie sahib. I am grateful." His eyes were sharp and searching nevertheless. "Were you seen by the soldiers?"

"I don't know," Ogilvie answered. "I saw no reaction from them, but something may have been seen and they may investigate."

"Truly they may do so, Ogilvie sahib—"

"So what will you do now?"

Razjah Shah shrugged. "One thing only is left to do! The defile is cleared, and we can go back much faster than we came."

"But then what? You said this was the only way for Mana."

"And I spoke truly, for it is. There must now be more delay. We shall go back along the defile, and hide, and when the British have gone away we shall move again and descend into the plain, and follow behind them at a safe distance into Mana."

"But if they investigate, and overtake us in the defile?"

"What I have said is all that is possible, Ogilvie sahib." Razjah Shah paused. "Perhaps your eyes saw that a quarter of the way back from here there is a cave in the side of the hill?"

"I didn't see it."

"It is well hidden and my hope is that the British will not see either. I saw it and I looked inside. It is deep, and we can cover the entrance even more than it is presently covered. Come!"

The Pathan turned away; Ogilvie and the rest of the

bandits followed, making their way with the horses, back through the cleared passage in the scrub. When they reached the mouth of the cave Ogilvie failed to find it even though he now knew it was there: smiling, Razjah Shah moved some scrub aside and showed him the opening. The men and horses moved in, penetrating well back though slowly in the pitch dark. When they stopped there was complete silence, a silence broken only faintly by the plop of a water-drip coming through the rock from above. They waited in as much silence from outside as there was inside. But after a while the outside silence vanished in the sound of men making heavy weather of their search, and the sound of a truculent voice raised in exasperation that verged on fury when after passing on the sounds came back. For a second time the sounds faded. The men in the cave remained as still and silent as carven images for a long time after they had gone. Then they relaxed as Razjah Shah's voice broke the stillness.

"All is well, Ogilvie sahib. While the British were here, I could feel the rope about my neck . . . but they have gone, and we are safe."

* * *

Brora was in a savage mood when he rode in to report. "No one, Colonel. That is, no one I could find."

"You still think—"

"I *know*, Colonel, I do not *think*. The signs were plain to see. Scrub hewn down, and horse manure in plenty—and recently dropped. But no horses and no men."

"And your construction, Major?"

There was a loud laugh, a contemptuous and dangerous one. "My construction, Colonel? Why, I smell treachery, by God! The filly that was taken . . . who's to say Ogilvie doesn't lust for her flesh? Who's to say that if pushed to the point he wouldn't put her before the Raj—or even throw in his lot with the damn Pathan and decamp into Afghanistan and thereby put her before his cousin, her lawful husband, as well? Who's to answer with certainty, Colonel?"

105

10

WHILE DORNOCH UTTERLY rejected the Major's insinuation, and said so unequivocally, it remained in his mind as an accusation, not against Ogilvie, but against Brora himself. Brora's arrogance and egotism had caused almost the whole regiment to fall foul of him from the start; Ogilvie had never been the sort to put up with bullying either of himself or of his men, nor injustice to boot. And whilst earlier in the year Dornoch had been on the sick list and the command of the battalion had passed temporarily to Lord Brora, the latter had managed to make a considerable fool of himself. His conduct at the Court Martial proceedings against Ogilvie on a charge of cowardice in the field had been a sorry exhibition. This episode Brora had not cast from his mind, and it looked as though he never would. In Brora's view, James Ogilvie in particular would never put a foot right.

In the meantime Brora's remark, uttered in the Major's usual hectoring and ringing tones, had been overheard by the rank and file. There was a good deal of adverse comment on Brora when the word spread like lightning down the column, and the colour-sergeants turned deaf ears to mutinous rumbles: Captain Ogilvie was a well-liked officer, and the Major was a bastard. . .

When the nil report was made to the Brigadier-General, he passed the order for the column to move out. There must be no more delay for wild-goose chases now: the safe delivery of the High Commissioner to Mana was of paramount importance and the arrival was to be made before the situation could deteriorate further.

* * *

At dusk the British brigade had vanished into the distance. Razjah Shah announced that the time had come to move out behind; with Ogilvie he led the way down the steep track to the flat ground, walking the horses so as to relieve them of their burdens. As he said to Ogilvie, they must not make too great a speed yet, but must remain well behind the British column.

"Yet, Razjah Shah? Will there, then, come a time when we can move faster?"

"There will, Ogilvie sahib, but not tonight and perhaps not tomorrow. Many miles ahead there is another track, another pass through the hills. By using this we can outflank the British force."

"And overtake? But won't they use it themselves, Razjah Shah?"

"No. It is narrow and twisting for most of its length, and while it will not delay us, it would be almost impossible for a large force with guns. Never fear, by taking this track we shall reach Mana on horseback before your Brigadier-General sahib."

Ogilvie nodded. The need to linger for the time being was hard to endure, for he felt in his bones that the arrival of Sir Lawrence Bindle to start his duties in Mana would prove the time of real danger for his cousin's wife. He believed that pressure would be put upon the High Commissioner to make his decision in Murrum Khan's favour at once, rather than to delay in order to hear all the pleas and arguments of the various *maliks,* the headmen with fingers in the pie of land division. The *jirgahs* at which these local leaders would talk so endlessly could go on for many months, as they had done in the past. Angela Ogilvie was there to ensure that they did not. Ogilvie spoke of her once again to Razjah Shah. The Pathan said, "You should not think too much, Ogilvie sahib. It does not help. The mind should be clear for action to come."

Ogilvie gave a short laugh. "That's when I'll stop thinking! Without action—"

"Without action it is hard. I know this. I wish to be reassuring, but also I must not raise false hopes. We men of the hills know much about false hopes . . . perhaps as a result we have grown hard and bitter—"

"Against the Raj?"

"Against the Raj many times, yes, but not of necessity against the officer sahibs, many of whom are such as you— honourable men and accustomed in their own land to a high station, such as gives them an inherent quality of mercy and compassion for those not so fortunate as themselves. You understand me, Ogilvie sahib?"

Again Ogilvie laughed. "We call it noblesse oblige . . . yes, I understand very well! We don't all follow it, I must confess," he added, thinking of Lord Brora. "Something of the same thing applies to the Pathans, I fancy? I believe you to be a good man, Razjah Shah. Murrum Khan is a Pathan of a different sort."

Razjah Shah spat on the ground. "An Afridi! Yes, a different sort, and that is why I cannot in honesty be reassuring."

They trudged on in silence, Ogilvie's thoughts growing gloomier and harder to bear. At dawn Razjah Shah called a halt, and they snatched some sleep under the watchful guard of a man who remained awake as sentry. Then more rice was eaten, and more berries. In a grey cold day they moved on; there was a bitter wind blowing free across the mountains as they began to climb, and ahead there was a covering of snow on the hills, lying red beneath an angry, cloud-strewn sun that hung large and watchful like the eye of the Prophet. All that day they trudged with the horses, not yet daring to move too fast, the ragged Pathans striding out hard-faced and with rangy limbs that seemed not to feel the terrible cold of the stark Waziri hills. Shortly after the next night had come down to bring out the stars to hang like lanterns close above, and as the air grew wickedly colder and sharper, good news came from the leader.

"The side pass, Ogilvie sahib. It is now but two miles ahead of us."

Ogilvie let out a long breath of relief. "Thank God! Shall we mount now?"

"If you wish, Ogilvie sahib." Razjah Shah turned to his

men and passed the order. Legs were swung over the horses' backs and there were happy grunts from the bandits as the weight was transferred from sore feet. Now there was no more delay: they rode for the pass as fast as the rough ground would allow and within the next few minutes were inside its high walls and making good speed towards Mana. By the next nightfall, Razjah Shah said, he expected to reach the city and come within striking distance of Murrum Khan.

"But do not hope too much, Ogilvie sahib," he said warningly. "If Murrum Khan should get word of our coming in time, he will move to another hiding place."

"Or stay and fight."

"I believe not," the Pathan said sombrely. "Murrum Khan is a warrior indeed, but has never been eager to cross swords, as you would say, with myself."

"And *badal,* Razjah Shah?"

"Murrum Khan's brother was killed by the father of Dostman Khan, Ogilvie sahib, not by one of my family. *Badal* is not directed against me."

"But Dostman Khan—"

"I understand your mind. Dostman Khan is also an Afridi. Nevertheless he may be of assistance to us against Murrum Khan. Of this I am hopeful."

Ogilvie, though full of questions, forebore to press: all along, Razjah Shah had been unwilling to elaborate much, and to that extent Ogilvie felt that the Pathan did not trust him fully but had reservations when it came to outlining plans in any detail. This was fair enough in one respect at least: matters could easily go wrong and if captured by an enemy, he who knew could be forced to reveal. That was a fact of life along the North-West Frontier that had constantly to be borne in mind, and the hill tribes were ever suspicious, confiding usually only in their own close family or in their brothers-in-blood, a status which Ogilvie had not remotely attained with Razjah Shah, though there was undoubtedly a mutual respect as between men of war.

They rode through the night, battered by the wind blowing

cold and eerie, sighing along between the hillsides, the horses stumbling now and again over the rocks in their path.

* * *

Twenty-four hours after they had entered the side pass Mana lay visible ahead, a city set in a surround of jagged peaks, starkly silhouetted beneath the moon: it was a romantic sight and a beautiful one, but also currently a foreboding one, since the city held the crux of the present trouble. As they came within sight of the clustered buildings beneath the minarets, Razjah Shah halted his followers and sat for a while looking down deep in thought, as though only now at this late stage formulating his final plan for the approach, the infiltration and the attack. After his thought he reached out and laid a hand on Ogilvie's bridle.

"The moment for decision, Ogilvie sahib."

"I wait your word, Razjah Shah."

There was a silence; the Pathan's eyes seemed to glitter in the moonlight. "I have your trust, as you have mine?"

"Yes, Razjah Shah, you have my trust."

"Then you will follow orders without question, taking me as your leader?"

"Without too much question, yes!"

"Here, then, is my decision." Razjah Shah spoke quietly but with firmness and an expectation of obedience. "For all to ride down into Mana would be foolish. The moon is such that we must be seen, and I find no approach uncovered by the moon's light. Therefore one man will go, and he shall be followed by one more. These men will go on foot—there is cover enough as far as the outskirts for two widely-spaced men moving carefully. Do you agree?"

"Perhaps."

"Then you shall be the first to descend, Ogilvie sahib, and I shall—"

"Why me? On my own, I'll stand out a mile in uniform—even under the goatskin!"

"You have answered your own question," Razjah Shah replied with a low laugh. "Ogilvie sahib, you are the target,

110

the magnet that will attract the attention of Murrum Khan. When he gets word of you, as undoubtedly he will very quickly, he will know who you are and why you come to Mana—"

"And he'll have me taken to him?"

"Exactly, Ogilvie sahib! And my man shall follow discreetly, and then return here to tell me where you have been taken. You are willing? I shall come fast to you, I give you my word."

There was a pause; the breath steamed from the horses' nostrils as they snorted, their hooves pawed impatiently at the ground. All the men waited for Ogilvie's answer, their gaze upon him expectantly. The British were brave, sahibs had no fear in their minds or bodies. Ogilvie looked Razjah Shah in the eye.

"It shall be as you say," he told him. "I'll go."

Razjah Shah reached out his hand and took Ogilvie's. "I shall come. I have promised. You will say nothing of me to Murrum Khan. You have made your way alone from your regiment to seek the wife of your cousin. Murrum Khan will not believe this, but it is all you will say to him." The leader reached into a leather holster attached to his horse's harness and brought out the British Army revolver that he had lent Ogilvie for the assault on Fort Canning. "This you shall take again. It will be expected of an officer sahib who has come from his regiment."

"Thank you, Razjah Shah."

"Now go. My man will be behind, though you will not be aware of him."

Ogilvie dismounted, handed over the horse to one of the tribesmen, and turned away, making down the track beneath the moon. As Razjah Shah had said, it was easy enough for him to keep in reasonable cover on his own. It was a long descent through scrubby ground dotted with rock, a progress similar to their earlier route. There was no indication at all of the man who would be following him down: the Pathans knew well how to shadow. As he entered the sleeping city Ogilvie felt the presence of watchful eyes, of men lurking in the alleys and the doorways, or watching from the minarets with the special purpose of reporting any movement of strangers to Murrum Khan in his hideout. It was an eerie advance into the cluster of mean dwellings, into the varied smells of the city, into the enclosed spaces of the filthy alleys and their few nocturnal wanderers. As in all cities of the sub-continent, there were many sleepers in the open, the men and women and children who could find no abode and must needs use their pitiful scanty garments as bed and bedclothes while the cold wind blew through to the bone. None stirred as he passed by them: they could have been the corpses of the dead. Now and again a mangy dog scavenged or cowered from Ogilvie's approach in avoidance of the anticipated heavy kick or the wielding of a stave. There were few lights: no more than one or two flickering oil lamps behind the glassless holes in the walls that did duty as windows to admit air and release smells. Two Indias, if not three, Ogilvie thought as he passed: the India of the great princes, the rajahs and maharajahs, the gaekwars and the nabobs with their unmeasurable wealth in diamonds, rubies, gold and emeralds; and this India of the natives who lived in poverty and deprivation and stinking squalor, diseased and in constant fear of death . . . and superimposed on both lay the third India, the India of the British Raj and Her Majesty the Queen-Empress and her armies and administrators who did their best in an impossible environment to hold some sort of balance, however rough and incomplete, between high and low. At least if the British had not been there, matters would be far worse and the sub-continent would be continually in a state of turmoil and murder and civil war. . .

Ogilvie became aware of footsteps padding the earth behind him. He was about to turn and confront the follower when from a doorway a little ahead of him a man materialised, a curved dagger in his hand, and stood in his path.

Ogilvie stopped. He asked in Pushtu, "What do you want?" Behind him, the padding footsteps also stopped, and he felt the second knife-blade press against his spine. He smelled dirty flesh and clothing, an appalling smell to add to all the others. He repeated his question, adding that he came in peace to Mana.

"Peace," the first man said, "yet you come dressed as a soldier of the Raj. Why is this?"

Ogilvie shrugged. "Soldiers of the Raj can come in peace as well as in war. Why do you stop me?"

"I stop you only to move you in another direction. Come." The man moved to his side and thrust the dagger close. Razjah Shah's revolver was removed from him. The knife in his back remained in position as the walk proceeded. They went ahead, then turned down one of the alleys, and after that they twisted snake-like so that soon all sense of direction was lost. They passed only one other wakeful man, a man who stared briefly and then vanished, presumably lest harm should come to himself. They stopped at last outside great gates of iron worked into strange shapes and topped by massive balls that could have been solid gold. Inside a man stood guard, a man who appeared to be of some private army, a man who at a word from Ogilvie's escort opened the gates to admit them. Two more men came from a guardroom inside the gate and held Ogilvie at rifle-point while his captors spoke in low voices to the sentry. A moment later, after handing over Ogilvie's revolver, the men went away and the gates were shut behind them. Ogilvie was pushed ahead of the rifles, through another gateway and into a large square courtyard around which a building like a palace rose in majesty, its towers seeming to probe the bright clusters of stars and to challenge the moon itself. Ogilvie was pushed up a flight of steps carved out of marble and from there into a magnificent hall, filled with light from oil lamps and candles burning in crystal chandeliers that hung from a ceiling patterned in gold with clusters of jewels sparkling red and green, white and blue and purple in the lamplight. Great marble columns climbed to this ceiling, and from one end of the apartment a staircase rose with wide, deep steps covered with a crimson carpet. Ogilvie was marched across the hall and through another door where, abruptly, the scene of splendour changed. Here he was in a bare, functional passage with dirty walls of rough stone and an uneven stone floor. Ahead of the rifles he went to the end of this passage, through yet another door, and down a greasy flight of steps that spiralled into the depths of the palace. At the bottom was another passage, at its end a trap-door.

Events had come full circle, though the venue had changed: the trap-door was lifted and Ogilvie was pushed to the brink of a black hole from which a vile smell rose. The goatskin coat was torn from him. Then a heavy blow landed in the region of his kidneys, a smashing blow from a rifle-butt, and he doubled up in pain and dropped like a sack through the hole.

* * *

As snow began to fall Razjah Shah's man threaded his way back through the maze of alleys and reached the perimeter in safety. He left the city, heading for the track into the hills, moving at a loping run as soon as he was away and clear, unseen and unremarked as he had been throughout. He was breathless when he reached the heights and answered the challenge, to be brought to Razjah Shah. "Ogilvie sahib has been taken to the palace of a merchant friendly towards Murrum Khan," he reported. "I followed all the way, but was not seen."

"And you can find this palace again?"

"With no difficulty. It is big, and I have the way in my mind, Razjah Shah."

"You have done well and I am pleased."

"Then we go down again to Mana, Razjah Shah?"

"I have given my word that I shall come to Ogilvie sahib, and come I shall, but not yet. We must wait and find out more things first, and when the dawn comes I shall go alone into Mana."

When the first streaks of morning lit the peaks, now snow-covered, around the silent city, Razjah Shah was as good as his word. His orders given, he rode alone down the track, out of the hills to the flat lands. He rode openly and arrogantly, and swaggered his way into Mana, riding slowly through freezing alleys already starting to teem with native life, heading for the bazaar quarter, where he dropped the word that he wished a meeting with a one-armed man, a *fakir*

114

named Zulifiqar. As he waited beneath the snowflakes' fall for the *fakir* to be found, he heard a sound from the distance, a sound that slowly swelled and, as it was heard by the townspeople, brought conflicting emotions to the dark faces around him: the evocative and often terrible sound of the wailing pig, the stirring warlike sound of the instrument beloved of the soldiers with skirts like Captain Ogilvie sahib, a sound that also stirred the hearts of the Pathans themselves. As this sound grew louder a thin man approached Razjah Shah's horse and caught his attention, bowing low.

Razjah Shah stared down. "Well?"

"The *fakir* Zulifiqar waits, Razjah Shah sahib."

"Where does he wait?"

The thin man bowed again. "I will take you to him."

"Then quickly! Time passes, and the sounds of war beyond the city tell me that certain threads may cross to the disadvantage of many people."

* * *

The wind had died, but now the snow had come in earnest; it lay white and deep over the peaks and drifted down to cover the countryside, the great plateau in which Mana was situated, to bring more discomfort at the end of a long and weary march, a march that had seemed to bring all the varied fortunes of the Frontier. Hunger and thirst and cold, and the fording of rivers during which in some cases men had had to wade through rushing waist-deep water with their rifles held above their heads. The guns had been sent across on rafts while the transport mules were made to plunge in and swim with their loads, and the camels pushed through with dignified faces above the bow-waves at their breasts. The wet clothing had to dry as best it could on the soldiers' bodies as they marched on, and the soaked kilts brought chafing and sores to the thighs. Now the marching feet lifted and came down soggily in the snow's muffling silence, making it almost impossible to keep the step despite the exasperation of Captain Black who rode down the column like a snowman on horseback, snapping at the colour-sergeants. As the covering deepened the order was passed back by the Colonel for the battalion to break step; much relief was brought thereby. The pipes and drums continued, sending their message ahead towards Mana that the High Commissioner was approaching under escort of the power and panoply of the Raj to see justice done in the name of Her Majesty Queen Victoria.

From Brigade, the orderly officer came riding down the marching, weary line with orders for all commanding officers to report to the Brigadier-General for briefing. The orders were concise: the brigade would make camp two miles outside Mana to the north and never mind the snow. It would be warm enough inside the tents. Full defensive precautions were to be taken: the perimeter to be strongly protected by a rampart faced with a ditch, the guns to be posted along the perimeter itself with the horses, mules and camels held in the centre with the camp followers. Guards and sentries would be maintained all along the perimeter, with warning posts established a hundred yards outside for the shoot-and-skedaddle men.

The Brigadier-General pointed ahead with his riding-crop, indicating a ravine that ran out across the plateau from the mountains. Along it marauders could descend in cover from the heights and lie nicely concealed until the moment came to spring out and attack. "I don't like that *nullah,* but it's going to be difficult to avoid unless we skirt the town and come up round the southern side. I don't like that either! It puts Mana between us and our line of communication to the north." He frowned. "What d'you think, Brigade Major?"

"I'd risk the *nullah,* sir. Provided we make camp so as to leave enough space between the perimeter and the *nullah,* we should not be easily surprised."

Norris agreed. "Very well, gentlemen, but see to it that your sentries are vigilant." He turned to the High Commissioner, who was in fact only just visible beneath an immense fur coat that covered his horse's rump as well as his own body, and a heavy fur cap with ear-flaps. "There'll be a fluttering in the dovecots of Mana now, Sir Lawrence, and I expect a visit shortly from a representative *malik*. When do you wish to start your business?"

"As soon as possible," Sir Lawrence Bindle answered through chattering teeth and blue lips. "I shall be ready for the *maliks* whenever they wish, and propose to hold a *jirgah* in the first place."

"Talking-shops!" the Brigadier-General said with a snort.

"A very necessary preliminary, I fear, General."

"Well, Sir Lawrence, I trust you'll not lose sight of two facts: the bayonets are ready if and when you want them, and the men of my brigade are made of flesh and blood—and both can freeze in this damnable climate!" The Brigadier-General turned back to his colonels. "Thank you, gentlemen, that's all for now."

Salutes were exchanged and the officers rode back to their battalions, where the temporarily halted men were stamping feet and blowing through mittened fingers to keep the horrors of frostbite at bay. The brigade moved on, to be halted in their appointed position below the hills now white and bleak with the falling snow, some of them bearing the dark green of pines that were becoming invisible as the flakes drifted down. As the order to halt was given, the pipes and drums fell silent and the men were fallen out and at once set to the task, a busy one, of making camp. Parties were marched away to dig the perimeter trench and throw up the rampart while other men shook out the tents from the backs of the mules and under the direction of the Regimental Sergeant-Major and the Regimental Quarter Master Sergeant began to peg them out in their strictly measured lines, scooping the snow from underneath with shovels. It was a warming task and the men had no objection to that, and in all conscience it was little colder than the depot at Invermore in Scotland, little worse than the route marches through the wild Monadhliath Mountains or the Grampians. . .

Cunningham, marching about his duties, was hailed by the Adjutant. He halted, making a personal snow-flurry beneath the swirling pleats of his kilt, and saluted.

"Sir!"

"Tents up—but we must still consider warmth, of which there will be little enough. What there is must be self generated." Black stared down from a greyish face, the dark moustache flecked with snow that, melting, ran into his mouth. "Do you take my meaning, Mr Cunningham?"

"I think you mean drill, sir."

"I think I do too, Mr Cunningham. See to it that the drill-sergeants are instructed."

"Aye, sir. Begging your pardon, sir, the men will be kept busy with guards and sentry duties and providing the out-post—"

"Not all the time, Sar'nt-Major. When not employed on guard, they are to drill. Sleep will take second place—in their own interest, as advised by the Surgeon Major."

"Aye, sir." Cunningham hesitated. "Is there any word yet of Captain Ogilvie, sir?"

"None." Black swung his horse round and moved away, his trewed thighs damp with the snow. The Regimental Sergeant-Major marched off to inspect progress at the perimeter ditch and reflected sardonically on drill in two feet, maybe more, of snow... not that he disputed the doctor's dictum, for sleep could bring the frostbite if the temperature fell low enough—but drill! The men would be better employed shovelling the snow than tramping it into hard-packed ice, and Cunningham made a guess that drill was not the doctor's panacea but one hatched up in his name by the Major and the Adjutant. Meanwhile, what in God's name was Captain Ogilvie undergoing?

*   *   *

The holy man, the *fakir* named Zulifiqar, was as brown as a nut, as bald as a coot, as thin as a stalk of wheat, and, despite the cold, almost as naked as a baby. Dressed only in a dirty white loin-cloth, he sat cross-legged in a fireless room into which blew eddies of snow through the hole in the hovel's cracked wall. It was a desolate and unpropitious sight, but it was somehow warmed and lightened and made to glow with hope by the eyes of the *fakir*. Holiness and goodness shone like a lantern in the darkness of a mountain pass, and gladdened Razjah Shah's heart.

"Whence do you come, Razjah Shah?" the *fakir* had asked.

"From Afghanistan."

"And your purpose?"

"To watch boundaries, O Zulifiqar, holy one. And in watching, to frustrate the schemes of another, an Afridi who would bend affairs to his own ends to the detriment of not only myself and my tribe of Mahsuds but also to the detriment of the townspeople of Mana." Razjah Shah paused, watching the *fakir* closely. "I think you know to whom I refer, O Zulifiqar, holy one, beloved of the Prophet and of Allah."

The eyes shone with benevolence. "This is possible. The one to whom you may perhaps refer is of the faith, a believer, and is beloved of Allah also, as much as you, Razjah Shah."

"Neither Allah nor his Prophet is blind or deaf, O Zulifiqar. Because of this he loves some less than others."

"We do not presume to know the mind of Allah," the *fakir* said with a hint of a reprimand.

"But we are permitted to guess." Razjah Shah shifted slightly on the earth floor, which was abominably cold when a man kept his body so still, and his attitude of obeisance was uncomfortable also. "This man is rich, and rich men are not beloved of Allah so much as poor men. In addition he is a murderer, and the son of a murderer—"

"All Pathans kill, my son."

Razjah Shah was momentarily nonplussed: what the *fakir* said was the truth. But he turned the statement neatly. "When the cause is good," he responded with equal truth, "the crime is less heinous in the eyes of Allah." He said no more; a case could be too strongly pressed and he needed, urgently, the help of the holy man. Humble silence was better now, and the *fakir* could be left to his digestion of utterances made. Digestion took a long time; Razjah Shah, growing restless, became seized with impatient and unworthy—and unholy—thoughts. The holy one was a holy old faggot, an old idiot to whom all men were in basis good—a stupid

119

philosophy and demonstrably, at any rate in non-Prophet terms, a false one. Razjah Shah shifted again, anxious to interrupt the processes of thought with further evidence of Murrum Khan's many iniquities, but fearing still to do so. At length patience and humility were rewarded. The *fakir* spoke.

"Razjah Shah, all men are brothers and must be treated as such. Yet within the family are the unruly ones together with the obedient and peaceable ones."

"Your words are true, O Zulifiqar, O holy one."

"The wise father admonishes the unruly sons for their own good."

"Yes. This is what the wise and good father does, O Zulifiqar."

There was another pause, a lengthy one again, and cruel for the spirit to bear in abjection. And prostration was becoming most painful . . . before Razjah Shah was forced to groan aloud, the *fakir* spoke once more. "My son, we must follow the teachings of the Prophet and the good example of his holy master's fatherhood."

"And admonish the unruly son, O Zulifiqar?"

The bald head inclined slightly. "So. You must tell me more, and then I can consider the admonishment, and how much of it there should be."

"Your wisdom is great, O holy one, beloved of Allah, seer of seers, in touch with heaven, doer of much good in the name of the Prophet Mahomet. The man of whom I speak has seized an officer sahib, a white officer of the powerful Raj . . . and also a mem'sahib, wife of a high official of the civil power, one who in India speaks for the white queen who presides over the world from the great castle at Windsor. This will bring much trouble and the shedding of rivers of blood to Mana, the more so since British soldiers now sit waiting outside the city. I, Razjah Shah, an unworthy man in the eyes of Allah but a loyal one and one well disposed towards Mana and its people, offer help. This help will not be enough without your help. O holy one, O great thinker, O man of much humbleness and goodness. . ." Razjah Shah most mightily abased himself, speaking almost automatic-

120

ally whilst his mind roved busily over more mundane matters: the *fakir,* who was of the *Ba Shara* class, and therefore one who was 'with the law' according to the faith, was undoubtedly good, undoubtedly holy and wise; but he was also practical, and his poverty was more apparent than real. Zulifiqar could help much; Zulifiqar was a power of his own, with call upon the services of many, many men and guns in the name of Allah, and was indeed something of a rabble-rouser whom almost one might call a lost *mullah.* After the help had been rendered, Zulifiqar would not be found unwilling to receive a reward. His price would be high, even if it were never mentioned in so many words, but it would prove well worth a large number of sheep and goats laced with just a little virgin gold, and a promise that Razjah Shah would, if ever called upon to return favour for favour, be at the holy one's call beyond the mountainous border of Afghanistan. . .

Razjah Shah reached the end of his submission.

"You argue well, my son."

"You speak with kindness, O Zulifiqar."

"Unruly brothers disturb the family. . ."

"Truly they disturb it much, O holy one."

"I shall help as you ask, and you will be grateful."

"I will be very grateful, O Zulifiqar." With a wince, Razjah Shah straightened his aching body.

*　　*　　*

In its long journey on the wings of the wind from the peaks and foothills of Himalaya in the north, the snow had passed over the splendid buildings of Division in Nowshera, and over Peshawar. It had whitened the cantonments and the garrison lines, the roads of communication, the Quissa Khawani Bazaar or Street of the Story-Tellers, the Mochi Lara with its dazzling displays of embroidered sandals, and all the spider's-web of alleys of the old native city. It had ceased its fall when the horseman out of the south, a wild man out from the Waziri hills, rode in; but the flakes lay thick upon the ground and the hoofbeats were muffled as the rider cantered along the alleys, scattering the townsfolk who stared up at a wild and haggard face, dark with almost frozen and congested blood. The man, who was clad in a long cloak and wore a green turban, was well armed with knives and daggers and a *jezail* that lay ready to hand across his saddle. The rider turned aside quickly when a British military patrol came into view ahead, a corporal and four privates from a line regiment keeping the peace in the city, a peace that the lone rider seemed likely enough to shatter. But he passed through Peshawar keeping his weapons to himself, and no peace was shattered until he began to approach the outskirts on the Nowshera side and found a fat man squatting on a cushion in the doorway of a hovel that announced itself by a sign as being the shop of Sajjad Athar, trader in leathern commodities.

The rider pulled up his horse, and lying snow flew. He seized and waved his *jezail* and its rusty bayonet. "You!"

Politely, the fat man clambered to his feet, holding his stomach and a bubbling *hookah* pipe. "You wish harness, perhaps?"

"I wish you, fat trader. Come!"

The man approached a little fearfully. "What do you wish, friend?"

"You are Sajjad Athar?"

"Yes, I am he—"

"Good! And as a trader in Peshawar, one who gets his living from his shop, you will wish no interference with your custom. Do not trouble yourself to answer. I know your answer before your mouth opens. Catch this, fat trader."

He lifted his hand and threw something: a goatskin bag, rimmed with brass and with a hasp and small padlock, landed in the snow. The fat man bent and picked it up, staring at it in increasing fear and wonder.

The rider said, "The bag you will take unopened to Nowshera, and you will deliver it to the Lieutenant-General sahib commanding the First Division of the British Army. If there is any failure, your trade will vanish in the burning down of your shop and the removal of your tongue, fat trader. You have a horse?"

"Yes—"

"Then mount and ride, but not before two hours have passed. In the meantime remain as usual in your shop and communicate with no one." The wild man brought his horse round, its hooves slipping and sliding on the packed snow. He rode away, leaving the fat man to stare after him and quake for his family and his living.

11

IN NOWSHERA BLOODY Francis Fettleworth raised his eyebrows at his Chief of Staff. "A trader, from Peshawar?"

"With this, sir." Lakenham held out the goatskin bag.

Suspiciously, the Divisional Commander took it, laid it on his desk and stared at it. "What is it, d'you suppose, Lakenham?"

The Chief of Staff explained the circumstances of the bag's delivery to Sajjad Athar, and added, "I take it as containing a message, sir."

"Then we'd better look inside! But it's padlocked."

"Allow me, sir." Lakenham took possession of the bag again, brought out a pocket-knife with an attachment for removing stones from horses' hooves, and inserted this steel probe into the hasp. He twisted, the hasp parted company with the brass rim, and he upended the bag. A piece of parchment, covered with thin spidery writing, fell out upon the General's desk. Fettleworth picked it up, his expression distasteful, stared at it doubtfully as he had at its container, then laid it on the desk and told his Chief of Staff to smooth it out; which was done.

Fettleworth then read the words aloud: "I have in my power the mem'sahib from Nowshera also her kinsman Captain Ogilvie, son of the Lieutenant-General sahib at Murree. Both will die unless the British High Commissioner is ordered to decide the boundaries as drawn on the other side of this parchment." Fettleworth pulled a red silk handkerchief from his pocket and mopped at his face: he had begun to sweat badly, and his eyes were staring. "It's signed Murrum Khan. God in heaven! What do we do now?"

"It's not unexpected, sir, when all's said and done—"

"No, but—"

"I suggest we turn the parchment over for a start, sir, and see what the actual demand is."

"Yes, yes." With shaking fingers, Bloody Francis turned the parchment over and swore again. "Good God, Lakenham, just look at that! The bugger wants all the damn territory from a little north of Mana to the damn Afghan border! All the way north to the Kurrum River and the damn railway line from Kohat to Parachinar! It's monstrous, Lakenham, absolutely monstrous!"

Lakenham took up the roughly-drawn map and studied it. "I agree, sir. What do you propose to do about it?"

"Do?" With glassy eyes, Fettleworth stared. "For a start, reject the bugger's impudent demands, of course! He must be mad! What does he think I can do for him anyway? I'm the military. It's not for me to attempt to sway the High Commissioner's judgment, is it?"

"No, sir. I suggest Murrum Khan will be expecting you to pass on his message to quarters that would be in a position to accommodate him . . . if they were so minded."

"Which of course they damn well won't be!" Fettleworth said energetically. "Damn impertinence, I've never heard the like! I suppose you mean the Government in Calcutta, don't you, Lakenham?"

"Naturally," Lakenham answered with a touch of impatience. "But you'll have to go through the proper channels first, sir."

"What?" Fettleworth seemed dazed.

"The Army Commander, sir. And Sir Iain's going to be mightily concerned in a very personal way, is he not?"

Fettleworth sucked in breath and rose to his feet, his large stomach, scarlet-clad, rising over the edge of his desk. He went across to the wide window and stood looking out at the lying flakes and the Divisional flag drooping from its staff, its colours lost in a covering of frozen snow. However expected the demands had been ever since the disappearance of Mrs Ogilvie, their actual arrival was still a shock and the more so since the son of the Army Commander was also now a prisoner of the damn heathen: much trouble would now fall upon the luckless Divisional Commander at Nowshera, and Bloody Francis, not so far off retirement, had no wish to have his copy-book blotted at this late stage. Fettleworth stood and quaked, felt a shiver in his spine and a queasy visitation of his stomach: Sir Iain Ogilvie was far from being an easy man to suffer under, and never mind that their military ranks were the same—the Army Commander was his superior and that was that. The loss to the evil machinations of the Pathan of not only his nephew's wife, but also his own son, would certainly not incline Sir Iain towards reasonableness . . . but as Fettleworth turned from the window and his protuberant blue eyes met, across the long room, the portrait of Her Majesty the Queen-Empress, he stiffened himself. That stern, autocratic face, the down-the-nose look, the neat bun sticking out a little way behind the lace cap, the plump and motherly breast, the firm rat-trap mouth the utterances of which scared the bowels out of the Prince of Wales . . . it all added up to a tonic, a sort of distillation of the enormous power of the British Raj. Fettleworth's chest went out: Murrum Khan was nothing but a damn native, an ill-kempt Pathan ridden out from beyond the Khyber, an upstart with crazy demands upon British territory, scum that would shortly be despatched with his brigands back whence he had come, unless his head first rolled bloodily in battle or his wretched body dropped limp from the scaffold in the civil jail in Nowshera! How could such scum dream that they could challenge the might and authority of Her Majesty Queen Victoria! Really, there was no cause at all for alarm.

Fettleworth once again seated himself behind his desk. "That trader, whatsisname. Better send him in, Lakenham. Lily-livered bugger should have raised the alarm before the damn messenger got away."

The Chief of Staff went to the door and beckoned. In came Sajjad Athar, trader in leathern commodities, a frightened fat man cringing between an armed escort of a corporal and two privates of the King's Regiment. His eyes were closed, so great was the glory of the Commander sahib of Her Majesty's First Division in Nowshera and Peshawar, Her Majesty's own representative, very God of very God to poor

126

traders whose service to the Raj was but humble. Sajjad Athar quaked but began in a high voice to justify himself: his business, his living were at stake, so was his family of a wife and fourteen children and a mother and a mother-in-law and many aunts, uncles and cousins and cousins' children. All would have suffered, and in an agony of remorse he had obeyed the wild-looking nomad and had remained in his shop for the appointed time. He was most humbly sorry, he was abject, prostrate and most loyal to the Raj.

"Take him away, for God's sake, Lakenham, he makes me sick. Not a thought for the Raj! Get a description of the damn Pathan, for what it's worth, and notify Brigade at Peshawar. Then you shall inform Northern Command— and I'd better have a word with Mr Hector Ogilvie, I fancy. . ."

*   *   *

All night Ogilvie had lain in the hole's blackness, assailed by the terrible stench of drains and putrefaction, and by more: by the attentions of rats and smaller things that crawled and bit, and by puddles and trickles of water, and at one moment, a terrifying moment, by something cold and smooth that wriggled across his neck—a snake, but one that had not attacked. After that, the place held sheer horror and Ogilvie scarcely dared to breathe unless he should attract the snake. But as all things come to an end, so did this: as he began to give up all hope he heard the opening of the trap-door above, and yellow light came down, and in the glow he saw a man's face, evil and bearded and scarred with the cuts of knives or bayonets.

A moment later a rope's-end was trailed down and the man said, "Come."

Ogilvie grasped the rope and climbed. As he came through the hatch his body was seized by two pairs of hands and he was set on firm foundation. The lantern's light gleamed on three men, well armed. Not another word was said; the point of a knife in his back gave him his marching orders, and he went ahead along the passage which he had traversed the

127

previous evening, up the spiral steps and along the second passage; but not through the door at the end that led to the richly-decorated state apartments. Instead he was halted at a door half-way along, and one of the men knocked with the butt of a *jezail*. From inside heavy bolts were drawn and the door was opened.

Ogilvie was pushed in. Entering, he was at first blinded by sudden brilliant light, light from what seemed like thousands of candles burning in crystal chandeliers and reflecting off polished silver that surrounded many mirrors built into the walls of a great room. As his eyes became accustomed to the glare, Ogilvie saw that this was no ordinary room: at one end was a raised dais, and on this dais stood a number of gilded chairs like thrones, only one of which was occupied. Along the side walls stood benches; it was like a courtroom or an auditorium. Running almost the length of the room, and some twenty feet wide, was water. By the look of it, deep water—a kind of sunken bath of vast proportions. The atmosphere was warm and humid. Across this curious pool, some half-dozen feet from the far end, ran a barrier, a wooden boom with a strong wire-mesh net stretching down from it, a net that seemed taut as though it were held fast at the bottom. From beyond the pool, from the single man seated on the dais, there came a laugh that echoed round the high walls, a hand flashed, something flew through the air, and landed with a splash in the water beyond the barrier. On its heels there was a sudden flurry in the water, then a larger disturbance that made small waves run, and from a dark round hole just below the water's surface a thing emerged at speed, long and scaly and with enormous snapping jaws and big eyes: a crocodile.

Ogilvie shivered, a prey to sudden hopeless fear, but clamped his teeth hard. Behind him, the knives pushed him towards the dais and the seated man whom he guessed to be Murrum Khan. The description as given him at Fort Jamrud fitted in every detail: the gold-worked cloak of maroon cloth, the exceptional height of the man, the gold earrings with dangling medallions. Ogilvie could not see the boar's head motif but had no doubt that it was there. Halted by his escort, he stared upwards at the Pathan, and there was another laugh.

"How neatly you have dropped into my hands, Ogilvie sahib!"

"Not for long. The Raj never sleeps, Murrum Khan."

"So you know my name."

"As do others. I think your time will be short, Murrum Khan, now that you have transgressed the law of the Raj."

The man gathered saliva and spat. The gob landed on Ogilvie's tunic and drooled down. "That is what I think of the Raj. That is what I think of your Queen-Empress, who is fat with age and inactivity and who has reigned for too long, and who is greedy, and who must now shed land to those who dwell upon it. When the news that you are in my power is told in your garrisons of the Raj, especially those of the north, then I believe negotiations will start. Do you not agree?"

Ogilvie said, "The Raj always negotiates, Murrum Khan, but from a position of justice. The High Commissioner is coming for that purpose, as you know well, but there will be no shedding of land on the part of the Raj—"

"I spit on your High Commissioner as I spit upon the Raj itself," Murrum Khan said, and again spat. "It is not your High Commissioner who concerns me, but the General Officer Commanding your Northern Army of the Raj."

Ogilvie nodded. "I expected that, naturally. But I think you misunderstand the Raj and underestimate my father. What would you do, if your son were held as hostage by the Raj, Murrum Khan? Would blood weigh more heavily than what you saw as your duty?"

Murrum Khan smiled. "I answer that it would not, Ogilvie sahib."

"Exactly! On the other hand, you would use all your strength to get your son back. That's what my father will do. I am not so much a hostage, Murrum Khan, as a millstone round your neck, and your neck is a fragile thing when set against the regiments and brigades and divisions of the Raj."

"Brave talk," Murrum Khan said sneeringly. "It is you who fail to understand *me*, not I you. I do not expect the

General sahib to urge surrender on the Government in Calcutta for his own sake or yours, but I think the Raj will accommodate my wishes nevertheless. What is a mountainous track of land when set against a man's life?"

"Frontier land is much valued for defence against the Afghan tribes, and in any case it's a matter of principle, Murrum Khan. If a thing is done once, it can be done again. That is why there will be no surrender, no matter how many men's lives are threatened."

The Pathan lifted an eyebrow. "Then a woman's life?"

Ogilvie caught his breath: that Angela was in this man's hands he knew, but the utterance of the threat was hard to take. He asked, "My cousin's wife?"

"The same." Murrum Khan got to his feet, and stood tall and commanding. He clapped his hands twice. "Turn round, Ogilvie sahib," he said.

Slowly, feeling as cold as death, Ogilvie turned. The door was thrown open by a man standing just inside. Something like a procession came through, led by a man with the holy air of a priest. After him came two young women, heavily veiled in accordance with the teachings of the faith of Islam; after them two armed men in ragged garments, looking strangely out of place in the mirrored room with its chandeliers. Behind them Angela Ogilvie, calm seemingly, but with a face like ashes. Behind her two more guards and finally a bent and shambling old beldame, veiled like the young women, and clad in deepest black all over so that she looked like a slow-moving, earth-bound crow.

Ogilvie opened his mouth to call out to Angela, but the words stuck in a dust-dry throat and mouth. As for the girl herself, she seemed not to be registering or to have even recognised her husband's cousin; her eyes were dull, lacking all life. As the procession came forward and halted at the doorward end of the pool of water, Ogilvie turned on Murrum Khan, fists clenched, and took a step forward. At once he was seized by his escort and a knife-point nicked his throat, drawing blood, while another pressed against his side. Again the words would not come: there was little point in the utterance of them in any case.

130

Murrum Khan spoke: "The way out is open. It calls only for the compliance of the Raj. Let this be understood."

Again he clapped his hands, and there was a stir behind Ogilvie, and then a cry of terror and despair. He swung round. Angela had been lifted high by the guards and was being borne past the veiled women. A moment later her body was swung, and thrown, and spread-eagled she splashed down into the water of the pool. Immediately she touched, and for a moment sank, the flurry came again from behind the barrier and an armoured tail was flailed, battering at the net, and cruel jagged teeth in the long jaw cracked harshly at the wooden boom and splinters came away. There was a violent thrashing, and as Angela, screaming in terror, put up her hands to grip the sides of the pool, the guards moved towards her with their knives. Blood trailed in the water thereafter and the scaly creature, which Ogilvie recognised as *crocodilus porosus,* a native of India, a species known to be capable of growing to a length of thirty-three feet and to have a voracious appetite for flesh, hurled itself again and again at the net, almost lifting the boom in its sockets and bringing a terrible hollow sound to echo about the apartment.

12

THE COLD IN Mana was intense: the wind bit to the bone and the snow lay to freeze the feet. But the *fakir* Zulifiqar seemed possessed of an inner fire. His nakedness covered only by a white cloth like a sheet that fell from his bald head to enfold his body, he went out into the alleys seated on a board carried by four men, pausing at corners and in the wintry bazaar to talk. His words spread; men gathered in groups in the alleys, or sat huddled in hovels out of the snow's searching wet fingers. The *fakir's* words were pondered: the great one in the palace, Murrum Khan, was about business that would bring much trouble to the city, and the Prophet would be displeased thereby. Already outside the city—and this they knew without assistance from the Prophet or his henchman Zulifiqar—the power of the Raj was manifest in the presence of many soldiers and weapons. Soon there would be discussions between the Raj and the *maliks* from the neighbouring tribes, and it would be well if these were peaceable. The British were on the whole just, and at times were merciful, but there were the other times when they reacted with fire and sword and put entire communities to the flame of the torch by way of punishment for crimes committed against the almighty Raj. Murrum Khan was of course powerful, but on a much more localised scale than the Raj that stretched from Cape Comorin to Himalaya, from Karachi to the Bay of Bengal and the Sundarbans of the Brahmaputra, embracing Muslim and Hindu, Sikh and Jain and many other religions, and enjoying the support of all the great princes of India. Against this, so said the *fakir* Zulifiqar, Murrum Khan was no more than the flea upon the dog. Yet Murrum Khan was here in Mana, while so far the main power of the Raj was not . . . a problem existed, and many were the mutters as the dictum of the *fakir* spread.

* * *

Lieutenant-General Fettleworth's urgent despatches sped to their destinations and Hector Ogilvie was summoned to Division and given word of his wife: Fettleworth promised that everything possible would be done, but refused to be drawn on specifics. The matter, he said, was moving out of his hands and the orders would now be given by the Army Commander after decisions had been made at Viceregal level in Calcutta with the advice of the Commander-in-Chief. Hector, almost distraught by now, unable to eat or sleep since his wife's disappearance, demanded audience of his uncle, who had remained on in Nowshera; but found little help from that quarter.

"My dear boy," Sir Iain said sympathetically, "I'm as worried as you are, but what more can I do than send out patrols to cover as much territory as possible?"

"It can be settled easily enough, Uncle Iain—"

"Pray tell me how!"

Hector's lips trembled. "The message to General Fettleworth. It offered a way out."

"I disagree," Sir Iain said frostily. "It did no such thing."

"But—"

"The integrity of the High Commissioner cannot possibly be compromised, and will not be by any order of mine. I hope that's clear, Hector."

"Your own son!" Hector put his head in his hands.

Sir Iain caught Fettleworth's eye and read understanding: it was always the very devil when one's own flesh-and-blood became involved, and it was when such happened that those who held high command were put to the ultimate test. Sir Iain, who had already faced his own wife, James's mother, stiffened himself. He said quietly but formidably, "Yes, Hector, my own son. I know. And I'm very fond of Angela as well. You must never doubt that. But you must remember my responsibilities. I have the whole future of the Raj to consider."

133

Hector burst out, "One wretched little boundary dispute, a parcel of barren land . . . how can anyone be so damn stupid!"

"Barren land yes, but strategically vital. It must be held by those the Raj can trust. It can never pass to a border bandit such as Murrum Khan. Wretched it may be, but little it is not! You of all people, Hector, should know the balance for the Raj is knife-edged . . . that there are many dissidents waiting their chance—"

"In other words, Uncle Iain, the integrity of the High Commissioner doesn't exist!"

Colour mounted in the GOC's cheeks. "I beg your pardon?"

"It's already biased, isn't it? His decision must be acceptable to the Raj—"

"As must that of a judge be acceptable to the law. I see no difference. The Raj must remain faithful to its friends or it is lost. I shall not aid its enemies, Hector. I'm sorry, but if you've come here to persuade me to use my command for personal ends, you're wasting my time and yours."

"Then you'll do nothing?"

Sir Iain's mouth opened, then closed again. He turned away and walked to the window, where, like Fettleworth earlier, he remained staring out at the symbol of the Raj, the standard of the First Division hoisted to the head of the flagstaff. There was a massive lump in his throat and he wished himself back as a regimental officer in the Royal Strathspey, a position where it would not be inconceivable that he could make a personal foray against the tribesmen, strike some personal and private blow in support of his own kin without it becoming a matter for rising murmurs in headquarters and messes and barrack-rooms as well as in the places of civil power and the echoing halls of government. As General Officer Commanding, the envy of many of lower rank, he was hamstrung, tied up in his own conscience and his own appointment, as it were the unfreest soldier in all Northern India after the Commander-in-Chief himself. Without turning, he spoke: "I shall do all possible, Hector. Extra patrols, wider probes . . . someone shall be taken, and will talk of

134

Murrum Khan. He'll be found, never fear!" He had control of himself now, and he turned to face Fettleworth. "I believe the most likely area is the Afghan border itself, Fettleworth, the area where Murrum Khan's interest lies."

"From Jamrud down to Mana?"

"Yes. These bandits prefer to keep within the limits of their own influence—where their support is. I suggest you saturate the area and if necessary deplete the Nowshera and Peshawar garrisons, the others too. I've already asked for reinforcements from Southern Army, and don't tell me they'll take the devil of a time being trooped by the train from Ootacamund—I know it! It's the best we can do."

"And Mana itself—and Sir Lawrence Bindle?"

"Bindle has Norris's brigade as escort and I consider that force enough, though you'd better hold some cavalry in reserve to reinforce if necessary. Norris may have reached Mana by now—we must await further word before we make more dispositions." Sir Iain put a hand on Hector's shoulder and said kindly, "It's hard to bear, Hector, but be assured everything's being done that can be done. I suggest you occupy yourself in work—it's the only way."

* * *

Andrew Black made for the Colonel's tent, returned the salute of the sentry, and ducked down through the flap. "Your pardon, Colonel. There's a mounted party approaching from the town, under a flag of truce."

"Brigade's been informed, Andrew?"

"I understand so, Colonel."

Dornoch reached for his Sam Browne and buckled it on. As he took up his glengarry the bugle sounded from the brigade tent, ordering the stand-to. No chances were being taken, it seemed, and never mind the flag of truce. With the Adjutant, Dornoch left his tent. He looked towards Mana, as white as the surrounding hills. The air was bitter, with a rising wind blowing the lying snow and the falling flakes into whirls and flurries. There was quite a procession coming out: a troop of native horsemen, wild and ragged so far as could

135

be seen beneath their covering of snow, twenty riders escorting a party of old, bent men, the *maliks* coming out for the *jirgah*.

"They appear as old as Methuselah, Colonel," Black said.

Dornoch laughed. "Then they should have much collective wisdom!" He turned and strode through the regimental lines towards the perimeter and its ramparted ditch. There was bustle outside the brigade tent, where Brigadier-General Norris was mounting with his Brigade Major and orderly officer to ride to greet the *maliks*. Around the perimeter the soldiers waited with rifles and bayonets, British and Indian together, fingers half frozen as they gripped their weapons, bodies a-shiver beneath the greatcoats. Inside the entry to the camp, where a drawbridge of wooden planks had been thrown across the ditch, a ceremonial guard found by the Border Regiment waited with rifles at the slope. Snow settled upon their helmets, edged the shining bayonet blades with white. The Brigadier-General rode through, behind a mounted *sepoy* of the Punjab Frontier Force bearing a white flag. A hundred yards from the perimeter he halted, and waited for the *maliks* to ride up.

Dornoch was joined by Lord Brora.

"Good morning, Colonel. Here beginneth the verbal diarrhoea. There'll now be delay . . . the damn natives'll be here till next week and beyond!"

"Possibly, Major. Decisions can't be arrived at in haste."

"With respect, Colonel, I think they can and should." Brora waved a hand around. "I don't like that damn *nullah*. It gives too much cover for attack, especially after dark."

"I agree with you there," Dornoch said, "but it's out of our hands, and Brigade knows the risk." He turned as a runner approached, with orders for all commanding officers to attend at Brigade for a ceremonial meeting with the *maliks*. Black and Brora stood watching as the Brigadier-General formally saluted the native party and spent some minutes in apparently friendly conversation, then turned his horse back for the encampment with the newcomers. As the party rode across the makeshift bridge, one at a time and carefully, the guard was ordered to the Present: the *maliks* were to be treated with respect. Into the camp rode the motley collection of tribesmen and elders, old men with wizened faces like nuts, many of them bearded, all of them armed to the teeth.

"Some truce!" Brora said in a loud voice. "I'd not trust the buggers with a dead nanny goat!"

At the brigade tent the *maliks* dismounted and went inside to meet the High Commissioner while their escort remained upon their horses, forming a warlike force by the entrance. As the guard was fallen out and marched away, the bugle sounded again to disperse the men from the stand-to position, and the normal routine was taken up again, parties returning to complete the defences before night should fall and bring the time of danger, though it was unlikely any attack would come while the *maliks* were present in conference.

* * *

Ogilvie was held under guard, sitting in the middle of one of the rows of seats by the side of the water. Angela was still immersed, the ravening scaly brute at the other end still thrashed in frustration behind the mesh barrier. Murrum Khan had departed; before leaving he had told Ogilvie that the water was warm from fires that burned beneath its stone base and the mem'sahib would come to no harm by remaining in it. He expected word before long as to the British response to his message; if that word was favourable, then the mem'sahib and himself would both go free. Should it be unfavourable, the barrier would be lifted. As for Ogilvie himself, he would accompany Murrum Khan into Afghanistan by a devious route; in Afghanistan a resistance to the Raj would be organised, and Murrum Khan would lead an army against the Raj, with Ogilvie still a hostage. Word would be sent to Peshawar of the fate of the mem'sahib, as a terrible earnest that Murrum Khan kept his word and carried out his threats, and Ogilvie himself would testify in writing as one who had been a witness. In the meantime Ogilvie was not left for long with his cousin's wife: soon after Murrum Khan's departure men came for him and

137

once again he was dropped through the stinking hole below the palace, back to the utter darkness of the cell and its crawling, slithering denizens. Here all hope seemed at an end, and Ogilvie was left with his last image of Angela, of the appeal in her eyes as he was taken away leaving her without even the small comfort of his physical presence. Razjah Shah, it seemed, had let him down after all, though in all conscience there must be little the Pathan could do against the solidity of Murrum Khan's palace and his watchful guards.

* * *

The *fakir* Zulifiqar was back in his hovel, bald and bony and bare but still, apparently, not cold. The inner fire burned yet and his eyes gleamed at Razjah Shah. His words, he said, had borne fruit: the townspeople of Mana were anxious, fearful of the British brigade that waited below the hills. Without Murrum Khan, perhaps, the British would go away. Without Murrum Khan their wives and children would not be put to the sword.

"Yet they are a warlike people as are all Pathans, O holy one," Razjah Shah said with a touch of disbelief in the *fakir's* confident words.

"True. But when the Prophet speaks..."

"And the Prophet has spoken?"

"Yes. He has spoken. He has uttered a warning, and his people will heed. It is written."

"What has the Prophet advised, O holy one?"

"That the faithful of Mana turn their hands and their weapons against Murrum Khan and that the hostages be released and returned to the British, who will then heap rewards upon Mana and its people."

"They will attack the palace of Murrum Khan, O Zulifiqar? In that I am ready to assist, since I gave my promise, the word of my honour, to Ogilvie sahib. You have only to say and I shall bring my men."

The holy man lifted a hand, and smiled. "Do not leap ahead of events, Razjah Shah. Your help is needed, but not yet. My ears have been assailed by other tidings, which are these: in the hills is Dostman Khan, and with him his men in much strength." He stared at the Mahsud quizzically. "You have heard of the paw of the cat, Razjah Shah?"

"The paw of the cat, O holy one, leader of the faithful?"

Zulifiqar inclined his head. "To draw from the fire the nuts for others is thrust the paw of the unsuspecting cat, who burns while those whom he benefits remain unscathed." He closed his eyes for a moment. "Dostman Khan, the sworn enemy of Murrum Khan his kinsman, shall be the paw of the cat. A message will be sent, and down from the hills will come Dostman Khan with his armed men."

"To attack the palace of Murrum Khan!"

The *fakir* gave no direct answer to that; he smiled enigmatically and said, "I return to the unfortunate cat, of whom there are said to be more ways than one of killing when desired. There will not be an attack on the palace of Murrum Khan by his kinsman, for if that should be allowed, then the hostages might merely change hands, and much trouble would still come to Mana and its faithful. Better ways are known to the Prophet, my son, and you shall give ear to his wisdom. . ."

Razjah Shah bent a ready ear, and was soon open-mouthed in wonder at the *fakir's* inspired strategy, and his fingers began itching for the fight even as his mind roved busily over the necessity of retaining the hostages, not for Murrum Khan nor for Dostman Khan nor yet for the British, but for himself and the grinding of his own axe. When the *fakir* had finished Razjah Shah's praises were many. Leaving the hovel he made his way, silent in the snow, out of the city and back into the hills to rejoin his patiently waiting men. When he made his contact in the heights he lost no time in briefing his followers; already the night was falling, dark and ghostly yet because of the lying snow not entirely dark, and already a message would be on its way to Dostman Khan, lurking with ready knives and rifles in the hills behind the British brigade encamped and in conference below. The Prophet's strategy, though of course wise beyond worldly wisdom, was simplicity itself: Dostman Khan was to be urged to mount by stealth a raid on the British and capture the arguing *maliks* who the *fakir's* message would say—were known to be about to settle against his interests. Razjah Shah's task was equally straightforward: he was to mount his own attack upon Dostman Khan before the latter had reached the British perimeter. True, his available force was small compared with Dostman Khan's, which was a strong one of a size that should give it the capability of cutting right through the camp's defences before the British had collected their wits; but Razjah Shah's sudden foray would deprive Dostman Khan of the vital element of surprise—and the delighted British, Zulifiqar had said with obvious truth, would return his loyalty with much good will. More importantly they would be certain, as a result of his submissions, to march at once upon the palace of Murrum Khan and release the hostages. It was this last part of the plan that had given Razjah Shah food for thought, thought that had proliferated during his journey back into the hills and, by the time he had reached his tribesmen, had crystalised into firm if dangerous decision: *fakirs* were not to be trifled with, but the prize was great, and afterwards much abasement would be made to Allah in propitiation of his wrath; and Allah's mediator the Prophet, who by virtue of his very calling must ever take the long and broad view of worldly events, would surely proclaim the wisdom of his, Razjah Shah's, act of deviousness . . . if one thing was certain, it was that neither Allah nor the Prophet would wish to assist the infidel British.

"Gather round me," Razjah Shah adjured his followers. "Our difficulties are all but over, so long as our knives are sharp, our rifles loaded, and our wits keen."

*   *   *

The argument in the brigade tent had been long, and was still continuing. Each *malik* in turn had harangued with passionate conviction for his own cause. Each was in conflict with his neighbour, each had his own territorial demand that must be resisted by all the others. Knives had been produced in support of argument and on three occasions troops had

had to be summoned to restrain the headmen and avert the shedding of blood.

Through it all Sir Lawrence Bindle, representative of the Queen-Empress, sat almost motionless but for a head that either nodded or shook as the arguments were presented, sometimes many arguments simultaneously since the *maliks* were not susceptible to the disciplined approach. His mind wandered as the affair grew more and more tangled: long experience of his office as High Commissioner had taught him that tribal arguments could never in fact be untangled and that it was pointless even to try to do so. Before his eyes, as before the eyes of Lieutenant-General Fettleworth, there was ever an image of Her Majesty in the dignified, secure fastness of Windsor Castle: hers was the glory, hers the way all decisions must eventually go. The Raj was paramount, and the judgment of the Raj, like the cleaving of one of Her Majesty's ships of war through the restless seas, was sharp and clear and must cut cleanly through all the arguments, imposing a just solution to all problems. None of the *maliks* would be satisfied as a result of Sir Lawrence's judgment, but all would be dissatisfied together so that in a sense none would be the loser. Why, then, strain oneself by listening? Sir Lawrence listened in fact for one thing only: a mention of the hostages. None came.

The interminable hours dragged past, the atmosphere in the crowded tent became thick and smelly, a horrible cold fug that was oppressive to the senses, senses already battered by the excited, passionate voices of dissent. From outside the ordinary sounds of an encamped brigade followed one upon another: the shouted commands of NCOs, the crunch of marching feet on crisp snow as details and guards and picquets moved about, the notes of the bugles sounding the men to supper and the officers to dinner; and then, as Sir Lawrence yawned mightily, the sad notes of Last Post followed by the solitary piper of the 114th Highlanders. Sir Lawrence pulled out his watch surreptitiously, and sighed. It looked like extending all through the night, but he must not be seen to be hurrying justice yet: the *maliks* must be given their say in the hope that very many words would ease pressures. It had not been unknown in the past history of the Raj for the tribes to talk themselves through unaided to a settlement . . . Sir Lawrence's white head sank to the prop of his left hand, and his eyes gently closed as the waves of argument washed over him like a lullaby. He had had a very tiring journey and he was no longer young.

* * *

The first shot shattered the peace and calm of the mostly sleeping camp. For a moment it seemed to hang in lonely suspension, to be somehow unreal, then it was followed by others, and by shouts of war, and pandemonium seemed to break loose as a rush of feet crunched through the lying snow. In the brigade tent the High Commissioner awoke with a start to find the court in utter confusion, the assembled headmen trying to fight their way out while a guard of the Punjab Frontier Force under a *havildar* tried to push in through what had already become a mob. The *havildar* shouted at the High Commissioner sahib, but his words were lost. Sir Lawrence left his seat of judgment and burrowed through the mass of natives, largely on the ground like an urgent mole, his chest heaving and his eyes staring and a cry of alarm forming in his throat. As he reached the exit he was yanked to his feet, unceremoniously, by the *havildar*, and taken outside. He heard bugles and shouts and rifle-fire and looking towards the south-eastern perimeter he saw men outlined against the snow, leaping and bounding like stags over the defensive rampart and the ditch.

13

LORD BRORA'S FACE was almost black with fury. "I damn well told you so, Colonel! That damn *nullah* was made for the purpose! By God, the Brigadier-General shall lose his balls over this!"

Dornoch took no notice of the Major's outburst. He ran ahead for the breach in the defences, the spot where natives were pouring into the camp undeterred by the rifle and Maxim fire. There was noise everywhere, and a degree of confusion as the various regiments tumbled out with their rifles. Ready dressed and armed as they were, it yet took some minutes to deploy them for the counter-attack, valuable minutes that were a gain for the enemy. Already, and in silence, the perimeter guard and the shoot-and-skedaddle men in the warning outposts had seemingly been attacked and overcome: at any rate they had given no warning of the assault, which had come from the point where the *nullah* ran closest to the perimeter. As Dornoch watched, his revolver in his hand, the whole of the south-eastern defence line became alive with dark bodies that poured across the ditch to hack and stab. Dornoch lifted his revolver and emptied its chambers point-blank into a horde of men closing him, then went down with blood spurting from the shoulder of his already wounded and splinted arm. Feet trampled him as he lay, and he was aware of Brora cutting into more men with his broadsword. Dornoch staggered to his feet and sent out a rallying cry to his Scots: the Regimental Sergeant-Major, running past, checked when he saw the bloodstained figure.

"You'll be best taken to the medical tent, sir."

"I'm all right, Mr Cunningham. Unless Brigade orders otherwise, fan the battalion out along the attack sector —

concentrate the Maxims there too. Where's the Adjutant?"

"Coming up now, sir." Cunningham went off at the double as Black approached, wild-eyed and covered with snow.

"Colonel, they've come in like the tide—"

"I realise that—"

"The Gurkha battalion's being cut to pieces. Their tents were facing the wind, so they laced them up, and were caught like rats. The Pathans have cut the guys . . . the Gurkhas are being slaughtered beneath the folds."

Dornoch swore. "What's Brigade doing, I'd like to know!" A moment later Brigade appeared to react: from the mountain batteries star shell sped into the air, and burst, and in the sudden brilliant light the extent of the attack was seen clearly. The whole camp was alive with tribesmen out of the hills, and with bodies and much blood. A tight formation was moving towards the tent where the High Commissioner had held court; the *maliks* were bunched together, jabbering in terror, while their own guards attempted to fight back but were clearly about to be overwhelmed by sheer numbers. Dornoch shouted into Black's ear above the noise. "Pass the word to all company commanders, Andrew: the battalion to fall back on the southern perimeter and then form into line. They're to move through the camp with bayonets fixed, and clear the ground as they go. No quarter, Andrew. Send a runner to Brigade to inform the Brigadier-General."

Black doubled away, sending out blasts from the whistle on the lanyard round his neck. As the fighting continued in the centre where the Gurkhas and the men of the Punjab Frontier Force were still under heavy attack that amounted to bloody slaughter, the Scots companies began to withdraw to the ditch. They were joined by the Borderers led by their Colonel, who had assessed Dornoch's intentions and had reacted swiftly. When both battalions had formed line with their backs to the defences, Lord Dornoch gave the word, blood pouring down from his shoulder. On a grim, long front the Scots and Borderers advanced at the double behind the shining steel of their bayonets, sweeping the camp from side to side, ready to return slaughter for slaughter. As the tribesmen continued their hacking at the helpless, canvas-

144

bound Gurkhas, the bayonets took them from the rear, slicing savagely into writhing bodies, to be twisted cruelly and withdrawn and sent plunging into the next man.

All through the history of the Raj the Pathan had been a brave fighter against the guns and the rifles, but always the naked steel of the bayonet had been a different story and one that struck dreadful fear into the native mind, and as close upon twelve hundred bayonets came down upon them, they broke. Pursued by a savage vengeance, they ran screaming for the far side of the camp, falling along the way in scores as they were overtaken. Behind the advancing line of Scots and Borderers the *sepoys* of the Indian Army re-formed and were ordered by Brigade to outflank the centre fighting and mass along the tribesmen's escape route. As the attackers flung themselves across the ditch and up the rampart, rifle and Maxim fire stuttered out, tearing into the mass of bodies and sending them in heaps into the ditch as they fell in mid air or slid dying down the slope of the rampart. The rout was total. The last remnants fled before the gunfire, and then there came a curious silence; almost one of thanksgiving for deliverance. This silence was broken by an outburst of cheering, and in the middle of it the Brigadier-General was seen riding towards the Scots line. Dornoch, his face white and pinched in the light of the guard lanterns, saluted.

"Well done, Dornoch." Norris was himself wounded, a wide patch of blood showing through his tunic. "Your order was the right one, and I'm to blame for not having given it sooner. Had I done so... there might have been less slaughter."

"I doubt it, sir." Dornoch swayed, feeling faintness overcome him. A corporal took him and supported him, and the Brigadier-General himself passed the order for the medical orderlies and a *doolie*.

As Lord Brora came up still brandishing his highland broadsword dangerously close, Norris addressed him. "Major, you must take over as battalion commander for the time being. Your Colonel's to be placed on the sick list."

"Very good, sir." Brora smiled, and in the lanterns' light

the smile was somehow devilish. He flourished his sword. "Your further orders, if you please?"

"First of all, kindly control your broadsword, Major. It's an instrument out of hell—"

"One that has proved effective, sir."

"I dare say! But I am not the enemy. All battalions to muster their men and report casualties as soon as possible, and then remain standing-to until further orders."

"Standing-to, sir? May I ask why?"

"You may, Major. The attack was not in fact unsuccessful. The prisoners we took during the attack in the pass have been released, and more importantly all the *maliks* have been cut out from under our noses. For a British force to fail to provide protection for the headmen will not be popular with their tribes, and I expect a reaction. That's all, gentlemen." The Brigadier-General turned his horse, then paused and spoke over his shoulder. "One thing more: the tribesmen, the dead and wounded. They are to be sorted out and the survivors are to be questioned. I wish to know by whom the attack was mounted and what is intended for the *maliks,* and I also wish as much information as possible as to the hostages, of whom we have so far heard nothing. Lord Brora?"

"Sir?"

"I am not disposed to be squeamish. Are you?"

"I am not, sir."

The Brigadier-General, his face grim, nodded. "Then I shall leave the details to you, Major."

He rode away to Brigade, leaving a somewhat tense silence behind him.

*   *   *

Razjah Shah had started down the hillside earlier, in dead silence, in the lead of his well-armed tribesmen, at about the same time as Dostman Khan's hordes had started their creep along the concealing *nullah.* As he reached the snow-covered plateau he heard the sounds of fighting from the direction of the British camp, and soon after this he saw the bursting shells and their brilliant stars falling over the embattled Dostman Khan. He smiled, and led his men on for the sleeping city, putting distance between himself and Dostman Khan, putting his deviousness into effect. Into the city like ghosts rode his bandits, the horses' hooves muffled by deep snow. They were not to be anonymous for long, as Razjah Shah had known and had indeed bargained for. The noise of the fighting was loud, the star shell was bright, the night had come alive. Men emerged from doorways to crowd the streets of Mana, and to wonder—and to fear. Razjah Shah, moving among them, fed their fear with clever and appropriately chosen words, words that inflamed and fanned. As the *fakir* Zulifiqar had said already, the hostages of Murrum Khan were likely to bring much trouble to Mana. If the hostages were found by the British, as of a certainty they would be, Mana would suffer cruelly, for it would be held to have tolerated Murrum Khan and even to have offered support and succour to him in his wickedness. Already the sounds of war held overtones of great foreboding. The British were under attack; when the attack was over and the British were victorious, they would seek revenge—and Mana was handily placed for the wreaking of revenge. Much blood would flow from the British bayonets, for when roused they were far from being merciful fighters, and the men in skirts and with the music of the unhappy pig were always without exception wild. All this Razjah Shah's audience, a growing one, could comprehend well: *badal* was a wholly natural thing, a very proper thing, and was always exacted...

"I, Razjah Shah, shall save you all in the name of Allah."

Murmurs rose round the tribal leader and his followers. "How can this be—you, one man with a few other men?"

"I shall take away the hostages held by Murrum Khan."

"And you? What will then become of you, Razjah Shah?"

Razjah Shah laughed. "I shall be helped by Allah, who is great and powerful and wise, also good, and I shall take the hostages far from Mana, and thus draw the British fire. It shall be easily done. The attention of Murrum Khan and his guards will be upon the plateau and the fighting, and a mob

147

can help much if it be determined to work the will of Allah. What say you, my friends?"

The murmurs grew louder, and swelled mightily, and fists were shaken, and the mob grew as the sounds spread.

*   *   *

Inside the palace the fighting had indeed been heard; Murrum Khan had climbed to his battlements to look out upon the plateau as the star shell burst. He didn't linger; he was deep in thought as he descended, and called down curses upon the head of whoever had attacked the British camp. He had received word that Dostman Khan had rallied forces in the vicinity, and ten thousand goats upon it that this was Dostman Khan attacking now! His ruminations ran closely along the lines of Razjah Shah's words to the mob in the streets: the British would seek vengeance and would mount a punitive expedition that would almost certainly attack Mana along with the isolated mountain settlements in the area. Panic, however, was not to be indulged in; the British would have suffered casualties, and they might well decide to send riders for reinforcements before moving further towards war. That, perhaps, was something that could be taken care of, and Murrum Khan gave his orders according-ly: risking the depletion of his palace guard, he sent a strong force riding fast for the hills, to outflank the British camp and come down to ambush the passes farther along and to cut any field telegraph wires that they might find, although the probability was that any such wires would have been cut long since, for few of the Waziri tribesmen could resist the cutting of British telegraph lines.

Thirty minutes after Murrum Khan's descent from his battlements, Ogilvie's trap-door was opened and once again the dim flaring light showed the rope's-end coming down. Ogilvie grasped it and climbed; he found it an effort, for he was weak now from lack of food. This, however, was to be remedied: at the top a meal of a sort awaited him—rice and mashed corn, some goat's milk, and some unidentifiable fruit preserved in sugar. He ate under the watchful eyes and the rifles of two Afridis, and he ate in silence, his questions remaining unanswered. When he had finished he was taken again to the great chamber with the pool of water. Angela was there still; not in the water, but standing with a rough garment thrown round her shoulders, under guard beside the pool. The crocodile was sluggishly inactive behind its mesh barrier, visible just below the surface with its humped nostrils awash and its eyes like lamps, waiting for human movement.

On the dais at the end Murrum Khan stood, a hand on the haft of a jewelled dagger thrust into a crimson sash.

"Ogilvie sahib, the time approaches and I am ready."

"Ready for what, Murrum Khan?"

"I have told you. Now I tell you more: outside the city to the north is a British force. A brigade, I believe it to be. And there is fighting in their camp."

Ogilvie's heart beat faster: the brigade, then, had arrived . . . the regiment was not far away, and that was truly wonderful news that brought a sudden surge of hope; though Murrum Khan would scarcely have told him, of course, if the hope had been a high one. He asked, "Fighting? Your men have engaged?"

Murrum Khan shook his head. "Not my men. There has been an attack, and I believe it comes from Dostman Khan. I believe also that the British may come here. If they do, they shall find neither me nor you, but we shall not move too soon—not until I have word that the British are on their way. Nevertheless, I must be ready from this moment so that when the word comes, if come it does, you and I can be away on the route for Afghanistan." He paused. "That leaves the mem'sahib, whose fate also you know."

Ogilvie looked at Angela. She was deathly white and shaking all over, and still her eyes were dull and without register; she seemed almost to have stopped caring, as though already she had gone past the coming agony and had stepped behind the veil . . . Ogilvie said in a strained voice, "You'll be hunted down, Murrum Khan, never doubt that. You'll hang in the civil jail as a common murderer."

There was a sneer in Murrum Khan's voice. "The British

149

cannot find me when I go, Ogilvie sahib! I have known the hills and the passes all my life, as my father and my grandfather knew them before me. I know ways that the British would never find in a thousand years. I have no fear of being taken in the open by the Raj, Ogilvie sahib."

"I would not be so confident if I were you, Murrum Khan." Ogilvie licked at dry lips. "Why cast away a hostage who could yet be useful to you?"

"You I shall have yet. You refer to the mem'sahib, but she will not be cast away before her time—you shall see. For now, you wait, and so does the mem'sahib." Murrum Khan turned away and stalked through a door behind the dais, which was closed behind him with a thud, a sound of foreboding and doom. From the other door, the one through which Ogilvie had been brought, more men filed in—bandits carrying modern British Army rifles and many knives, and with bandoliers of cartridges across their chests. Ogilvie was made to sit on a bench at one side of the pool, and Angela at the other, each of them well guarded, and the wait began, a wait in enforced silence. Ogilvie tried to assess what might be in the air at Brigade, what the Brigadier-General might decide to do. A march into Mana was a possibility, if not to attack then at least to mount a show of strength, to show that the Raj was not going to have a snook cocked at it again. On the other hand the British presence was for talk and negotiation, not war. Norris might decide one way, he might decide the other, and a good deal would depend on the advice he was given by his colonels, Lord Dornoch in particular since he had many years of Frontier experience. And the High Commissioner would have his viewpoint: this was fairly certainly to be for the other cheek to be turned. One way and another it looked like being a long wait, and if the brigade made no move within, say, the next twenty-four hours, then Murrum Khan might put haste into reverse and maintain his low profile inside the security of his palace to await, as he had at first intended, some response to his message to Fettleworth in Nowshera. Meanwhile Ogilvie, wishing desperately that he could talk to Angela and try to bring her hope, had to be content to believe that his physical presence might of itself be some comfort.

*   *   *

He had fallen into a kind of reverie from sheer weariness when he heard the rifle-fire, and he came to in an instant to sit up fully awake. The guards looked at each other in alarm, while keeping their weapons closely upon the two prisoners. The firing seemed close; within minutes Murrum Khan came back into the chamber, his face furious.

"The brigade?" Ogilvie asked.

"No. A mob! There has been treachery." Murrum Khan shouted at his bandits in Pushtu and they ran from the room, hastening to their stations to repel the intruders, leaving two men each to guard Ogilvie and Angela. On the heels of his Pathans Murrum Khan departed again. Now there was considerable change in the air; much shooting came from outside, and there was the stutter of what sounded to Ogilvie like a Maxim, probably captured from the Raj on some raiding expedition for arms, or taken in the field. Which side was using it, he couldn't tell; but soon the sounds came closer and the fighting seemed to be taking place in the corridor outside. The guards were growing restive, anxious, beginning to show fear. Ogilvie felt excitement rise in him. He was fairly sure now that the intruder was Razjah Shah, honouring his word that he would come to his assistance. Now, then, was the time . . . once Razjah Shah's men were crowding the doorway, maybe sooner, the guards might shoot the hostages, for Murrum Khan would never allow them to fall to Razjah Shah, that was certain. Ogilvie took a deep breath and chose his moment when one of his guards had moved, rifle pointed, for the door. Lunging sideways, he took the other man with a heavy blow straight into the gut. There was a shout of pain and as the man doubled up Ogilvie wrenched away his rifle, took cover on the ground behind the benches and aimed at the man who had turned to run back from the door. He fired. The native fell with the top of his head blown

151

off, and from his cover Ogilvie swung the rifle on the two natives guarding Angela.

He spoke in Pushtu. "Move away from the mem'sahib. Then the rifles into the water or you die. I shall give you a count of five."

Staring back at him, the men moved aside and Ogilvie scrambled to his feet. The rifles were thrown into the pool. Ogilvie, catching a flicker in the eye of one of the men, looked round just in time. The man who had taken the fist in his stomach was back on his feet and moving for him. Ogilvie, with no time to take aim, swung the rifle viciously and its heavy steel muzzle caught the man in the mouth, tearing the lower lip from his face and smashing blackened teeth. The man yelped and staggered sideways with both hands to his mouth, then fell, slipping on the greasy edge of the pool, unable to stop himself before his legs went in beyond the mesh barrier. Screaming, he tried to drag himself clear but he had no hope. There was a flurry in the water, a sudden dash at immense speed, and the great jaws snapped. There came a crunching sound and the screaming grew more dreadful and the body slid further in. As Angela stared with every drop of blood drained from her face, Ogilvie brought up the rifle and put the man out of his agony. Blood coloured the water, drifting down in long streaks past the barrier. The great tail thrashed, sending up a red spray. Ogilvie instinctively emptied the magazine on to the armoured back with no effect at all: the bullets richocheted harmlessly away. Meanwhile the two remaining guards were running around the pool towards him, knives ready. As Ogilvie stood four-square with the rifle clubbed, the door at the end went back on its hinges and men crowded through, bringing with them the smell of smoke. One was Murrum Khan, carrying something in his hands, something that he threw towards Ogilvie as the two guards stood back. Along the floor of the chamber rolled the bloody, severed head of Razjah Shah until its own matted black hair halted its progress and it stopped with the sightless eyes seeming fixed upon Ogilvie's face. Murrum Khan gave a sign with his hand, the rifle was wrested from Ogilvie, and its butt was brought down in a wicked blow on his head. As he fell there was another commotion from outside, shouts and cries and gunfire, and Murrum Khan, showing incredulous fury, shouted an order for the woman to be removed under guard, then turned away himself and ran from the chamber. The shouts and gunfire continued in the courtyard. Ogilvie was still unconscious under two Afridi rifles and was about to be removed when, ahead of thickly billowing smoke, the mob poured in tumultuous and victorious noise into the room.

14

A DOZEN MAHSUD riders sped swiftly out of Mana, heading back into the hills whence they had come. Across the saddle of one of them lay James Ogilvie, still unconscious and with a large lump on his skull. During the ride no one spoke; it was a grim and sorry ride without their leader, who would of a certainty be revenged another day. Murrum Khan's partial victory would not last for many more suns to rise on the Waziri hills. Below those hills now, part of his palace smoked still, though the flames had subsided. The fire had not been a big one, though its spread had served to allow the cutting-out of Ogilvie sahib and the escape of the survivors of the raid. It was to be hoped that the Prophet would now intercede to protect the wretched townspeople of Mana, and the *fakir* Zulifiqar . . . Murrum Khan's raging fury would be terrible to behold!

In the comparative safety of the hills the riders halted and Ogilvie at last came round to a sick and dizzy headache. It was some while before he could understand his situation, and the tribesmen waited in patience until his head cleared enough for him to be told. He recognised the speaker as Razjah Shah's chief lieutenant, a Mahsud named Mohammad Yusuf.

"When Razjah Shah was killed, we grew more angry, Ogilvie sahib. Fire was set to the palace, and in the confusion many men fought their way into the room with the great bath, where you lay as if dead. You were lifted and taken from the palace. Not easily . . . many men died, but those of us who are here brought you safely into the alleys and then here into the hills where Razjah Shah had ridden with you from Takki, from the fort—"

"The mem'sahib? You have her too?" Ogilvie tried to sit up.

The answer was grave. "There was no sign of the mem'sahib, only of you."

"But she was there with me!"

Heads were shaken. "Not so. Not upon our arrival in the great room. We found the head of óur leader Razjah Shah, and we found you, Ogilvie sahib, with guards whom we killed. But not the mem'sahib."

Fear expanded, exploded in Ogilvie's head: could Angela have gone into the pool? This was doubtful, however; in the adverse circumstances of the sack of his palace, Murrum Khan would surely have felt it prudent to keep her alive for future use. He asked, "And Murrum Khan himself?"

"Sahib, we did not linger to find out. He was not then in the room of the bath. Razjah Shah had ordered that we take you from Murrum Khan, and this we did—"

"He also ordered you to take the mem'sahib, Mohammad Yusuf?"

"Undoubtedly, but I have said . . . although we searched as best we could, the mem'sahib we failed to find."

Ogilvie nodded dully; his head swam, he felt sick and parched. He asked for water, and it improved matters a little. "And the British?" he asked. "What are they doing now?"

"They are still in their camp, Ogilvie sahib. They have sent out patrols, no doubt to locate those who attacked them earlier, and that is all."

"You can see the camp from here?" The sun was well up now, and the sky was clear of snow.

"Yes, we see them well."

Ogilvie raised himself on one elbow, but the effort worsened his head and he fell limply back to the ground. "I must rejoin them. I must find the mem'sahib—"

"Sahib, with us you will be better able to search the city for her. The people of Mana may have heard whispers from the palace—"

"No! Murrum Khan spoke to me . . . he will have gone from Mana into the hills, towards Afghanistan, for now most assuredly the brigade in which I serve will move in. An attack on the camp, then a fire and fighting in Murrum Khan's palace . . . they must march, and Murrum Khan will

155

know this." Ogilvie pressed a hand to his aching head. "If she's alive, the mem'sahib will not have been left behind now Murrum Khan has lost his other hostage."

"Then we are still the better guide, Ogilvie sahib. We know the hills better than the British soldiers."

"There is much truth in that, but it is my duty to rejoin and give the Brigadier-General sahib full information. Of this there is no doubt. Besides, you will want your revenge on Murrum Khan for the killing of your leader—"

"*Badal* is much on all our minds, this is true."

"And I understand it. The brigade is strong, and also wants Murrum Khan—for murder now. We shall assist *badal*, and we shall succeed quickly where you might take many years. You must let me rejoin my regiment, and I give you my word that I shall not act against you."

There was a pause, then, with some reluctance, the new leader said, "We trust your word, Ogilvie sahib."

"There's yet a better way." Ogilvie looked up solemnly at the assembled, haggard faces. "If you throw in your lot with us, with the British brigade . . . if you also join, and act as guides . . . then Murrum Khan may be found the quicker. Is this not so?"

*   *   *

Below on the plateau, the bugles sounded to fall in the brigade by regiments. After due consultation with his colonels and his Chief of Staff, and with the High Commissioner, Norris had made his decision. With the heavy and callous hand of Major Lord Brora in the background, the prisoners taken had talked: although they knew nothing of Ogilvie, they revealed that Murrum Khan was present in Mana. That was good enough in all the circumstances; the brigade would march but would not strike camp. With the possible reprisals in mind from the villagers of the captured *maliks*, the Brigadier-General ordered that the Punjab Frontier Force together with the remnant of the Gurkhas should remain behind as camp guard while he took the Royal Strathspey and the Border Regiment into Mana. Thus

156

the battalions of the British Army formed column of route behind the Staff and marched away through the lying snow, with sloped rifles and fixed bayonets and the pipes and drums sounding loud and clear in the still air, marched to possible action and a warlike, rather than a peaceful, solution to the boundary problem. Only the High Commissioner had objected, and had been overruled on the grounds of present military necessity. As the pipes and drums at the head of the column came within the shadow of the city, the officer of the advanced guard came riding back to Brigade with something in his hand.

He saluted the Brigadier-General. "A body on the track, sir—an Afridi, dead but recently I believe. This was skewered to the body with a knife."

He handed up a large piece of skin, a square into which words had been crudely burned with an iron. The reading took some minutes and when he had read the Brigadier-General's face was hard. He folded the message, and beckoned to his ADC. "The commanding officers to Brigade at once. The column will halt." The ADC saluted and rode away and the bugle sounded. Wondering what was in the air now, the column halted and the men were stood at ease. From the Borderers Colonel Hinde rode towards Brigade, with Lord Brora from the Scots. The Brigadier-General lost no time. "A message from Murrum Khan, gentlemen. Mrs Ogilvie will be killed if we advance upon the city."

"So she's positively there!" Brora stood in his stirrups, a scowl on his face. "We must make all speed to her rescue, sir!"

"I don't think you took in the purport, Major—"

"Oh, yes, I did! Are we to be made lily-livered by a damn native's threats?"

Norris reddened. "It's scarcely a case of that. I have Mrs Ogilvie's safety to consider. I wish no bulls at gates, Lord Brora."

"What, then, do you propose to do, sir?"

Norris said, "The regiments will stand-to but will not march. I shall ride ahead with an escort and with my staff, and seek a parley—"

"And bargain with a woman's life?"

"It's what we've been doing all along, in essence. Melodrama won't help us, Major. We must face the situation as it is, and the situation happens to be that currently Murrum Khan has the whip hand." The Brigadier-General turned to the flank and was about to pass orders for an escort when his attention was caught by some movement below the hills to the south-east. Frowning, he pulled his field glasses from their case around his neck. Brora followed suit, and it was Brora who spoke first.

"A flag of truce . . . a bunch of damn tribesmen . . . and by God it's young Ogilvie with the buggers!"

* * *

There had been much explaining to do; Ogilvie felt that it was fortunate that the Brigadier-General was present in person when he rejoined. Norris, if with some difficulty, had a restraining effect upon Lord Brora, and Ogilvie was given a peaceful hearing as briefly he outlined the whole sequence of events since he had ridden back from Fort Jamrud in the Khyber many days earlier. He brought Razjah Shah's bandits before the Brigadier-General, saying that they had been of much service to the Raj and that he had given them his word that the Raj would not now lift arms against them.

"A somewhat large pre-emption of authority, Captain Ogilvie?"

"Yes, sir."

"And the immediate future?"

"They'll assist further, sir. They know the hills, and the routes into Afghanistan, where we believe Murrum Khan to have gone."

The Brigadier-General raised his eyebrows. "I think you're wrong, Captain Ogilvie." He quoted the recent message. "The man's still in Mana, evidently."

"With respect, sir, I doubt it. The message could be a ruse, a delaying tactic. Murrum Khan told me himself, when he had me prisoner and thought he could talk safely—he told me he intended going into Afghanistan to raise an army

158

against the Raj. He intended taking a hostage with him."

"Mrs Ogilvie?"

"Me, sir. My cousin's wife was to die at once if the British came."

"As the message says."

"Yes, sir. But I still don't give the message much credit. I believe that in the changed circumstances Murrum Khan will have taken her on into Afghanistan in my place, as a continuing hostage ... a continuing inhibition against our movement."

"Yes, I see." The Brigadier-General blew out his moustache, looking baffled. "You appear to have been at the seat of affairs, Captain Ogilvie, at the nub. What would you do now if you were in my shoes?"

Ogilvie said, "I'd first check the palace, sir, entering Mana in strength to make quite sure there were no prisoners—"

"And Mrs Ogilvie? If she *is* there as the message suggests, what happens to her then?"

Ogilvie bit his lip and felt the blood drain from his face: what would happen was clear enough and the mere thought was like a knife in his guts. But he said steadily, "I'd bank on it she's not there, sir. In any case. . ." He didn't finish: he had meant to say that in any case a British force could not be held indefinitely from its duty, but the words would have seemed like a betrayal. The Brigadier-General seemed to understand, however; he said, "Very well, what would you do after that, assuming nothing was found?"

"I would hold the brigade in camp, sir, and despatch someone who knew the hills, with a small and fast escort, to find Murrum Khan, and bring him back before he could muster support."

Norris smiled. "I think I know who you'd send!"

"Yes, sir. With Razjah Shah's men, I'd have a fighting chance. I could get through much faster than the brigade."

Norris glanced at Lord Brora. "Major?"

"A fool's errand, sir." Brora seemed nettled that a junior officer should be consulted at all. "We should not forget the attack upon us last night. You made the point yourself, that the villages would be up in arms about the loss of their

159

maliks. The whole of the damn hills will be alive with men looking for vengeance."

The Brigadier-General nodded. "A point indeed. Well, Captain Ogilvie? What d'you think?"

"I take the point, sir, but the attack came from Dostman Khan—Murrum Khan's enemy. There will be divisions of feeling, since some of the *maliks* will have been for Dostman Khan and some for Murrum Khan, and others for their own communities alone."

"Well?"

Ogilvie smiled. "Razjah Shah's men, as I said, know the hills and the hillmen. We may be able to take advantage of the rivalries—"

"Find help to put you on Murrum Khan's track, d'you mean?"

"Yes, sir."

"You may be right," Norris said. He rode his horse a little way from the group of officers, looking thoughtfully towards the city, and at the bleak surround of hills beneath the snow, and back along the halted column with its greatcoated men and its mountain guns; back towards the camp with its transport animals and followers. To send a small party of men to penetrate the hills and passes in the snow, to offer themselves as targets for the sniper's bullet ... it was to send them to likely death. On the other hand, every patrol that had ever been sent out from Peshawar or Kohat, Bannu or Mardan had faced a similar situation; and a brigade with all its impedimenta was certainly slow on the move by comparison. . .

Norris rode back. "Very well, Captain Ogilvie. Your suggestion's a good one. Lord Brora, if you please, make the arrangements within your battalion ... Captain Ogilvie should be given the choice of men."

"As you say, sir." Brora stared at Ogilvie. "Well, what's your wish, Captain Ogilvie?"

"Half my own company, Major, volunteers, with Colour-Sar'nt MacTrease as second-in-command."

"Subalterns are available," Brora snapped.

"Yes, Major. But MacTrease is better acquainted with the

160

Frontier. He's been out here as long as I have, ever since the regiment arrived."

Norris interrupted as Brora's mouth opened again. "Give him what he asks for, Major. Time's short. Captain Ogilvie, take your volunteer detachment back to camp and see it fully provisioned and mounted. You'll ride out the moment you're ready. Brigade Major?"

"Sir?"

"The column is to move on as soon as Captain Ogilvie has detached his men, with the guns brought forward to the van."

*   *   *

Ogilvie's whole company had volunteered and selection was difficult. On arrival in the camp, Ogilvie went at once to the Colonel's tent to report to Lord Dornoch. He found him pale and weak but in fair spirits though full of frustration at being out of action on the Brigadier-General's order. However, he had no intention of remaining long on the Sick List, much to Ogilvie's relief: one spell of Brora as acting commanding officer had been more than enough. Dornoch wished Ogilvie well. "You'll be out of communication, James," he said, "but every man's thoughts will be with you and your half company."

"Thank you, Colonel." Saluting smartly, Ogilvie left the tent and crunched through the snow towards his company's lines where the men were making ready under MacTrease's orders and with the assistance of the RQMS and his staff. Enough dry provisions and water were being taken for fourteen days and the half company, formed into Mounted Infantry, would take transport mules to carry the stores and the ammunition for the rifles and a stripped-down Maxim gun. Mr Cunningham, who had been retained in camp as senior warrant officer of the brigade to stiffen defence, marched up as the small force made ready. He was delighted to see Ogilvie back. His eagle eye scanned equipment and weapons without seeming to undermine Colour-Sergeant MacTrease's authority.

161

"A hard task faces you, Captain Ogilvie, sir."

"Yes. But we'll survive!"

Cunningham smiled. "I know you will, sir. And I'll be praying you find the lady—and you'll do that too, with God's help."

Ogilvie nodded; he was not too sanguine about his chances, though he believed, as he had told the Brigadier-General, that he would have the best hope possible. The Frontier was vast and wild and full of hiding places; but men and animals left spoor that could be read by the experienced. In a little more than an hour after reaching the camp, Ogilvie was ready to ride out. With MacTrease on one side of him and Razjah Shah's successor Mohammad Yusuf on the other, he led his troop across the ditch and the rampart and headed on the bandit's advice towards the north-western edge of the plateau. Here the party was unavoidably obvious to any watchers and the word of their coming would be sent ahead; but Murrum Khan would be expecting some sort of pursuit notwithstanding his message, and it could be presumed that little would be lost. Before they reached the shelter of the mountains a horseman was seen behind, riding hell-for-leather from the direction of Mana: Ogilvie's field glasses identified him as the Brigadier-General's orderly officer and he halted his troop for the rider to reach them. The orderly officer reported a peaceful entry into Mana and the palace; the latter, void of any of Murrum Khan's followers, and of Murrum Khan himself, had been found sacked by the mob on the instigation of a one-armed *fakir*. There had been no trace of Angela Ogilvie.

"The pool?"

"No one there. There was blood in the water, and the upper half of a man's body, a native, beside the pool. That's all."

Ogilvie watched the orderly officer ride back at the gallop. Later when he began the climb into the hills, he heard from far behind the skirl of the pipes and the beat of the drummers sounding clear across the plain as the brigade marched out again from Mana. Then the snow began falling once more and the sounds were muffled behind a screen of white that blotted out sight as well.

*   *   *

In Nowshera, as the days dragged past without news from the south, faces had grown longer. Fettleworth's Divisional Headquarters were like a mortuary, albeit a gilded and busy one. No one liked to think of a woman helpless in the hands of bandits, and there were other considerations too that weighed like lead upon highly-placed military minds: the Civilians were always a damned nuisance but when the military failed to come up to expectations they became incomparably worse and their memoranda, issuing in streams from Calcutta, developed a cutting edge that infuriated Bloody Francis and Sir Iain Ogilvie alike. Fettleworth knew that only the latter's presence in Nowshera kept from his own head the strictures of clerkly pimps in Calcutta and Whitehall who, having never in their miserable lives wielded anything more lethal than a pen-nib, which in all conscience could be lethal enough when dipped in poison, attacked with file and paper-clip any general whom fate had unkindly delivered into their hands. Fettleworth writhed beneath it all: the telegraph lines across the ocean from Whitehall had borne his discomfiture and the next mail from home would bring copies of *The Times* and *The Morning Post* to make him writhe more. The Prime Minister was deeply concerned, so was Her Majesty, and the latter had prodded her Viceroy with a personal cable, clearly against Lord Salisbury's advice, stating baldly that she was shocked and dismayed and expected much better news before Christmas.

"Christmas my backside," Sir Iain said when word of the Queen's expectations reached him in Fettleworth's headquarters. "She ought to try the passes herself, with a full pack and rifle!"

Fettleworth was shocked at such a thought. He coughed and said sharply, "My dear Ogilvie, Her Majesty—"

"I wish she'd damn well keep her mouth shut. She often

163

does more harm than good. Can't you see the damn newspapers, Fettleworth? The Queen's Christmas spoiled by lack of news from India. Why bring Christmas into it? You know how damn sentimental the public are! Why focus attention on *Christmas,* for God's sake? Don't you see what I mean?"

Fettleworth nodded reluctantly. "Yes. But we shouldn't make too much of that. Her Majesty has the very best of intentions, she always has."

"Which doesn't help my son and my niece."

"Er—no. No, of course not." Fettleworth hesitated, cleared his throat, coughed; he was debating within himself whether or not to offer his panacea, the one thing that in his view solved everything along the North-West Frontier: a massive show of strength, a review by the General Officer Commanding of the power and might of the Raj, a great assembly of infantry and cavalry and field guns, the combined divisions of the British and Indian Armies of the North marching past the dais behind the pomp of the brass bands and the rolling thunder of the drums. The natives had to be shown the tremendous power of the Raj and of Her Majesty, and then, by Gad, they became willing to talk turkey! Fettleworth's chest swelled behind the scarlet tunic of the General Staff, and, almost without volition, he said, "Ogilvie, why not put on a show to impress the natives, let 'em see what's what—hey?"

"One of your parades, Fettleworth?"

"Yes! Since you're here, you're available to—"

"You're as bad as the Queen." Sir Iain turned away angrily and stalked from the room, leaving Fettleworth to simmer and wonder if personal anxieties could have unhinged the GOC's mind. To talk like that . . . and everyone knew the efficacy of parades! Apart from anything else, they put heart into the garrison. The men loved the splendour and the smartness and the music of the regimental fifes and drums— loved it! Fettleworth banged at a bell on his desk; a native entered, salaaming.

"*Chota peg.*"

"Yes, sahib."

164

"Quickly."

"Yes, sahib." The bearer backed away from the Divisional Commander's august presence. When the next person entered, it was not the bearer with his silver salver and the whisky, but Fettleworth's Chief of Staff.

"What is it, Lakenham?"

"Bad news, sir."

Fettleworth looked bleak. "Well, out with it, then."

"The husband—Hector Ogilvie. He's disappeared. We must inform Sir Iain." As Fettleworth sat with a sagging jaw, wondering what the Civilians would say now, Lakenham put the facts before him concisely: there had apparently been no disturbance of Hector Ogilvie's quarters and no evidence at all of any penetration by natives. Hector's horse had also been found missing from its stable and his *khansamma* had reported a quantity of basic foodstuffs missing from the kitchen. "I don't know what all that suggests to you, sir," Lakenham finished, "but I know what it suggests to me."

"Gone looking for his wife?"

"Yes."

"Poor fellow—poor fellow! He'll not stand a chance—a very foolish thing to do, if natural. And I wish he hadn't done it." Fettleworth put his head in his hands for a moment and when he looked up his face was haggard. "Take word to Sir Iain, Lakenham, and then come back here."

* * *

"I'd never have thought it of him," Sir Iain said. "My own flesh and blood, I know—but his own father would say the same. Dreadful as a boy—one graze on a knee and he'd run indoors blubbing! Must be some guts somewhere, give him his due, but it's a confounded bloody nuisance. What are you going to do about it, Fettleworth?"

"I'm waiting for your orders, Ogilvie."

"Are you?" Sir Iain stared. "Then here they are: have him found, bring him back, tell him to report to me! I'll handle it from there. See to that at once."

Fettleworth went speedily into action, ordering mounted

patrols to scour the open country around Nowshera, and alerting the provost corps to go through the town with a fine-toothed comb. Lakenham saw personally to the close questioning of Hector's domestic staff and of all other persons who might have had some knowledge of the missing man's movements. Fettleworth waited in severe agitation for the reports to come in; by the end of the day it was clear that Hector Ogilvie had vanished somewhere in the snow that lay around Nowshera and Peshawar and had left no traces as the flakes continued to fall and the bitter wind blew out of the north.

15

FOR OGILVIE'S HALF company, it became a desperate business as, slowly, they penetrated the little-known passes of the northward-leading Waziri hills. The snow came intermittently ahead of blizzard force winds that drove the bitter flakes into men's eyes and made it painful to face their front as lips and cheeks froze blue. Ever present was the nightmare thought of frostbite. Only Mohammad Yusuf and his tribesmen were able to face the terrible ride philosophically; and in so doing proved an encouraging example to the soldiers. If they could survive, then so could Scots.

Now and again when the snowfall eased and the skies cleared to reveal the sun, wild men were glimpsed along the crests that ran across the border into Afghanistan, figures that quickly vanished, though occasionally there was some exchange of fire. They were close now to Afghanistan and Ogilvie's hopes had begun to fade.

"It's no use, Colour," he said to MacTrease. "He'll have crossed the Frontier by this time."

"He had little start on us, sir."

"Enough, probably!"

"Never say die, sir." MacTrease hesitated. "You'll follow into Afghanistan, sir?"

"Follow what?" Ogilvie responded with bitterness. "What *are* we following, when all's said and done—other than Mohammad Yusuf's nose?" He waved a hand around. "The snow's blotted out all tracks even if they existed in the first place!"

"Aye, sir," MacTrease said quietly, "but yon's nose is a good one. There's a purpose about the man, sir. He's not riding blind."

Ogilvie nodded: that was true. Razjah Shah's successor

was a man of few words but firm action; all along his guidance had been positive and he seemed to know well what he was doing. There was no hesitation; it was as though he had an inbuilt compass the needle of which indicated not north necessarily but the lodestone of Murrum Khan, the killer of a revered leader. As to a penetration of Afghanistan, this was something Ogilvie had pondered much, knowing that it would be on the cards. Once into Afghanistan they would find few friends: they would come firmly into the territory of the wild men whose whole way of life was the antithesis of the Raj, the territory of the border raider and the thief in a much more positive sense than was Waziristan. Murrum Khan would be the one who was at home. There was another consideration as well, an important one: Calcutta might have reservations about the crossing of the North-West Frontier in depth. It was not normally up to an officer of captain's rank to take it upon himself to pre-empt government decisions and the repercussions of action inside Afghanistan could be serious. Nevertheless, Ogilvie's decision had been made already: he would follow Angela to the death.

*   *   *

Many miles to the north and east of Ogilvie's blind advance into the snows, Hector Ogilvie, now riding south by way of a pass leading from the Peshawar-Fort Jamrud track, was facing similar conditions and facing them alone. His equipment for his self-imposed task was entirely inadequate. He had coffee but no means of heating the water for it; he had food but no means of cooking, and the food he had brought in his panic haste was not of a sort that lent itself to eating raw: packets of porridge, of flour . . . even a jar of marmalade had found their way into his haversack and saddle-bags. Such might provide some energy but would scarcely prove sustaining. Something else was providing Hector Ogilvie with courage and a crazy determination: a flask of whisky that could be refilled from half-a-dozen bottles of Dewar's that he had found in his allotted quarter, which was normally inhabited by a major of Probyn's Horse temporarily absent on detachment to Quetta. In his anxieties for his wife, Hector had discovered belatedly the anaesthesia to be found in a bottle of spirits. . .

Desperation had been his driver, whisky had been his final impeller along a chaotic course. He had no plan in mind other than to find Angela—simply that. In a confused way he had thought that he might fall in with natives who could be bribed into his service, men who might form a force to attack Murrum Khan and release Angela. He was not unimportant in the governance of the Raj and his promises would carry weight. He rode on into the whitened hills and behind him the snow covered his horse's tracks. The cold was intense and terrible but was held at bay by Dewar's whisky, and over the horizon was a vision of Angela . . . tears flowed down Hector's face until they froze and formed icicles that cracked away as he drank from the flask and filled out his cheeks. He knew a moment of terror as a bank of snow crashed down the hillside and almost submerged him. It worked down his neck in freezing rivers and he cried out aloud to the unfriendly, uncaring immensities of distance.

*　　*　　*

In camp outside Mana, Brigadier-General Norris, after long and earnest consultation with his Brigade Major and Sir Lawrence Bindle, had reached a decision. The High Commissioner had admitted that he saw little point in remaining immobile in the hopes of being able to convene another *jirgah*; the *maliks* had been kidnapped and that was that. A peaceful solution now seemed unlikely in any case, though it was manifestly no fault of his. Shivering and miserable and far from the comforts of Calcutta, Sir Lawrence had no objection to withdrawing from the Mana plateau and advancing northwards and thus coming gradually into rather more friendly territory; the closer one got to Peshawar and Nowshera and the seats of the military power of the Raj, the less one needed to be in constant fear of the natives. The Brigadier-General, however, having drawn

169

these admissions from the High Commissioner, had then proceeded a step further during his later briefing of his colonels. It seemed that he intended advancing, not safely upon Peshawar, but dangerously upon the entry to the notorious Khyber Pass. . .

"We're serving no useful purpose here," Norris said. "It's still true we'll be slow and ponderous on the move as compared with Ogilvie, but he may have a need of us, and unless we're coming up behind him he'll remain out of communication. In the absence of any orders from Division, I propose to march my brigade towards Fort Jamrud. Not as a tight formation, however. I shall split the brigade into three groups." Using a pointer, he indicated the positions on a large map hung upon an easel. "I myself, with the two native battalions or what's left of them, will advance centrally along this line." He traced it with the pointer. "Colonel Hinde with the Border Regiment will advance towards Kohat and then close the Khyber after crossing the railway line from Parachinar. Lord Dornoch and the 114th will make their advance on the west flank, keeping as close as possible to the Afghan border. That will give us a reasonably broad and comprehensive sweep, I fancy." Norris raised his eyebrows. "Yes, Brora?"

"Lord Dornoch is not yet fully fit. *I* command the 114th Highlanders."

"Indeed you do—a slip of the tongue. Is there anything else?"

"Yes," Brora said arrogantly. "You speak of a comprehensive sweep, sir. I fail to find it such. If Murrum Khan backtracks, which I would gather is what you have in mind—"

"It is."

"Well, then he'll find it abominably easy to slip down between the three lines of advance, will he not?"

"Very easy, I regret to say! However, I'm in no position to block him entirely—"

"I think you could split your brigade more, sir. Why not advance in half battalions?"

Norris frowned. "For many reasons, Brora. For one thing, I haven't enough guns to distribute between six columns. For

170

another, the front would still not be anything like fully covered and to split the brigade too far would leave each sector severely weakened with no useful result brought about."

"Your plan's nothing but a compromise," Brora said loudly and contemptuously.

"Compromise is what war is all about," Norris said, "as you will find if you reach the Staff. In the meantime, since you've not yet achieved that, you'll kindly see your regiment prepared to move out in accordance with my orders." He pulled his watch from a pocket. "Camp is to be struck forthwith, gentlemen, and the three columns will march out with the divided artillery in two hours from now."

*　　*　　*

For a while now there had been no fresh snow; Ogilvie's Scots crawled out from their bivouacs after a few hours' respite to find the day clear and bright as the sun came up, thinly enough to be sure, over the eastern peaks to spread soft colourings of gold and pink and green. Ogilvie, up and about before his men and standing with MacTrease scanning the summits of the hills, heard his Colour-Sergeant's sudden warning.

"A horseman, sir, approaching from the north."

Ogilvie brought up his field glasses. "Mohammad Yusuf, Colour. He must have scouted ahead on his own."

"Then the picquets should have reported, sir. I'll be having a word with them." MacTrease sucked at his teeth, angrily, as the horseman rode in. Mohammad Yusuf seemed pleased with himself, grinning all over his face as he pulled his horse up before the two men.

"Good news, Ogilvie sahib!"

"Well?"

"Over the hills lies a village, a small place which I know and where I have a kinswoman on my mother's father's side, an ancient woman but with all her wits—"

"You said nothing of this?"

"No, Ogilvie sahib. A visit by myself alone was better for many reasons, chiefly for the sake of the village, also because

171

my kinswoman would not have talked to the British—"

"But she has talked to you, Mohammad Yusuf? What did she say?"

The smile was broad; the face showed excitement and the lust for blood. "Murrum Khan passed through yesterday, Ogilvie sahib. He demanded food, which was provided, and he left in peace. He did not say where he was going, but he was seen to ride westerly from the village."

"And the mem'sahib, Mohammad Yusuf?"

"There was talk of a woman, Ogilvie sahib, a woman closely veiled who seemed to be captive and whom no one was permitted to approach, nor to see her face or hands."

"And Murrum Khan's route? It leads into Afghanistan?"

"Assuredly, Ogilvie sahib. It is a route well known to me. Murrum Khan must have been in much need of foodstuffs, and therefore had to ride into the village. Had this not been the case he would assuredly have taken another track, one that branches off before the village—"

"A shorter one, Mohammad Yusuf?"

"Much shorter. Farther to the north-west, it joins the one now taken by Murrum Khan. And that is the track we must now take, Ogilvie sahib, for we may cut across in front of Murrum Khan, and turn him aside from entering Afghanistan."

"How far ahead is this shorter track, Mohammad Yusuf?"

"Little more than a mile, Ogilvie sahib."

"And how far from there to the point where it meets the track Murrum Khan has taken?"

"About twenty-five miles more, sahib."

Ogilvie swore. "Almost a day's ride in these conditions! At what hour did Murrum Khan enter the village?"

"Towards last sunset, Ogilvie sahib, and he left within the hour. But by the track he has taken, he will have twice the distance to ride."

"Touch and go," Ogilvie said, and turned to MacTrease. "We'll take breakfast quickly, Colour, then mount and ride at once."

*　　*　　*

172

By now Hector was in a bad way. Weariness and the whisky had forced him to halt for rest, and left him with wit enough to tether his horse to a jag of rock that thrust up from the snow like a stalagmite. There, he had virtually collapsed; but his clothing had been thick and he had enveloped himself from head to foot in a vast cloak of heavy tweed from Harris, and he survived to wake into total darkness and an eerie silence, a silence so complete that it came close to unnerving him to screaming point. But once again Dewar's had come to his aid and had calmed his nerves and brought to his body a comforting if misleading sensation of warmth.

He pulled himself together, got to his feet, stood swaying for a while and half crying, then remounted his horse and once again set out along the pass, quite fortuitously choosing the direction in which he had been headed earlier, deeper into the hills and treacherous rocks of Waziristan, his mind beginning, although he was unaware of this, to slip its moorings. Soon, he began to feel almost warm, and there was a stupid grin on his face as he lurched onward.

*   *   *

The Earl of Elgin, Her Majesty's Viceroy of India, faced the Commander-in-Chief, Sir George White, and Colonel Durand the Military Secretary, across the fireplace where the coals blazed in red and yellow flickers to bring perhaps the one piece of Christmas cheer to Government House. Outside as the guard was changed, a splash of colour was provided by men of the Viceregal Bodyguard in scarlet and gold, shining leather thigh boots, and striped puggarees. Inside, all except for that warming fire seemed dour and bodeful. As His Excellency had already said, the stability of the Raj was threatened by the news, such as there had been, from the North-West Frontier—always like tinder, always the weak spot from which trouble might emerge.

Lord Elgin lifted a hand and ticked off the points in summary. "*Item,* where's Mrs Ogilvie? *Item,* what's become of Norris's brigade and the High Commissioner? *Item,* has Mr Hector Ogilvie ridden slap into the hands of more

173

bandits, and if so, are we shortly to be faced with another demand with him as yet another hostage? Finally, where's young Ogilvie? Sir George?"

White shook his head. "He was last reported as being in Murrum Khan's hands. No answer's been given to Murrum Khan's demands, as you know, Your Excellency."

"Not good for Ogilvie or the girl."

"Indeed not, but we know the alternative only too well, sir." White pulled his shoulders back, and met the Viceroy's eye. "We can't concede, sir. We can't possibly."

"Yet to leave them will be nearly as bad."

"No, sir. I must disagree."

"What will be the view of the tribes? That we left a white officer and a white woman to be slaughtered . . . it diminishes the Raj, Sir George. It diminishes our honour."

"Not as much as concessions made under duress, sir. We must never allow the Pathan to find hostages effective—if we do, it'll become a daily occurrence and we shall never rule again. It would not be the first time sacrifices have been made, and made willingly too." The Commander-in-Chief shrugged. "Nevertheless, like you, Your Excellency, I shrink from leaving them to it. That was the whole point of my submission that an expeditionary force should march at once."

"I don't wish to inflame the situation. In any case, I can't move without Whitehall's approval—"

"For which there is no time, sir!" White's voice rose, urgently. "The telegraph's fast enough, no doubt, but Whitehall is not! Cabinets . . . a fuss in parliament, and a debate . . . Lord Salisbury going down by coach to Windsor, and being kept cooling his heels while Her Majesty—"

"Yes, yes. I take your point." Morning-coated, Lord Elgin paced up and down before the fire, his hands clasped beneath the coat tails. Minutes passed, and then, with clear reluctance, he reached a decision. "Very well, Sir George, you may assemble troops as you wish so that they're ready, but the GOC in Murree is to be instructed beyond all doubt that they're not to move until they have my personal order as from the Governor-General in Council. Is that clear?"

"Quite clear, sir. It's not, frankly, enough but—"

"I can go no further. Where, pray, are the Ootacamund drafts now?"

"One day by train from Peshawar, Your Excellency." Sir George reached for his ostrich-plumed cocked hat. "I shall see personally to the despatches," he said, bowing formally to Her Majesty's representative and at once taking his leave. Half a loaf was better than no bread. Within the hour the word had gone westward by the telegraph. Nowshera and Peshawar and all other garrisons and outposts along the North-West Frontier were to be brought immediately to a full war footing. The regiments about to arrive from Southern Army as reinforcements would be further stiffened by yet more drafts from Ootacamund; and from Bombay within the next few days would come two battalions of infantry and a cavalry brigade with field artillery attached, all newly trooped from home. Units of all arms due for relief would have their home drafts stopped until further orders. The Pathan was to be made to realise that the Raj would move in strength to protect its own, and the Raj was now almost committed to the brink.

"And about time," Sir Iain Ogilvie remarked to Fettleworth in Nowshera when the orders reached Division.

"What's HE's intention, precisely? Has he been specific?"

Sir Iain chuckled. "I doubt it, but I understand White's pressing him."

"How far?" Fettleworth asked.

"All the way to Kabul! White wants HE to put pressure on the Amir . . . in short, to announce that if the Amir doesn't round up his bandits and deprive Murrum Khan of succour, then the Raj will march through the Khyber. That's what we've to be ready for, Fettleworth "

Bloody Francis nodded, his chest swelling. "D'you think it'll happen?"

"At the moment," Sir Iain answered, "it's a threat. A counter-threat if you like, such as should have been made much earlier. No more than that. Officially the next step's up to Whitehall, and HE will stick to that." He paused. "I'm not sure I shall! Nelson used his blind eye in the hour of his country's need and I call that a very good precedent . . . but that's between you and me, remember."

"Of course. . ."

"In the meantime you'd better mount that parade of yours."

* * *

The short cut towards the track taken by Murrum Khan had considerably lessened the distance but the conditions had been extreme and the progress slow, and it had been necessary to make many halts. However, Ogilvie felt there was good hope that they might reach the main track before Murrum Khan. As before, occasional ragged figures had been glimpsed against the snow along the crests until the light had gone; two had been shot down, their bodies falling outwards, arcing down into the pass to shatter on the jags of rock. As the next day's dawn came up Mohammad Yusuf announced that the track into Afghanistan was some three miles ahead. Ogilvie kept up the pace until the junction was in view, then he ordered his small force to halt.

He turned and rode down the line. "Into cover," he called. "Dismount and get in the lee of the rocks and bushes. See the mules and horses hidden as best you can. Colour Mac-Trease?"

"Sir?"

"A lance-corporal and three men to climb the eastern side and act as scouts. They're to watch for Murrum Khan's party and report the moment he's seen."

"Sir!"

"I'll ride ahead myself to reconnoitre while they're taking post."

"Aye, sir." MacTrease, with his rifle at the slope, marched away to detail the scouts. Ogilvie lifted a hand to Mohammad Yusuf, who joined him for the ride down towards the main pass. They dismounted a little way short of the junction, and moved ahead on foot, carefully and watchfully. Ogilvie looked each way along the pass: there was nothing moving. The track was under lying snow and at first sight there were no traces of men or horses. Closer inspection, however, showed some faint indentations almost filled by a fall of snow that had come since the last travellers had gone by.

"What d'you think, Mohammad Yusuf?"

"The direction is towards Afghanistan—"

"Yes. I saw that. How likely is it that Murrum Khan has gone through already?"

The native shrugged. "The possibilities are equal, Ogilvie sahib."

"Do many people use this pass?"

"Not very many, but some. The tracks may not be those of Murrum Khan."

Ogilvie nodded, frowning, in a quandary. The tracks were not very recent or they would not be snow-covered; when the dawn had come up, there was no snowfall either upon his force or ahead. But there was no knowing when, before that, the snow might have fallen again in the main pass; and there was nothing to be gained by entering the pass ahead of Murrum Khan and in effect preceding him and his bandits into his own land. Ogilvie put a hand on Mohammad Yusuf's shoulder and they turned back towards the south. "It's a guess and no more than a guess," Ogilvie said, "but I'm going to assume he's not gone through yet. In the meantime I'll move the men down closer to the junction." He indicated a big bluff at the westward end of the side pass, a mass of overhanging rock that circled back to form first-class natural cover. "I'll hold them in there, and we'll have plenty of warning from the scouts." He had seen for himself that the pass was clear and open, with no twists or turns, for a good distance along to the east. "All right, Mohammad Yusuf?"

The Mahsud, who had been looking doubtful, shook his head. "I am sorry, Ogilvie sahib, but I think such a place would appear natural for an ambush, and Murrum Khan will be ready."

"True. But what's the alternative?"

"A little way to the west there is a better place. It may be known to Murrum Khan or it may not, but what is certain is that this place here will be known to him."

"And this other one?"

"A false front of rock, detached from the side of the pass,

177

that forms a long and narrow *nullah,* open at both ends. There is much room. Come and I will show you."

They went back towards the junction, with Mohammad Yusuf in the lead. Although the way from the east was clear and open, the pass turned a little as it left the junction behind it, leading around the rock bluff which had to be negotiated before the route ahead could be seen: which, as it turned out, was just as well. As Ogilvie began to move round the bluff, Mohammad Yusuf stopped very suddenly and waved him urgently back. Ogilvie asked no questions until they were both safely in the side pass. Mohammad Yusuf said, "There was a man, a Pathan—an Afridi, Ogilvie sahib. His back was to me . . . but he was on watch!"

"What does that mean, Mohammad Yusuf?"

"Perhaps that Murrum Khan has reached there—certainly that the place is occupied."

"Murrum Khan . . . in ambush waiting for us?"

The tribesman nodded. "This is possible, yes. The men on the peaks may well have passed on word of our coming, and the word has reached Murrum Khan, and now he waits. The boot is on the other foot, Ogilvie sahib—but perhaps not for long?"

Ogilvie grinned. "Perhaps not for long!" With Mohammad Yusuf he went back towards MacTrease and the half company and told the Colour-Sergeant the facts. "I think we must attack, Colour, though we can't be sure it's Murrum Khan "

"With respect, sir, I'd suggest we wait a wee while to see if he shows up from the east. We can't afford to lose men by engaging other persons who may not be him, sir."

"We can't afford to be caught on two fronts if Murrum Khan does turn up from the east, Colour, that's for certain. It's not likely the men in the *nullah* are friendly to us, and I "

He broke off sharply: a shot had come from one of the scouts positioned on the eastern heights, and the man was calling down urgently. His voice was lost in more rifle fire from high up to the west, and then the side of the pass seemed to come alive as wild-looking men poured like a wave over the crests and bounded down behind puffs of smoke.

16

IT WAS COLD to be standing around, but pride was keeping
Lieutenant-General Francis Fettleworth warm on the
windswept dais. With him was the General Officer
Commanding, Northern Army, to take the salute as the
reinforced garrison marched past, the infantry with fixed
bayonets and lively tunes from the fifes and drums boosted
by the brass of the headquarters band; the cavalry behind the
kettle-drums on the drum-horses and their somewhat muted
wind instruments; the artillery with the thunder of the guns
and limbers, the wheels of which sent up the snow in great
gouts behind them. Snow was again falling, but thinly before
the wind, powdering the uniform greatcoats, the dais itself,
and the *maidan* upon which the great parade was being held.
It was different from previous parades: for one thing no
spectating women were present, partly because of the cold
but principally because Sir Iain Ogilvie had expressed the
view, irritably, that no damn women should stare and
chatter at what was a soldier's occasion. For another, this
was more a review and inspection of men going to their war
stations rather than a pure parade: action was in the air and
from the *maidan* the soldiers would march into cantonments
to be on stand-to, with all arms and equipment ready, to
await the orders from Calcutta.

When the review was over and the last files had marched
off parade into the falling snow, there were *chota pegs* at
Division. Sir Iain was morose, taciturn; the lack of news
wrenched at his nerves and for the first time he wondered
what he was doing in Nowshera when he might have been
better employed in Murree comforting his wife—but it had
been partly to avoid the look in his wife's eyes that he had
come to Nowshera to sit upon the back of Bloody Francis

Fettleworth ... and he wished to God His Excellency the Viceroy would stir himself and act before it was too late! So often, as he remarked now to Fettleworth and Lakenham, no news along the Frontier was bad news. Lakenham agreed, but was about to utter some comforting platitude when Fettleworth's ADC entered the room looking portentous.

"Sir—"

"What is it?" Fettleworth demanded, putting down his glass of whisky.

"Word from Fort Jamrud, sir. They've received a report from some friendly Waziris of a body of tribesmen, Afridis, having crossed the border into Afghanistan with prisoners."

Sir Iain crossed the room and stood in front of the ADC. "Where was the crossing?"

"A pass south of the Khyber, sir—that's all that's known, apparently."

"No distance given?"

"No, sir."

Sir Iain waved an arm at Fettleworth. "Maps, and quickly!" He turned back to the ADC. "These prisoners. Is anything known about *them*?"

"Largely men of a Highland regiment, sir."

"I see." Sir Iain whitened for a moment, then his mouth set hard. "Any officers?"

"That was not reported, sir." The ADC added, "There's believed to have been a woman, sir. A veiled figure that *could* have been a woman."

The GOC swung round on his heel, saw that Lakenham had unrolled maps and was hanging them on the wall. He marched across, a mist before his eyes but otherwise in full control. For a few moments he studied the border area south of the Khyber, then swung round to face Fettleworth. "I'm about to make assumptions, General. If there are Scottish troops taken prisoner, then I shall assume Norris's brigade has been under further attack and has again been cut up. The 114th are the only Scots currently south of the Khyber, are they not?"

It was Lakenham who answered: "Yes, sir."

"I further assume the bandits to be Murrum Khan's

Afridis and the veiled woman to be Mrs Hector Ogilvie."

"A large assumption—"

"No! A reasonable one!" Sir Iain blew through his moustache, angrily. "If my assumptions are correct, as I believe them to be, there is little time left. From now, gentlemen, we must consider the Raj to be under extreme threat and to be at war—"

"Sir, I am forced to protest. The Viceroy—"

"The Viceroy fiddlesticks. He is in Calcutta, the Queen awaits Christmas in Windsor. I am here. General Fettleworth, as Commander of the First Division, you will at once march out all available men. Barrack guards only will be left in cantonments. You are to march your division upon the Khyber, and I shall accompany you myself. I want a message sent ahead by the field telegraph to Fort Jamrud: they are to pressure the men who brought word of the crossing, and when I reach the Khyber I shall expect to know precisely where the crossing was made."

Soon after, Nowshera was in a state of controlled turbulence as the regiments made their final preparations for action. The many hundreds of animals—riding horses, pack mules, ponies and camels—that accompanied a division on the march were made ready and loaded with their burdens by detachments of the Supply and Transport; the final touches were put by the Ordnance to the guns and the ammunition trains, and the field ambulance sections were checked over for full complements of supplies and spare horses. In the infantry lines rifles were given one more pull through with four-by-two dipped in oil, and the bayonets were given an extra shine so that they might the more easily slide into native bodies.

*   *   *

The ride to the west was ignominy, utter failure. The assault had been well conceived and Ogilvie knew that he had been guilty of over-confidence. The attackers had poured down upon the Scots before the Maxim could be assembled and at the same time more men had come in at the

181

rush from the main pass and the Scots had been open to enfilading fire. In fact not many casualties had been suffered: two men dead and eight wounded, only one seriously. Not one of the attackers had been accounted for. They had come too suddenly and they had come in overwhelming numbers and it had all been over in less than two minutes. Murrum Khan, it seemed, still had plenty of willing support in the Waziri hills! Ogilvie and his Scots now rode with ropes bound tight about their arms and bodies, and their mules led by armed tribesmen, as did Mohammad Yusuf's men: the latter were clearly terrified of the vengeance that would be wrought upon them by Murrum Khan. They had proved brave in action but had been as helpless as the Scots in the sudden fury of the onslaught.

Behind Ogilvie, in the centre of the mounted bandits, was Angela, still veiled from head to foot. Gloatingly, Murrum Khan had confirmed to Ogilvie the identity of the shrouded figure. Ogilvie's thoughts were in tumult: Murrum Khan now had his two hostages back and they would be used against the Raj. And Ogilvie had no doubt that the whole affair had now gone far beyond the original boundary dispute and that Murrum Khan's ambitions would have grown bigger. Unless the British reaction to stepped-up demands was extremely cool and cautious, the Raj might become drawn into war. A rising all along the Frontier was a different kettle of fish from a boundary dispute in the localised area of Mana. There might be many pressures, particularly from Whitehall with world power alignments in mind, to concede enough to avoid the bigger risk. Ogilvie found this unwelcome. Anxious enough to live himself and to see Angela freed, he disliked the notion of being returned to the Raj like a parcel by a triumphant Murrum Khan to become a person to be stared at and even cold-shouldered as the officer who had dropped into enemy hands and become a pawn of natives to be used to discomfit the mighty Raj. An officer's career was always strewn with impediments to honour and promotion and this could certainly be considered one of them.

The ride continued, painfully and in biting cold that was

the worse for the fact that he was bound and therefore unable to move to circulate the blood. The nearer they approached the Afghan border the worse the weather became. They advanced through a blizzard; exposed areas of flesh lost all feeling. Murrum Khan, however, was stopping for nothing now. The ride continued. After a long time the track took a downward slant, ziz-zagging through the mountains, and the blizzard eased. Murrum Khan rode ahead to come up alongside Ogilvie.

"Now we are in Afghanistan," he said. "We have left the Raj behind."

"Where are you heading?"

"For a village where I am known and expected."

"How far?"

"A long way yet. Soon we shall rest. It is quite safe to do so now." Murrum Khan turned his horse away, and rode back down the line. Shortly afterwards he passed the word to halt, and his men dismounted and led the animals off the track into a deep cleft in the hills where they were protected from the weather. Ogilvie and the other prisoners were lifted down and, under strong guard, their hands and feet were untied so that they could stamp and flail the blood back into circulation, a process slow at first and painful. The horses and mules were fed from nosebags, and a meal of rice was given to the men. They drank from melted snow. After a four-hour halt during which the guards snatched sleep in watches, they were ordered to mount again and they rode deeper into the wild Afghan hills, coming at nightfall into a broad plain, a kind of bowl with more hills rising beyond and extending all around into immense distances, range upon range of utter loneliness and desolation. The wind howled and the cold was bitter but now the snow had stopped falling. A village lay ahead, a place with a remote look as though it had withdrawn from the world. As the bandits rode on, shadowy figures were seen ahead in the dimming light, men riding out in welcome. There was noisy acclaim for Murrum Khan, shouts of anger and derision against the bound natives, the Mahsuds of Mohammad Yusuf, traitors to the Pathan cause: it seemed that the bush telegraph had already brought word ahead that Razjah Shah had taken up arms against Murrum Khan and before dying had rendered assistance to the British Raj.

In the middle of an excited throng, they moved into the village, riding past rude huts and hovels and a mixture of wild-looking, ragged men and women, children, goats and domestic animals. Hands reached out, plucking with interest at the British uniforms, pulling at the cloak that covered Angela until the villagers were pushed back by the armed riders. There was a wait while Murrum Khan dismounted and went into the headman's hut, a long wait in the freezing cold under the light of flares that smoked and flamed eerily. Then Murrum Khan came into view again and called orders, and the prisoners were removed from the mules and horses. All except Angela were led under guard of the *jezails* and the knives to a hut larger than all the others, a place that looked like a meeting hut. The interior, as Ogilvie ducked down below the lintel of a low doorway, was seen to be completely bare of any furnishing. It had a floor of well-trodden earth, and the walls were of wood and stone and looked strong. Two Pathans remained inside as guards and the door was shut upon them, and a heavy beam was set in place outside. Light was given by a flare set in a metal holder on an upright pole that stood in the hut's centre and helped, presumably, to support the roof. The place was at least warmer than the outside air and gave full protection from the wind. Ogilvie tried to keep a cheerful face for the benefit of his Scots, but when he offered some words of encouragement he was at once stopped by one of the guards, speaking roughly in Pushtu: "There will be no speech." To lend emphasis to his words, the man darted across like a snake, squatted before Ogilvie and laid the tip of a dagger against his throat, remaining for perhaps half a minute staring into his eyes from behind a mass of facial hair and sweeping his nostrils with foul breath.

By now an intense weariness had set in and some of the men had fallen into sleep already, heads lolling and shoulders slumped one against another. It was not long before Ogilvie joined them, totally unable to keep his eyelids

184

from closing. When he woke he felt much refreshed, though hungry and thirsty. Dawn was showing through the crack above the top of the door, and the guard had been changed while he had slept. Soon after he had woken, the door was opened and Murrum Khan came in. With him were four of his tribesmen. These men, ignoring the Scots, went across to Mohammad Yusuf and dragged him to his feet. As he was pushed towards the door, the Mahsud met Ogilvie's eye and smiled.

"*Salaam*, Ogilvie sahib, and farewell. We shall not meet again—" He staggered as the butt of a *jezail* took him a viciously heavy blow in the side. Ogilvie called out to him; as he did so Murrum Khan came over and struck hard with the back of his hand, a blow that left red weals and blotches on Ogilvie's cheek. Mohammad Yusuf was taken outside, dragged along by the Pathans. A rising murmur was heard as he went out, a murmur that grew to an angry baying sound, a sound of blood-lust and savage cruelty, then this sound was stilled as Murrum Khan began haranguing the mob. Ogilvie was unable to catch his words, though he picked up an occasional reference in Pushtu to the Raj. After this there came a hush, and the hush was broken by a faint swishing sound, a sound of displaced air followed closely by a long drawn scream, and then another swish, then silence, then a noisy outbreak of savage pleasure. As the happy shouts continued, the door came open again and, as in the case of Razjah Shah far to the south and east in Mana, the bloody head of Mohammad Yusuf rolled along the floor beneath the flare's flickering light.

*   *   *

Murrum Khan did not come back. Ogilvie sat on with his Scots and the natives of Mohammad Yusuf, all of the latter at least now clearly facing something similar to their leader's execution. Rice was brought, and water-bottles, and all were fed by a veiled woman while the armed guards stood ready. There was no word of Angela. But as the day wore on into evening, tremendous news reached the village. From the hut

185

Ogilvie heard the galloping hooves of horses: two riders, he fancied. The hoofbeats slowed and stopped not far from the hut, and Ogilvie heard the excited voices clearly, speaking in Pushtu and asking for Murrum Khan.

"A great British force has passed Fort Jamrud and is within the Khyber ... many, many thousands of soldiers and beasts and heavy guns ... and with them is the great warrior, the General sahib who commands in Murree..."

17

SIR IAIN OGILVIE was in an angry mood: the men who had brought the word to Fort Jamrud, those friendly Waziris, had been of no further help at all. They did not know the route Murrum Khan had taken; their message was in fact at second hand, and their own informant had not known or would not say. But they had a grudge against Murrum Khan whom they would like to see brought to British justice and Sir Iain, who had spoken to them himself, had seen that they were speaking the truth. Had they known—having reported in the first place—they would have told all they knew. All they could say was that there were very many avenues into Afghanistan for those that knew them, and Murrum Khan could have taken any one of these.

"What do we do now?" Fettleworth enquired anxiously, but not as anxiously as he would have done had he had the responsibility himself. "Where do we march?"

Sir Iain pointed ahead. "Into the Khyber. Where else?"

"The weather's putrid "

"I've marched in worse."

"But what are you going to *do*?"

"I'm going to damn well advance into the Khyber!" Sir Iain snapped.

"But really—"

"We may get further word at Ali Masjid or Landi Kotal. If we don't," Sir Iain said with grim passion, "it'll be the bloody Amir who'll get word from *me* by the time we reach Fort Dhaka at the western end!"

Fettleworth blew out a long breath that lifted the trailing ends of his moustache. "What word, sir, pray?"

"That I intend marching on Kabul if he doesn't have Murrum Khan arrested and handed over with his hostages."

Sir Iain passed the order for the long column to get on the move, and somewhat cumbersomely it did so. Regiment upon regiment, squadron upon squadron, battery upon battery with all the paraphernalia of supply and its hundreds of camp followers, the latter ragged and unkempt and dirty, the low caste sweepers who did the housework of any formation on the march, an appallingly spread-out mass of men and animals for a winter advance through the terrible mountains of the Safed Koh. Fettleworth muttered and rumbled unavailingly: Sir Iain was set upon his madness and that was that. Not that Fettleworth ever shrank from a fight; he certainly did not. But in the circumstances the wrath from Calcutta would be terrible and Sir Iain was putting his head firmly on the chopping-block. His career in the army was virtually finished from this moment, in Fettleworth's view. Generals, however highly placed in their commands, did not declare war on their own, and this was war. Some of the opprobrium would rub off upon himself—bound to! Part of the column was formed by his own First Division, indeed all of it since the reinforcements had been incorporated. He was the Divisional Commander . . . well, he had already protested, of course! Lakenham had heard him do so, and would have to testify. But he tried again. Sir Iain wouldn't listen, merely set his face ahead and rode on before his massive force, into the gathering gloom beneath the enormous jagged peaks that rose in some cases 3,000 feet above the pass—14,000 feet above sea level—hostile and cruel even in summer, grim and grey and concealing tribesmen with rifles who would snipe continually from their safe vantage points above.

*　　*　　*

Pushing north, the three separated columns of Norris's brigade had made fair progress, mostly unimpeded by the Waziris although there had been a handful of attacks, as always expected, upon all three columns. These had been fought off without loss. The Royal Strathspey had followed the route taken by Ogilvie and his half company: having noted the position where Ogilvie had entered the hills, as reported by the Brigadier-General's orderly officer, Lord Brora had made for the same spot and from there had followed willy-nilly, hemmed into the pass by the hills to either side. Later, the battalion had had a stroke of luck: a native had been brought before him by the Regimental Sergeant-Major—a boy searching for strayed goats in the snow.

"What's this, Mr Cunningham?"

Cunningham explained. "You may wish him questioned, sir."

"I may, and indeed do, Mr Cunningham! You shall ask the questions. If he's slow to answer, prod him."

"He's but a child, sir."

Brora stared down from his horse. "Don't argue with me, Mr Cunningham, if you please. Child or not, he's to answer fully. Where's he from, has he seen Murrum Khan, has he seen Captain Ogilvie?"

The boy was cheerful under Cunningham's questions and answered willingly. He came from the village that had been visited by Mohammad Yusuf, and had heard talk of both Murrum Khan and of British soldiers. He was able to tell the Sergeant-Major sahib which track Murrum Khan had taken; but, because the Major sahib on the horse had spoken with an arrogance that came clearly through the foreign tongue, and because the Major sahib looked down at him with disdain and contempt, the boy did not point out the short cut that lay ahead and which could have saved the Major sahib many miles of dreadful progress. Released, he skipped through the snow after his goats and not until he was a long way off did he turn and put fingers to his nose towards the Major sahib.

Lord Brora spoke to Andrew Black. "That was helpful. Move the battalion out."

Black, who had been studying a map, said, "I believe the track that boy indicated leads into Afghanistan, Major."

"No doubt. And no doubt that was why Murrum Khan's taken it."

Black looked nettled. "Quite. My point was, are you going to ride across the border?"

"I don't know till I get there, my dear fellow. We may overtake Murrum Khan on the way, may we not?"

"I think not, Major. As for entering Afghanistan, our orders from the Brigadier-General are for Fort Jamrud, and—"

Brora interrupted rudely. "You have no damn initiative, I think, Captain Black. I am Lord Brora. I shall act as I think fit when occasion demands." He rode forward, large, handsome and dark, somewhat obviously making no reference to the Colonel, still under Corton's orders and being borne along in a *doolie* in the centre of the advance.

*   *   *

Murrum Khan himself brought the already overheard news of the Khyber penetration to his prisoners. "There is no cause to rejoice, Ogilvie sahib, even though your own father marches with the soldiers. None of you shall benefit. If the British happen to come this way, all of you will die before they reach the village."

"So you're not moving on, Murrum Khan?"

"Not moving, no." Murrum Khan waved a hand, airily. "The village is in fact quite safe from the British, and will not be troubled. The British are many miles away."

"And you?"

"I?" Murrum Khan stared down, eyebrows lifted. "I do not understand."

"What can you achieve from here, from your safe isolation, Murrum Khan? How do you propose to make use of hostages?"

The Afridi smiled and shrugged. "I have messengers, Ogilvie sahib. Soon the Raj will know that you and the mem'sahib are in Afghanistan and beyond reach of the British Army—and will know also, as indeed they know already, that both will die if my demands are not met . . . my demands for the cession of the border lands. More than this I have no need to do. I wait, and all will come to me."

More, perhaps, than you bargain for, Ogilvie thought; but without real hope. Murrum Khan went away, refusing to

190

answer questions about Angela beyond saying that currently she was safe and well and recovered from the rigours of the journey through the passes. Ogilvie eased his neck in his uniform tunic, trying to shift the headache that had come with the increasing fug in the hut. The many exhaled breaths, the smoke from the ever-guttering flare on its pole, used up the air faster than the chinks in the walls and the occasional opening of the door could replace it. The men, both British and native, sat about listlessly, unable to move hand or foot. Helplessness was becoming hopelessness ... Ogilvie looked across at MacTrease, too far off for any exchange of talk, of views and plans that might have led to some sort of concerted action. Ogilvie bared his teeth in a savage, self-rebuking grin: how could action of any kind come from bound men, with a vigilant armed guard watching every movement? Yet action there had to be if they were to avoid the slaughter that if it didn't come sooner was certain to come when the Raj rejected Murrum Khan's demands.

Something had to be thought of, and quickly. Clearly it could not at this moment be physical. Unless their situation changed dramatically, and this was improbable to say the least, Murrum Khan had to be countered by other means, the means of the mind. Ogilvie sat with closed eyes, trying desperately to get his brain working along constructive lines, but found himself unable to see the wood for the trees, the trees of the actual military and political situation as he saw it. It was known now that the Raj had entered the Khyber in strength; that must mean the First Division under Fettleworth, possibly with reinforcements from Murree. As for his father's presence ... it was not the Army Commander's proper duty to leave his headquarters for the field, but James Ogilvie knew his father's often impulsive reaction and his liking for a fight. It was many years now since Sir Iain had been promoted from command of the Royal Strathspey to the Staff, but at heart the old man was a regimental soldier still and chafed at the restrictions of high command. With his son and his nephew's wife in tribal hands, he was likely enough to cut right through the red tape and put himself at the head of the expeditionary force. . .

Ogilvie's thoughts flew on: what would be the purpose of a penetration in strength, a penetration that seemed likely to go beyond the boundaries of the Raj, though the Khyber itself was British territory? Was the First Division marching upon a needle-in-a-haystack chase, a mere hope that they might fall in with Murrum Khan or be led to him by bandits taken along the way? Again—if indeed Sir Iain was with the column—James knew his father's way. Often bull-at-a-gate, he was inclined to charge past the small fry and attack the pinnacle of power. In Afghanistan the pinnacle was the Amir, and the power lay in the city of Kabul. If you took Kabul, you took Afghanistan. The Amir would not wish that; the Anglo-Afghan border had been satisfactorily settled by the Durand mission as recently as 1893, in which year the Amir's subsidy from the Queen-Empress had been increased from twelve to sixteen lakhs of rupees. The Amir Abdur-Rahman had effectively broken the power of the tribal chiefs—all except Murrum Khan, it seemed now—and had since maintained a standing army of some 80,000 men with many thousands of horses and a respectable number of field guns. There would be a bloody battle if the Amir chose to resist, but he was well disposed towards the British and might be reluctant to jeopardise his position for the sake of a warring tribal leader.

All this, Murrum Khan must be presumed to know; however, there would be nothing lost by reminding him of it. Ogilvie reached a decision and called out in Pushtu, addressing the Pathan on guard.

"I wish words with Murrum Khan. The matter is important."

The guard came over and stood looking down at Ogilvie, the bayonet of his *jezail* pointed towards him. "You must wait. Murrum Khan has left the village."

This was contrary to what Murrum Khan had said. Ogilvie asked, "To go where?"

"I do not know."

"When will he return?"

"This also I do not know."

"I have said the matter is important. Murrum Khan

192

will have left a trusted tribesman in charge?"

"Yes."

"I must speak to this man."

There was uncertainty in the Pathan's dark, watchful face, and Ogilvie pressed. "If my words remain unsaid, Murrum Khan will be angry upon his return."

There was a pause; the man stared at Ogilvie, then shrugged and backed away towards the door. He banged with the butt of his rifle on the wood, and the door was opened. The Pathan spoke rapidly, and the door was shut again. All the men in the hut were watchful now, on edge, awaiting the next move. After a long interval the door was opened once more, and a short, thickset man came in wearing a filthy sheepskin coat with a round fur hat on his head. Ogilvie recognised him from their arrival: the village *malik*. Approaching, the man asked, "What does the British officer wish?"

Ogilvie answered as the *malik* had spoken—in Pushtu. "I wish to utter a warning. The British force in the Khyber is said to be strong. That means the Raj is marching upon Kabul. There will be war between the Raj and Afghanistan . . . between Her Majesty the Queen-Empress with her many divisions and guns, and ships to bring more men, and the army of the Amir. This you know?"

"It is possible."

"But more possible is this, my friend: the Amir will send his army to rout out Murrum Khan, rather than offend the Raj."

There was an oily grin. "Not so. Persons in Kabul who have the ear of Amir Abdur-Rahman promise help of his army for Murrum Khan. It is wished to push back the border into territory held by the Raj."

"So there will be war?"

"There will be war, yes." The headman spoke flatly. "You speak of nothing important, nothing new."

"Yet I think it is new that so strong a British force is on the march. I believe this will cause the Amir much thought and his mind may well be changed thereby. I believe you should consider this in the absence of Murrum Khan."

The *malik* shrugged. "It is not needed for me to consider."

"What happens if the Amir withdraws his support for Murrum Khan? What happens if the Amir sends men to take Murrum Khan, and then casts him and his tribesmen into jail in Kabul, or perhaps delivers them to the Raj for justice?"

"The Amir will not do this."

"I wouldn't be so confident were I in your shoes, my friend. Sixteen *lakhs* of rupees is much money, and this can be lost. The minds of princes are frequently changed when they see trouble coming for a way of life to which they've grown accustomed. They begin to think of the advantages of the *status quo*. And Kabul has many reasons to fear the Raj, as you know beyond doubt, remembering General Roberts sahib. You should think well, friend, in the best interest of your leader, Murrum Khan."

The eyes had narrowed to slits, and the face was watchful and tense. "And when I have thought—what then?"

"Come back, and I will offer you a solution."

"No. The solution now."

"Very well—the solution now, to aid thought." Ogilvie stared back at the squat, dirty headman, holding his gaze in his own. "I also have no wish for the Raj to involve the Amir in war. My reasons are personal . . . because I am told that my father marches with the British force. My father is a man of much impetuosity, who does not always follow the wishes or the commands of the Queen-Empress. He is liable to exceed his orders and put Kabul to the sword. This, the Raj may not want."

The headman seemed to understand, and grinned. "The great Queen-Empress will be angry?"

"Yes. My father may suffer much."

"It is an affair between him and the Queen-Empress."

"And Murrum Khan. Because of my father, I am willing to assist Murrum Khan."

"How?"

The crucial question that had to be answered; and the answer must convince beyond doubt. Ogilvie said steadily, "I am willing to go as an emissary to the British column and negotiate on Murrum Khan's behalf—"

He was interrupted by jeering laughter. "You are willing, Ogilvie sahib? Willing to be handed back safely to your Raj? Who would not be found willing for that?"

"You misunderstand," Ogilvie said quietly. "I am willing to go under escort, under a flag of truce, to talk at a distance to the commander of the column. I do not ask to be handed back. I shall tell the British that it is best for them to agree to Murrum Khan's demands and march back upon Fort Jamrud. And that when they have done this, and when the new boundaries have been drawn up, then the mem'sahib and I will be released."

"But already the Raj knows the terms of Murrum Khan! You suggest nothing different."

"Only that I shall myself be the envoy. I can convince them."

"And your father ... an illustrious soldier, a warrior, known along the Frontier and throughout the Raj, so it is said ... he will feel no shame for you?"

Ogilvie said, "I think not. I'll be acting for the mem'sahib ... who will remain meanwhile in your hands."

The *malik* said no more, but looked thoughtful and grave, and at the same time disdainful of the cowardice that allowed an officer of the Raj to leave a mem'sahib in hostile hands: neither side loved a traitor. As the headman turned and walked out of the hut, Ogilvie felt his contempt like a physical force. He found his forehead dripping with sweat as he caught the looks of his Scots. Many of them had enough Pushtu to have followed the conversation, MacTrease being one. MacTrease's face was scornful, his words cutting. "Man, I'd never have thought it of an Ogilvie."

Ogilvie flushed. "You'll kindly remember your rank, Colour-Sar'nt MacTrease."

"Aye! And more worthy, I hope, to hold it than you are yours, *Captain* Ogilvie!"

Ogilvie held on to his tongue and endured the bitterness that came across like knives to wound. It was better so; unprompted, unrehearsed reactions were always the more convincing if overheard. For the next hour or so he was subject to every kind of insult, some of them muttered, some

195

of them hurled openly. Had the men's hands and feet not been tied, he would, he believed truly, have been lynched. A Scots regiment was like no other, save perhaps an Irish one: the loyalty was intense and personal, but when it was flouted not even the hierarchy could hold the men down. They would have their say and make no bones about it: that was part and parcel of their race. Each man had his dignity as an individual, and in the Highlands there was no touching of the forelock to the squire and never had been. Army discipline they accepted up to ninety-nine parts in a hundred: today the hundredth part had been reached. Ogilvie sat pale-faced while the *malik* pondered and consulted his village lieutenants. The pressures upon him would be heavy: he must act for Murrum Khan and for his own headmanship, his own head too. He was being offered possible peace and a full acceptance of his leader's demands, and it must seem to him that he could scarcely lose by agreeing to Ogilvie's suggestion. Besides, the aspect of concern for a father would ring true: the Pathan understood and respected concern for the elders.

The headman came back and stood looking down at Ogilvie, alone but for the guard as before.

"I have considered, Ogilvie sahib."

"Good! And the result?"

"You shall go."

Ogilvie sat tensed, and more jeers came from the Scots. "I am ready as I promised."

"There will be an escort of twenty men, and you shall go mounted to the Khyber Pass."

Ogilvie nodded, licked at dry lips as he approached the next hurdle. "I am sore from the ropes, and my flesh has lost feeling. In the cold weather that is not good. I must be untied and not ride like a bound sack. If I am not freed, I shall not go."

The headman puffed out his cheeks, but after some thought nodded reluctantly. "You shall be untied."

"And my colour-sergeant, who is to ride with me."

There was an oath from MacTrease. The *malik* shook his head in refusal. Ogilvie said, "I must have corroboration for what I am to say. This is surely obvious. My colour-sergeant is a man of known sound character, and will convince."

"You ask more than you asked at first, Ogilvie sahib."

"Yes. But I offer much, and will go only on these conditions."

Once again, though reluctantly, the headman conceded the point. He gestured to the armed guard, who came across and held his *jezail* pointed at Ogilvie's chest. The headman himself bent and cut away Ogilvie's bonds at wrists and feet. The returning blood came painfully, and as MacTrease was freed Ogilvie lay working hands and toes, finding them useless for the time being, stiff as boards. MacTrease was cursing savagely across the hut. Leaving the guard on watch, the headman went to the door and called an order. A few moments later there was a sound of hooves on hard, icy ground —the horses mustering for the ride. When the headman returned both Ogilvie and MacTrease were getting to their feet, stumbling painfully. Movement was coming back. Ogilvie took a turn or two up and down the hut, watched by the Scots and the captured Mahsuds of Razjah Shah, and the terrible feeling of powerlessness vanished gradually.

"You are ready, Ogilvie sahib?" the headman asked.

"I am ready," Ogilvie answered. He caught MacTrease's eye. "*Craig Elachaidh!*" he called out, using the regiment's Gaelic battle cry. "Stand fast, Craigellachie!" MacTrease looked much puzzled, but only for a moment; then he gave Ogilvie a fractional wink. Ogilvie said, "The *jezail*, Colour." As MacTrease moved for the guard with his eyes shining, Ogilvie flung himself bodily against the central pole, sending it clear away from its seating. There was a creaking sound and the roof began to sag downwards; the flare shot off its hook and arced down into a corner of the hut, smoking and sputtering. Ogilvie recovered himself just as MacTrease's knee came up hard into the sentry's groin. As the man fell screaming, MacTrease grabbed the *jezail* and swung it on the *malik,* driving it deep into the chest and twisting the blade to withdraw it. Then with Ogilvie he moved back to where the torch was flaring and igniting the wood walls, firing towards a press of men coming in through the open doorway.

18

THE FLAMES AND the shooting so close at hand had panicked the horses: bucking hooves beat at the hut's walls, and there were cries from outside as the villagers were caught by flailing legs. While MacTrease covered him with the captured *jezail* Ogilvie used the headman's knife to cut the ropes binding the captives, working fast before the smoke could choke him. As the mob closed in, the Colour-Sergeant reversed the *jezail* and used the butt as a club, smashing heads. As the flames got a grip MacTrease burst backwards through the burning woodwork, clearing a way for the Scots and Mohammad Yusuf's bandits to be dragged out to safety. There were casualties but two of the Scots at least, quickly regaining circulation, were in action now; Ogilvie was aware of a lance-corporal and a private making short work of one of the villagers and getting possession of knives and another rifle. The lance-corporal tore like a maniac into the natives, thrusting with the snaky bayonet so that they pressed back, yelling and in disarray, to be taken in the rear by the flames. More and more of the ex-prisoners came back to vigour and joined in, two of them taking up flaming pieces of wood to bring fire to more of the huts before Ogilvie could stop them. MacTrease with a corporal and four men moved at the double for the compound where the mules had been tethered; within a matter of minutes they had the Maxim assembled. It began stuttering out fire, sweeping the village to leave bloodstained figures on the frozen snow. After that the former prisoners, under Ogilvie, ran for the headman's hut: on their first arrival in the village they had seen their captured arms being taken under the headman's charge. They were there still. As the rifles and bayonets were re-issued, MacTrease marched up to Ogilvie and saluted.

"God forgive me, sir," he said. "I thought you meant what you said."

Ogilvie smiled. "You were meant to, Colour. Part of it was genuine, the part that said I'd ride to join the advance through the Khyber and stop it before it goes too far."

"The lady, sir—"

"First the lady. She's not been found yet. Right through the village now, Colour, and let's hope she's not in any of the burning huts."

Saluting again, MacTrease turned about smartly and began shouting for the section sergeants and corporals to muster search parties and provide a perimeter guard. The men moved among the huts, some of which had already burned to the ground. It was Ogilvie himself who found Angela in a strongly-built structure with a stone floor and heavily bolted doors, a grain store in the centre of the village. Tied hand and foot as he himself had been earlier, and gagged, she was lying on a bed of sacks and matting. Quickly he released her. Bending, he kissed her cheek. Tears came. He said, "It's all right now. You're back . . . we've a long ride ahead, but you're back."

*   *   *

Most of the villagers had fled into the hills in the fading light, but they would return when the British had gone. In the meantime they had left some of the elderly and immobile behind, also some frightened children who had hidden when the fighting started and the huts had begun to burn. Mac-Trease asked what was to be done with them and with the village.

"They've asked for punishment, sir. They harboured Murrum Khan."

"Who has yet to be found . . . yes, they've asked for it, but I'll leave them in peace, Colour. *Badal's* for the Pathan, not for us."

"Aye, I dare say you're right, sir. Time moves on, and punitive expeditions don't look as right as once they did, though I don't know if Bloody Francis'll agree, sir . . . begg-

199

ing your pardon." There was an expression of innocence on the Colour-Sergeant's leathery face. "Is the lady fit to move out, sir?"

"Yes, she is, though the sooner we find a field ambulance section the better, both for her and the casualties. She and they will have to be carried as best we can manage on the mules and horses—and speed's the watchword now, Colour." Ogilvie paused, looking about him. "Talking of which, we'll move faster with a guide, I fancy."

"Razjah Shah's bandits, sir—"

"No. I've had a word—they intend to leave us at a crossing track once we're clear of the village and I can't say I blame them! Can you rustle up a guide from the people of the village?"

"Leave it to me, sir." MacTrease marched away. Ogilvie turned for the headman's hut, to which Angela had been taken. Darkness had come down now, thick darkness with no moon or stars to lighten it. Ogilvie feared more snow in the overcast sky. He prayed that it might not come to delay their ride upon the Khyber; once the British force had passed Fort Dhaka at the Khyber's western end, and there was no knowing when that might be, a boundary violation on the part of the Raj would have taken place and the results would be incalculable. A positive advance of a division was a very different thing from the inadvertent border crossing of a patrol . . . Ogilvie ducked down into the headman's hut and smiled at his cousin's wife lying on a more comfortable bed now, in the light of a flare. Rough food, and water, and a liberal amount of whisky from Ogilvie's flask, had brought improvement.

"Better?"

"Much, thank you, James." In fact she looked a very sick woman, he thought, and would need weeks of good care after they reached Nowshera. Hector was going to need to spoil her for a while. "Have we far to go, to reach Uncle Iain?"

"I don't know." He added, "You'll make it, Angela."

She answered in a whisper: "Yes. . ." Ogilvie looked at her narrowly: for his part he was not too sure, but he had no alternative but to head for the Khyber. Even had he not a positive duty to deflect the main advance, he could not remain in the village. His force was small, and before long the displaced villagers would gather support from neighbouring hill villages and a strong attack would come, and Angela would be worse off by far than if the ride to the north had been risked. But she was so frail and weak; her skin was almost transparent, her eyes haunted, dark and shadowed in a haggard white face. Her thinness was now skeletonic; a puff of the wind would blow her from her mule ... it would be tragic if she died on the march. Hector would never forgive him; he would never forgive himself, but what had to be, had to be and that was that. Ogilvie stiffened himself, gave her a word or two of cheer, and left the hut again to see to the preparations for moving out. The men were falling in, and a mount was being brought up for Angela while the wounded, the casualties from the hut action, were lifted as carefully as possible to the saddles of the fit men who would tend them along the way. Through the darkness came Colour-Sergeant MacTrease, pushing an old man and a young boy ahead of him.

"The guide, sir."

"Which?"

"The grandfather, sir—and that's what he is. The lad's his grandson."

"He knows the tracks?"

"He says he does not, sir, but I know well he must do, like all the villagers."

Ogilvie nodded. "Very well, Colour. Warn him of the consequences if he refuses to speak or leads us astray."

"Aye, sir. That I have! Not against himself."

"The boy?"

"Aye, sir," MacTrease said again, firmly. "A false move, said I, and the grandson's spitted like a pig by the bayonets. We need to be bastards, sir, at a time like this."

Murrum Khan would have done just the same thing: the knowledge made MacTrease's words no easier to stomach. Ogilvie, however, made no comment; the threat, he felt, would be an empty one, but should prove effective. In the

201

light from a flare held by one of the Mahsuds, he saw the boy's eyes. He had never before seen such hate in the face of a child; it was like a blow, a blow struck against the Raj by one who also had his loyalties. That child, for certain, would never point out the way; it was only to be hoped that the grandfather was made of lesser stuff! Ogilvie turned away and went back into the hut behind him, beckoning two privates to follow. Angela was lifted gently and brought out into the cold night's darkness, and set on the waiting horse, her rough cloak pulled up around her knees, awkwardly, as she sat stride. The two privates who had carried her out mounted to Ogilvie's orders and brought their mules alongside her, with a lance-corporal in rear, to act as close escort and to tend her along the rigours of the track.

As soon as the Scots and the Mahsuds were ready, Ogilvie passed the order to move out. They rode from the village, now almost deserted, in as much silence as possible: it was better that the scattered inhabitants should believe for as long as possible that they were still there. Ogilvie in the lead rode almost blind: the night's darkness was intense, still unrelieved by any moon. Beside him rode MacTrease with a hand on the bridle of the boy's mule. On Ogilvie's other side rode the ancient guide, muttering to himself as he indicated the way ahead. They made fair speed, but could have ridden faster had not the animals' hooves been impeded by the depth of the lying snow. After some five miles, appalling miles, they reached a cross track, the one expected by Mohammad Yusuf's bandits. The wild men broke off and rode away to the east, after each had gripped Ogilvie's hand; not for them the Khyber and the army of the Raj! Ogilvie's feelings were mixed: once, Razjah Shah had spoken of forming his own great army in Waziristan against the Raj. Now he was dead, and so was Mohammad Yusuf: had a dream ended with those deaths? And these men had taken part in the killing of his own patrol of Bengal Lancers in the Rahkand Pass, and this could not be forgiven though it had to be as it were pardoned since there was nothing he could do in the circumstances. There were too many to be arrested and escorted to justice, and in any case his word to Razjah Shah still held; and their subsequent help had been invaluable. He was sorry to see them go. The Scots rode on to their guide's instructions, taking the track that stretched towards the west—deeper for a time into Afghanistan, but soon they would turn to the north.

*   *   *

As dawn broke over the Khyber, the long divisional column from Nowshera began to come beneath the high-set fortress of Landi Kotal, pinnacled on the rearing peaks. From the fortress a man stepped into bold view, waving his arms, and was observed by Sir Iain Ogilvie.

"Fettleworth!"

"I've seen him," Fettleworth said grumpily, and turned to his Chief of Staff. "Semaphore, Lakenham. Fetch up the signallers."

Lakenham turned in his saddle and lifted an arm. Soon the acknowledgment was made from the column and the signaller of the Khyber Rifles in Landi Kotal sent the message, which was duly reported to Sir Iain by the Chief of Staff.

"From Calcutta, sir—His Excellency himself. No advance is to be made past Fort Dhaka—"

"Balls," Sir Iain said, "but that is not my official reply to His Excellency. I shall make *no* reply."

Fettleworth blew out his moustache and recalled an earlier conversation with the Army Commander. "My dear sir, Lord Nelson was in a somewhat different position. The confusion of battle at Copenhagen—"

"I am aware of Lord Nelson's position, thank you, General Fettleworth."

"As you wish, of course." Fettleworth shrugged.

A cough came from Lakenham. "There was more to the message, sir. Information has been passed that Amir Abdur-Rahman has word of our advance. He's already marching from Kabul towards the mouth of the Khyber."

Fettleworth cleared his throat and addressed Sir Iain with

203

much meaning. "I suggest we take note of that, General, and use caution."

"What sort of caution?"

"Heed His Excellency's orders," Fettleworth answered huffily.

Sir Iain gave a harsh laugh. "Damn it, the Raj wasn't built on namby-pambyism and running from a fight! I'm certain I shall have the Commander-in-Chief's backing. I'll make my final decision in the light of what we find upon reaching Fort Dhaka, as I indicated much earlier. There is no change in plan, General. The advance continues."

The column ground on behind the fifes and drums of the battalions. They moved over lying snow, through narrow gorges that extended the column's length but checked it like London traffic moving through the Marble Arch, under sheer hillsides and past long drops to sharp and jagged rock below. They marched on to a seemingly inevitable and un-authorised clash with the massed armies of Afghanistan as, around 150 miles distant, the 20,000-foot peaks of the Hindu Kush came up in clearing weather to the north-west of Kabul.

* * *

"A wrong direction somewhere, I fear, Major."

"Whose fault," Brora snapped, "is that, I wonder?"

Black remained silent: he had been reading the map, but the thick blanket of snow had confounded him by virtually obliterating all the landmarks other than the peaks themselves, and even they had seemed to lose their contours when they were visible at all.

"Halt the column!" Brora ordered sharply, swinging his arms and beating his hands upon the opposite shoulders. The liberal supply of blood always noticeable in his heavy face had turned blue, and the rest of him, like all the others, was white. "Damned incompetence, which shall not go unreported I may say—"

"The maps are seldom to be relied upon in Waziristan, Major."

"Nor, it seems, are adjutants. The bad workman always blames his tools, Captain Black, have you not heard that said before?"

Black scowled and once again remained silent. The column halted behind him. Cunningham, beaten by the snow as to his marching, clumped to the head of the column, lifting his feet high. Disregarding him, Lord Brora called loudly for all company commanders to attend upon him. When they had mustered the Major made no bones about their plight.

"Gentlemen, we've become lost. I have no idea where we are, Waziristan or Afghanistan. Let the blame for that rest where it sticks. As for myself, I accept no share. If any of you can advise the Adjutant, he will be happy to listen." He paused. "Yes, Captain Stuart, what is it?"

"We've been making a fair amount of northing, Major—"

"Until we turned to the west, yes. Well?"

"I think we're not far to the track for Peshawar . . . the track from Fort Jamrud—"

"Nonsense!" Brora interrupted tartly. "Damn it all, man, we've been moving *west* this last day and a night, as the compass bears witness even though the damn sun and moon have been hidden."

"I agree, Major. I think the basic error occurred farther back—"

"Farther back my arse. Where, pray?"

"After leaving the young goatherd. I believe we missed the right track soon after, and went too far north . . . or I should say north-east. You'll remember the track veered a little eastward for some way, Major."

Brora scowled and blew up the ends of his moustache in an angry snort. "Why didn't you damn well say we'd gone wrong at the time, Captain Stuart—if indeed we did?"

"I was not in possession of the maps. I assumed that whoever had the maps would—"

"Would know his job! There I'm in agreement with you! Kindly proceed, Captain Stuart."

Stuart said, pointing towards an outstanding peak in a great range lofting across the eastward sky, "There's a

205

leading mark that I believe I know, Major. That peak . . . it's visible from the Jamrud—Peshawar track."

Brora had turned and was staring, his face truculent. "Peaks can look very different, depending on the angle of sight."

"That's right, Major—"

"Does anyone else recognise it?" Brora called in a loud voice, pointing to the peak. There was no response, and he glared at Stuart. "Well?"

"I was about to say I'd seen it from this angle when on patrol. Not so far southward, that's all."

"How certain are you?"

Stuart said, "Pretty certain, but not positive."

"Ha!" Brora ejaculated harshly. "Well, Captain Know-All, you shall damn well ride out and take a closer look and come back when you *are* positive! Try not to lose yourself. If the peak is what you say, and can be used as a safe landmark, then I shall strike north for the Peshawar track and enter the Khyber where we're not likely to lose our way—are we, Captain Black?" Without waiting for an answer Brora turned upon the Regimental Sergeant-Major. "Mr Cunningham, I intend to fall out and rest while Captain Stuart makes his probe. See that the men are kept active, however, or they'll freeze.'

"Aye, sir." Cunningham saluted and started moving down the column, with difficulty. Robin Stuart rode to the rear, passing Lord Dornoch cocooned in thick clothing in his *doolie*. Dornoch called to him, and he dismounted and approached the *doolie*. The Colonel looked far from well; his shoulder was not healing, and there was some fever. If he should grow worse while Brora lost his way, there would be strong feeling throughout the regiment.

Dornoch said, "I have a suspicion we're lost. Am I right?"

Stuart hesitated. A white lie might be in order for a sick man, but the truth would out soon enough. He said, "Yes, Colonel, but only temporarily." He explained his present orders. "I shall be back as soon as I'm sure, Colonel."

"That peak. . ." Dornoch had lifted his body on the *doolie* to take a look. "I'm not familiar with it, at any rate with this aspect of it." He paused and fell back with a sigh. "The Major's not accustomed yet to winter in the hills, Robin. I feel the situation's unfair upon him. I'm not bad enough to be lying here so uselessly."

"All's well, Colonel, under full control."

There was a thin and shaky smile. "I take leave to doubt that, my boy! I'm getting out of this confounded contraption." He put a leg out, still booted and spurred and trewed. Stuart looked round somewhat wildly and with much gratitude saw the Surgeon Major tramping through the snow towards them. Corton summed up the situation quickly and acted with firmness: on no account was the Colonel to leave the *doolie*. If necessary, Colonel or not, he would be strapped in.

Stuart saluted formally and rode away to the north. Behind him the battalion settled down to rest, but it was rest according to Brora's orders, sensible enough ones, as given to the Regimental Sergeant-Major. Idle bodies were not permitted and the men were set to cleaning their rifles as if for an arms inspection in cantonments, after flapping the snow from heads and uniforms and the Slade Wallace leather equipment that hung from their shoulders in a spider's-web of belts; and meanwhile the field kitchen was set up and a makeshift meal was prepared, and steaming mugs of tea, strong and sweet, were sent down the line. There was a good deal of muttering and sarcastic comment: every man knew they were lost despite the maps and compasses and that the best hope of finding any track at all lay now with the eventual return of Captain Stuart. They were all anxious to be on the move, and their wishes went behind Stuart as he rode out. He rode until, bringing his landmark on to a more familiar bearing, he was able to make a positive identification and be sure that the Fort Jamrud to Peshawar track lay ahead. Before returning he rode a little farther to the north and east, coming up rising ground to look ahead through his field glasses in the hope that he might pick out the track itself so that Brora could be fully convinced. He was still too far off to identify anything beyond that one outstanding peak; the snow was an excellently covering blanket that deceived the eye. But something he did see as he lowered his glasses: not far ahead of him, a large hummock in the snow with a dark protrusion visible to the naked eye.

He rode forward, dismounted when he reached the hummock. The protrusion was a horse's hoof. Stuart scuffed at the snow with his hoot. The horse, a black one, was cold and dead. Something made him scuff around further, some feeling of eeriness that was making his hair rise. Then he found the body. A man, as cold and dead as the horse, lay against the animal's stomach, right between forelegs and hindquarters, as though he had crawled there hoping to find warmth and shelter. The body wore a fur hat and a tweed cloak and in the saddlebags of the horse Stuart found, incredibly, packets of porridge and a jar of marmalade. Beneath the body was an empty bottle of Dewar's whisky. Stuart reached into the pockets beneath the cloak and found identifying papers that caused his lips to frame a whistle.

He stood up: no point in taking the body back to the regiment. The regiment would march this way shortly, and Lord Brora could decide then what was to be done. Stuart mounted and rode back as fast as possible, bringing word that Hector Ogilvie was unaccountably dead in a Waziri pass.

* * *

As Ogilvie's half company advanced, they found a strange absence of any opposition; it was as though the men of the Afghan tribes were wary now, that the word of the great force in the Khyber had had its due effect. By the time the next day had darkened into evening, and still no further snow had come, they were not far off the Khyber—the old grandfather guide had confirmed this, and said that the track they were now on would bring them into the pass through the Safed Koh at a spot a little way to the eastward of Fort Dhaka.

"D'you think he's telling the truth, Colour?" Ogilvie asked MacTrease.

"There's no knowing, sir, but he knows what'll happen to

the lad if he's found to be lying. On balance, sir, I'd say he's not lying."

Ogilvie was dubious. "The boy's probably the key factor, Colour. The old man's fairly senile, I think."

"Being led by the nose, sir, by the lad?"

"He could be. The boy hates our guts, that's been obvious all along. It's possible he's blackmailing grandfather into resistance to threats . . . the boy's full of courage and I've no doubt he feels he holds the honour of every tribesman in Afghanistan in his hands! He's to be watched closely, Colour MacTrease."

"Aye, sir, he'll be that."

"Full alertness from now, Colour—we're coming into the most dangerous stretch and it'll last till we make contact with Division."

"Aye, sir. *If* we make contact with Division, sir." The Colour-Sergeant brushed the back of a hand across his moustache. "There's no knowing yet how far they've advanced."

"True."

"You'll march through the night, sir, I take it?"

"Yes, Colour." Ogilvie had halted his force a little before the light had gone; the horses and mules, even more than the men, needed a respite from the eternal slog through the snow, but after this there would be no more halts until they had reached the Khyber. With MacTrease Ogilvie walked down the resting line, having words personally with the men and stressing the need for every one to be watchful and ready for instant action. Ogilvie didn't trust the silence of the hills, the absence of tribesmen, the total lack of dark faces along the peaks. There was some falsity, some lulling. Once again he thought about the Afghan youngster. But now they were in the hands of the boy and his ancient grandfather and there was nothing they could do but advance and be on their guard. Ogilvie passed the word to MacTrease to move out the half company and maintain scouts and picquets. The Scots mounted again and rode into the darkness towards the Khyber, behind their officer and the old man and the boy. As they went along the skies started to clear a little, and stars were seen, though as yet no direct moonlight. Palely those stars shone down on the snow and the lonely hills, bringing a touch of silver and, almost, of magic. It was very lovely, and nothing moved except the men and animals who were the only things to break that intense and brooding silence that hung over the whole land to link the Scots as one with the distant ranges of Himalaya.

19

A MAN RODE back from the advanced scouting party to report to Ogilvie. "A fork ahead, sir."

"Thank you, MacKendrick." Ogilvie turned in his saddle. He spoke in Pushtu to the old man. "Which should we take, the right or the left fork?"

The old man mumbled something that Ogilvie didn't catch; it was the boy who answered in a loud, clear voice: "The left fork."

"That leads into the Khyber?"

"Yes."

"And the right one, where does that lead?"

The boy said, "It turns upon itself, leading back to the south by way of the east."

"If you speak falsely, you know what will happen. My Colour-Sergeant is ready with the bayonet."

The boy seemed about to spit, but changed his mind. He smiled sweetly. "I speak true words. You should take the left fork."

"I shall take the right."

For a moment hate showed again, then the boy shrugged with apparent indifference. "I have said. It is for the sahib to decide." The word sahib came out with a terrible disdain. Ogilvie stuck to his decision to move right, and instructed Private MacKendrick to ride back and rejoin the scouting party with his orders. MacKendrick rode away, his mule kicking up the snow in powder. The moon was up now and the whitened hills stood out clearly. The faces of the guides were clear also; the old man was registering nothing, continuing with a toothless mumble, chewing upon nothing. The boy's expression was calm, almost bored. Was there triumph in it? Worry and uncertainty nagged at Ogilvie. The Afghans were wily, and the boy's face was an intelligent one. Had he fooled his captors after all? Had he set them by contrariness on the path he, the boy, wanted?

It was only too possible; a toss of a coin would be as effective now as a considered judgment! Mentally, Ogilvie tossed one then spoke softly to MacTrease: "A rider to the scouts, Colour. I shall advance to the left."

"Sir!" MacTrease handed over guard of the boy to a private, then turned aside and rode down the small column. A man went ahead to overtake the scouts with the changed orders. Soon the main body came up to the fork: Ogilvie watched the face of the young boy as he moved into the left-hand track. There was a flicker, no more; Ogilvie was still unsure. Despite the change, the boy said nothing. The grandfather went on chewing, black eyes glittering from a mass of wrinkles in the moonlight. The advance continued; MacTrease rode again down the column to sharpen the men's watchfulness. No reports came back from the scouts or the picquets as they came between close-set hillsides, higher and steeper than hitherto. Underfoot the going became much rougher, and the mules's hooves slithered over rock, and jags rose up to impede their way. Ogilvie turned to look back at Angela: she was bearing up well enough so far, but Ogilvie knew she couldn't go on taking the ride for much longer. It was urgent that she should have medical attention and soon it might become necessary for her to be carried and a rough *doolie* fashioned for the purpose. That would slow the advance, and time was vital. But an impediment might have to be accepted. Another dilemma of command: was it more important to preserve the life of the woman who had set the Raj upon the march, or more important to preserve the Pax Britannica itself?

They rode on, deeper into the ravine. By now it was so precipitous that the picquets could no longer function, and had descended to join the main body of the advance. Ogilvie ordered them to fall back to form a rearguard five hundred yards behind.

The silence was there still, and was to Ogilvie still false. Somewhere the tribes must be in pursuit . . . Murrum Khan,

212

unaccounted for since he had ridden out from the village, must for a certainty be wishful to stop his hostages riding to the safety of the British column in the Khyber. And for an equal certainty the men of the tribes must, somewhere along the line, have noted the movement of Ogilvie and his men, and would have sent the word through to the right quarter. Icy fingers plucked at Ogilvie: everything, he felt, depended on whether or not his assessment of the boy's veracity had been correct. There had been ways of making more sure, but he had shrunk from the idea of torture upon a mere boy, and he had felt the boy wouldn't have uttered in any case. The face held dedication to the cause of his fathers. MacTrease, he knew, was silently critical of his officer on that score, but in any case it was too late now.

On and on beneath the moon, its light now largely obscured by the high hillsides. Still the silence, deep and foreboding, broken only by the crunch of the hooves, the rattle of arms and equipment and the occasional oath, almost involuntarily stilled before it broke right out, from a man whose mount had slipped on the snow or who had bruised a leg from a hidden outcropping of rock. It was as though all were trying not to break that quietness, as if to do so might bring a concealed enemy down upon them or, alternatively, overlay the sound of his approach.

Ogilvie watched the face of the boy as closely as he could: it might give some sign, the aloof coldness might well hide knowledge of where an attack might come. The boy gave the impression of knowing the wild tracks intimately; young as he was, he had no doubt taken part in tribal affrays, internecine battles or forays against the Raj. He was old beyond his years, but excitement and anticipation might show through in a boyish way. Meanwhile the soldiers were advancing towards a bend where the track ahead bore easterly, and always in the passes bends were dangerous. As they approached it Ogilvie sent back a warning for extra caution. Just here the sides rose higher, and the moon's light was taken away altogether; the boy's face was no longer visible. Flesh tingling, the half company of the Royal Strathspey rode on, into the bend.

213

Nothing happened: all was peace, and still the brooding silence. The track continued easterly. Savagely, Ogilvie swore. The sides lowered again, enough to admit the moon, and in the silver light Ogilvie saw the track extending ahead into the far distance, due east now by his compass, running more or less parallel with the Khyber and back towards Waziristan. The boy was grinning: he was delighted with himself. He had fooled the officer sahib, the colour-sergeant sahib, all the sahibs. They were idiots! He murmured in Pushtu to his grandfather, and the old man cackled suddenly. Ogilvie halted the advance and rounded on the boy. "The track," he said roughly. "It is this one that leads back upon itself?"

The boy's smile grew wider. "It leads east. You will not reach the Khyber."

"Where will I reach?"

"Not the Khyber. I say no more." There was an indifferent shrug.

Ogilvie turned. "Colour-Sar'nt MacTrease?"

"Sir?"

"We can go back to the fork. And still be lost when we get there! I'll take a gamble the right fork leads into this track — and it wouldn't have mattered which we took."

"But the boy, sir. *He* knows, the little bugger!"

"Yes. Find out, if you please, Colour. But be careful."

"Aye, sir." MacTrease dismounted and went over to the boy's mule. A strong arm wrenched the youngster from the saddle. Grandfartherly mumblings came but were disregarded. "Now," MacTrease said grimly, and marched the boy to the rear at bayonet point. Ogilvie sat waiting, keeping an eye on the grandfather. Minutes passed; there were no cries of pain. After almost fifteen minutes MacTrease marched back; the boy looked baleful but unharmed.

"Well, Colour?"

MacTrease gave a harsh laugh. "There's more ways than one, sir, of killing the cat. He's unharmed except in his pride, sir. The Pathan respects age, sir, and grandfathers are almost holy . . . and are not to have their guts disembowelled by the bayonet and taken into Peshawar to be fed to the pigs. The

214

track, sir, leads back into Waziristan, into the Rahkand Pass. And that's the nearest we'll get to the Khyber, Captain Ogilvie, sir."

Ogilvie let out a long breath of fury, frustration and self-blame: he had selected, or had allowed MacTrease to select, the wrong person as the lever and had been led astray accordingly. He said, "Thank you, Colour."

"Do we go on, sir?"

"We've no alternative, have we? The Rahkand leads north and the mouth's not far from Fort Jamrud. We must be content with sending a message on to Division from Fort Jamrud, and hope it reaches them in time—that's all!" He paused. "What about an attack?"

"He would not say, sir. It's my belief he has no knowledge of Murrum Khan's intentions, sir."

Ogilvie nodded. "All right. Move out, Colour. Keep up the best speed possible." Wearily, they rode on. It was, Ogilvie thought, coming full circle now in a geographical sense and was bringing him back to the wrong end of the Khyber. From Fort Jamrud he had ridden south along the Rahkand Pass himself; in the Rahkand he had been ambushed by the bandits of Razjah Shah, in the biting winds of the Rahkand he had lost a patrol of the Bengal Lancers. In point of fact he was probably even now not so far off the entrance to the Khyber as the crow flew, but by the time he reached Fort Jamrud via the Rahkand his father might well be past Fort Dhaka and deep into Afghan territory, and no one could forecast the reaction of the Amir in Kabul. Time pressed more urgently now than ever. Ogilvie dropped back towards Angela and spoke to her of the situation. He asked, "Can you go on, Angela?"

"I'll be all right, James."

"Truly?"

"Yes, truly. I've got to get there . . . and I will get there, James, I promise. Hector will be so worried."

Hector! Ogilvie caught his breath: he'd forgotten about Hector, anxiously pacing the corridors of Fettleworth's headquarters in Nowshera. Of course Hector would be worried sick, and would be making himself a confounded nuisance all round—naturally enough, but a worried Hector would be far worse an affliction to endure than would anyone else in a similar situation. However, Hector was having a useful effect now: Ogilvie believed that Angela was keeping herself going by thoughts of her husband's current purgatory; for his sake she must win through, and she would, and then she would give way to reaction. There was more steel in Angela than there was in Hector despite her surface frailty; Hector was a lucky man. After giving another assurance that her ordeal would not last much longer, Ogilvie rode back to the head of the column and they continued easterly through the night.

They made good speed as they came into easier ground, a wider track with less impedimenta. When at last the attack came it came suddenly and swiftly in unexpected surroundings, and it caught them with their defences lowered by sheer weariness and by an over-confidence that attack would come only in the narrow passes. It came before the dawn, when the moon was still bright: from points of cover on the hillsides rising gently to right and left of the track, tribesmen emerged behind a hail of bullets that cut down the picquets before they could give the alarm. Ahead, the scouts went down as though scythed like hay, and then bullets from more than a hundred *jezails* ripped into the riders. As Ogilvie shouted the order to dismount and scatter to the flanks but to have a care for the previously wounded men, he caught sight of the old grandfather's face in the second that it disintegrated into blood and shattered bone. The old man drooped sideways in the saddle and his mule took fright: it galloped ahead towards the ambushing tribesmen, dragging the body with the left foot caught in the stirrup. After it, as the Scots returned the fire from the cover of rocks and bushes, went the boy, head low, body held flat along the neck of his mule. Towards him streamed a horde of tribesmen, ragged garments and wild hair flying out in the cold wind, flashes of fire coming from their rifles as they stormed for the Scots. Ogilvie was firing his revolver point blank, reloading again and again as the attack came down and passed him to the rear. The moon showed the slaughter: Scots and natives together, in huddles along the track. Angela, in the care of her close escort, was in cover beneath a rock ledge like a roof, and behind the carcase of a mule. The lance-corporal and the two privates were firing into the howling mob over the mule's dead flank. Ogilvie ceased his own firing for a moment while he took stock: the men were in good cover now and this looked like becoming a battle of attrition; soon the natives would realise this and would themselves take cover, and both sides would become locked into a stalemate situation that could hold for days until one side or the other was starved out. That must not be allowed to happen: time was still vital.

Ogilvie saw MacTrease a little to his left, and called out to him.

"Sir!" Flat on his paunch, the Colour-Sergeant wormed his way to Ogilvie's side.

"We're going to be stuck here a while, I fancy, Colour. I have to get word through to Fort Jamrud."

"Aye, sir. Are you thinking of a runner, sir?"

"Yes. Two men, to outflank on right and left and join up farther along."

"I doubt if they'd have much hope yet, sir."

"No. But once the natives go into cover, as they must soon. It's the only way I can see, Colour. Detail two good men and have them report to me for orders."

"Aye, sir." MacTrease still sounded dubious: two men, riding out from cover, could not be otherwise than seen immediately, and brought down by the *jezails.* He said as much; Ogilvie was about to tell him, abruptly, to carry out his orders when he saw, clearly beneath the moon, a tall man riding fast from out of the native mass, making along the track towards Angela and her escort: a man of imperious bearing, with a cloak of dark, probably maroon, cloth worked with gold thread—Murrum Khan beyond a doubt. Gold fire flashed in the moonlight from the heavy, medallion-hung earrings...Ogilvie, disregarding MacTrease now, got to his feet, came out of cover and ran along towards where Angela lay, keeping on the high ground leading to the rock ledge. Bullets hummed and sang around him; he rushed

217

on. Murrum Khan seemed equally impervious to bullets. Beside Angela, the lance-corporal of the close escort gave a curious leap into the air, clutched at his throat, and fell back. Angela seemed to be screaming, though she remained unheard in the mêlée and the shouting of the tribesmen. Ogilvie and Murrum Khan reached her position simultaneously; Ogilvie halted on the overhanging ledge just as the tribal leader pulled up his horse by the mule's carcase, and reached down to slice at the two Scots privates with a bloody-bladed scimitar. As the arm lifted, Ogilvie jumped from his point of vantage. He took the native fair and square, coming down astride the man's shoulders. The scimitar blade dipped sharply and plunged into the horse's neck. There was a spurting fountain of blood and a high whinny, and the animal reared up, hooves flailing dangerously over Angela's head. As the privates of the escort opened fire into the body of the horse, Murrum Khan and Ogilvie crashed backwards, with Ogilvie underneath. Murrum Khan was like an eel, wriggling and contorting, his face almost black with fury as Ogilvie tried to hold his arms to his sides. He wrenched them free and got a grip around Ogilvie's throat, and squeezed. Fire from his tribesmen swept the ground all round, pinning the escort down in the lee of the dead mule. Ogilvie's eyes began to dim, then he became aware of MacTrease poised behind Murrum Khan. All at once there was a high shriek of agony, the grip of the hands relaxed, and Murrum Khan fell aside. As MacTrease grabbed hold of Ogilvie and dragged him behind the mule, the firing continued all around. Panting, drawing in air through a bruised throat, Ogilvie found that MacTrease had also brought Murrum Khan in. Murrum Khan looked dead, but MacTrease said he was only knocked out.

"The butt of a rifle, sir, in the kidneys. Mind, he'll not be the same man again, but he'll live long enough to swing in Nowshera." MacTrease brushed at his moustache. "I take it you wanted him alive, sir?"

"Yes, Colour. There's still a boundary to be sorted out!" Ogilvie grinned breathlessly. "That's if we come through this little lot, and. . ." His voice died away, and he cocked an ear to listen, looking at first puzzled, then incredulous. "Do you hear what I hear, Colour?"

MacTrease was grinning himself, and pulling his uniform straight. "I do, sir. The pipes an' drums, sir! And you'll recognise the tune I don't doubt, Captain Ogilvie!"

Ogilvie did. It was "Farewell to Invermore," Pipe-Major Ross's own composition, written when first they had sailed for India years before. As Ogilvie and MacTrease listened the tune shifted to "Cock o' the North," clear and totally unexpected signal that the 114th Highlanders, The Queen's Own Royal Strathspeys, were coming in to action. From all along the line of cover, a great cheer went up as the sound of the pipes and drums overlaid the diminishing rattle of rifle fire, and grew louder. The tribesmen began to stream away to the flanks, and the pipes and drums stopped abruptly, and from the advancing battalion, now coming on at the double, a great barrage of fire was opened upon the retreating backs. In the last of the moon's light before the fingers of the dawn spread over the waste of hills and the snow, the figure of Major Lord Brora was seen, swaggering into battle on his horse.

* * *

Brora was never a tactful man. The news having been broken, he elaborated in forthright manner. "We have your husband's body with us, ma'am. I'm sorry. I make the assumption he was looking for you. If that's the case, then it was remarkably foolish but he died well and you should be proud."

"Proud!" Angela covered her face with her hands and her body trembled. Ogilvie, at her side, held her close.

"Oh, no doubt you'd prefer him safe and alive—that's natural. But pride's no bad mainstay all the same." Brora began to look irritable: tears were not soldiers' business and failed to impress him. "Captain Ogilvie, we have much to discuss." He waved a hand towards Angela, and gave a jerk of his head as much as to say, get her out of my sight. "I wish no delay now."

219

Ogilvie handed Angela over to Robin Stuart, who, he had been told, had found the body. He might be of some comfort, or he might not ... when Ogilvie rejoined the Major, Brora was talking loudly to Andrew Black. "Women are an odd lot. I doubt if my words registered. Perhaps I should have buried the feller where he fell upon his Dewar's ... ah, Captain Ogilvie. Your cousin was of some importance. All Civilians rate themselves as such, anyhow—that's why I brought the body on. He'll have to have a proper funeral, I don't doubt."

"I think he's earned that, Major."

Brora sniffed. "I don't underestimate what he did, but he didn't do it with efficiency. Whisky and porridge are good Scots materials, and sustaining, but are not enough by themselves. Now, Captain Ogilvie, a full report at once, if you please."

"Very good, Major. It's a long one."

"No doubt! Kindly make it fast."

Ogilvie did so, and made representations as to the need for immediate contact with Division. Brora saw the point. Permission was given for Ogilvie to ride out independently with two mounted privates and head for Fort Jamrud with his urgent despatch to go by the telegraph to Fort Dhaka and the General Officer Commanding. Behind him as he rode away, the dead from the recent action were buried in shallow graves marked with roughly-made wooden crosses bearing names, rank and regiment to become yet another landmark of the Raj and the maintenance of the Pax Britannica. Ogilvie had gathered the facts from Robin Stuart before leaving, and could not but be thankful for Andrew Black's poor map-reading and for Stuart's sighting that in the event had brought the battalion within hearing of the rifle fire. Murrum Khan remained in the custody of the battalion, a man in much agony but a man who, according to the doctor, would reach Peshawar to face charges of murder and of conspiracy against the Raj. Ogilvie reached Fort Jamrud in good time and had his message passed on along the Khyber; and sent another to Peshawar asking for a field ambulance bearer company with attached transport to drive out and collect Lord Dornoch, who was still in poor condition but was expected to mend, and Angela Ogilvie together with the body of her husband, and the many wounded, plus a few men in danger of contracting frostbite. He waited for long enough to learn that the division had been contacted when just past Fort Dhaka, and to receive word back that Sir Iain Ogilvie had agreed in the circumstances to withdraw.

When many days later the huge divisional column had marched back through the Khyber and entered cantonments at Peshawar, Ogilvie was sent for to report at Brigade, where his father greeted him in company with Bloody Francis Fettleworth. "You don't appear too heartbroken by your cousin's death," were his first words.

Ogilvie was taken aback. He said, "He died well, sir."

"Certainly he did. But it's your uncle I feel for, James. Hector was . . . well, I'll not speak ill of him now." Sir Iain, showing signs of strain, coughed. "How's Angela?"

"Well, sir. That is, she's improving. The funeral was an ordeal."

Sir Iain's eyebrows went up. "She didn't attend?"

"She did, sir. She insisted."

"Not quite the thing, for a woman to attend," the GOC said grumpily. "However, that's her business. Now to the future: you did well, James, and I'm pleased."

"Thank you, sir."

"With Murrum Khan in custody, the tribal demands will collapse. I've read your reports . . . I'll see to it that the dispute's settled in favour of whatsisname's people—"

"Razjah Shah, sir."

"Yes. A bloody murderer and thief, but on the right side this time, apart from those poor fellers of the Bengal Lancers. I gather he was helpful."

"Invaluable, sir."

"Yes. Good! And the Raj always shows gratitude. So that's that. The High Commissioner will damn well do as I tell him. That village now, the one you were taken to by Murrum Khan. Know its name and location?"

"Not the name, sir. The location, yes."

"Good." The GOC rubbed his hands together and went across to hold them out to a coal fire burning beneath the portrait of the Queen-Empress. He glanced up at it. "It's not quite Christmas ... Her Majesty's got her wish. She'll be delighted with the news. Delighted! Won't she, Fettleworth?"

"Indeed she will." Bloody Francis met the Queen's eye; he gave a small inclination of his head. "The village, General. You mentioned—"

"Oh, yes. It'll receive a visit. A punitive expedition ... your report says much of it was burned down, James. They will have started rebuilding. That won't avail them for long."

"The village was in Afghanistan, sir."

"I know that." Sir Iain stared; his blue eyes bulged towards his son. "Beyond Fort Dhaka, I encountered Amir Abdur-Rahman in person, at the head of his army. Your message came just in time, James—*just* in time! Anyway, we had a parley afterwards, all very friendly. Abdur-Rahman's most obliging ... he's grateful for the subsidy and he doesn't want war. He'll see to the village, I'm certain." He broke off. "Care to spend Christmas in Murree? Your mother would like that. I'll speak to Dornoch, or Brora if Dornoch's not yet resumed command." Once again he coughed, and cleared his throat with a rumbling sound. "There's another thing your mother would be pleased about, but of course it's early days yet and no doubt indelicate. What?"

Ogilvie felt himself flushing like a schoolboy: he knew very well what his father's reference was and he considered it more than indelicate within a matter of days of the funeral. He said, "Really, I don't—"

"Don't argue, boy, don't argue. Think about Christmas. Off you go now." Sir Iain waved a dismissive hand, and James, saluting smartly, turned about with a crash of boots and marched from the room. Outside headquarters, Brigade's standard floated from the flagstaff, emblem of the power of the Raj and the Queen-Empress, symbolic of all the British Empire. At Brigade there was already a *soupçon* of holly and mistletoe, of whisky and plum pudding and crackers amidst the regimental silver, and loyal toasts and eyes misty when they thought of home beyond an immensity of sea. Christmas was a time for home. And Christmas, of course, was in the air. The Queen, who would be so delighted, was safe in Windsor Castle with her Guard outside. A village in Afghanistan was waiting for bullets and flame from its Amir. The dead were in their graves. Ogilvie mounted his horse and rode back to the 114th's cantonment.